these dirty
LIES

A DARLING HILL DUET : BOOK ONE

l. a. cotton

USA TODAY AND *WALL STREET JOURNAL* BESTSELLING AUTHOR

Jeanette

&

L·A·Cotton

THESE DIRTY LIES

A DARLING HILL DUET: BOOK ONE

L A COTTON

Whatever our souls are made of, his and mine are the same

EMILY BRONTE

Chapter One

Harleigh

"HEY, I thought I'd find you up here." Celeste joined me on the roof terrace, choosing the egg-shaped chair. "How are you feeling?"

"Will you believe me if I say fine?" My brow quirked up, and she chuckled.

"Nope, but I won't tell if you won't."

"God, I love it up here." A sigh escaped me.

It was the only place where I could breathe. The highest point in the house with an incredible view of Old Darling Hill. The lights of the town twinkled in the distance, like the stars winking above us.

"I think you'd live up here if you could."

She wasn't wrong.

The house on the edge of Old Darling Hill was practically palatial with its gated access, long winding driveway, and perfectly tended lawns. It reminded me of a small-scale White House, fronted with pristine alabaster columns and rows and rows of symmetrical windows. It was grand and beautiful and the epitome of the American dream.

But it wasn't *my* dream.

Instead, it was a nightmare I'd found myself trapped in. A warped reality where I was supposed to forget about my Darling Row upbringing.

I shut down *those* thoughts. It never did me any good going back to that time of my life. Those memories.

I wasn't that girl anymore.

My life was with my father and his wife Sabrina now and their children: my half-sister Celeste and her brother Max. Michael was my guardian, this mansion my prison.

"Are you ready for school on Monday?"

"I don't think I'll ever be ready," I admitted.

Celeste made it easy. Too easy sometimes. I liked her a lot. She was kind and funny and she didn't take herself too seriously, which was a small miracle given that she was half Michael Rowe and half Sabrina Delacorte. But their icy cold genes had obviously skipped their firstborn, passing Celeste and planting themselves firmly in Max. He was barely sixteen and one of the meanest kids I'd ever met.

And I'd gone to a school full of mean kids before being ripped from my life and implanted here.

"DA isn't so bad, you'll see."

DA: Darling Academy, my new school starting Monday.

Celeste gave me a reassuring smile. "At least I can show you around. And I'm sure Nate will be happy to—"

"I'd rather not talk about Nate Miller."

He'd been one of the first people to approach me at the mixer last month with his smug smirk and cocky attitude. It was my first 'appearance' at one of my father's events. What a disaster that had been.

"You mean you aren't fooled by his dashing charm and riveting conversation?" She rolled her eyes playfully. "The guy is a douchebag."

"Kind of? He tried to feel me up the first time we met."

"Is that why you stabbed him with the fork?"

"I didn't stab him... it slipped."

"Slipped, right." The corner of her mouth twitched. "You're so bad, Harleigh."

I managed a small smile in return. It wasn't like I went out of my way to be bad. But these people were... so not my people. Celeste was okay. She wasn't driven by how much money daddy had in the bank or who was wearing the latest designer label. She was normal. Well, as normal as you could be when your parents were filthy rich.

"I wish you were a senior too." I let out a heavy sigh, staring out at the view. The Rowe estate had a natural perimeter marked by the tree line. I'd spent weeks dreaming of escaping over the fence and making a run for it. Of course, my father's housekeeper and security guy had been briefed to 'keep an eye out for me.'

Everyone knew I was a flight risk. That one way or another, I was determined to leave this place. But that was *before*... Now it was different.

I was different.

At least, that's what everyone thought. That's what I let everyone believe.

They thought I'd been fixed. That the months and months of pills and therapy and time had cured me.

"We might have a class or two together. I'm taking some AP classes."

Celeste was smart, like MENSA smart. But she didn't flaunt it. In fact, she tried everything she could not to draw attention to the fact she was basically a teenage genius.

"I can't believe we have to wear a uniform," I said.

"It isn't so bad. At least you won't have the headache of deciding what to wear every morning."

"I guess." I got up and went to the glass balustrade, running my fingers along the polished chrome handrail. The balmy air kissed my skin as I tilted my face to the night sky.

For as long as I could remember I'd always loved the nighttime. There was something beautiful about when the world went to sleep, and darkness reigned. Even now, I felt more grounded once the sun had set than I did at any other time of the day.

Sabrina called me a night owl, but it was more than that —the strange affinity I had with the dark.

"It's late. I should probably turn in before Mom comes looking for me. You'll be okay?"

"I'm fine. Go. I'd hate for Sabrina to catch you up here again."

"Ignore her. We're sisters." Celeste shrugged. "Nothing

she does or says is going to change that. I want you here, Harleigh."

"Thanks." My smile didn't reach my eyes. It never did these days.

"See you tomorrow. Good night."

"Night."

Celeste went inside, leaving me alone. Sometimes, I didn't know what I would do without her. She was the only thing that made this—being here in this strange place—bearable. God only knows, it wasn't being reunited with my father. If you could even call it a reunion. I'd barely seen the man since returning from Albany Hills a month ago.

I exhaled a long breath, gripping the handrail tighter. Sometimes, I sat up here and stared out into the distance, trying to see past the trees and the town, all the way past the reservoir right to Darling Row, the trailer park where I'd grown up.

If this house was the epitome of the American dream, The Row was the place dreams went to die. But it had been more to me than this place ever would be.

It had been home.

And I knew why. It always came back to *him*.

With Phoenix by my side, it hadn't felt that bad at all.

Phoenix Wilder.

My best friend. The boy who had owned a piece of my heart since I was old enough to know what giving your heart to a boy meant.

There was a time I'd thought he would be mine. That we'd survive The Row, *life*, together. But that was the funny thing about dreams… they either came true, or in my case, they went up in flames.

Phoenix Wilder had been everything to me.

Until he wasn't.

Until he'd left me when I'd needed him most.

And now he was like everything else in my life that had existed before my father brought me here.

Gone.

"Harleigh," Sabrina's usual harsh greeting made me bristle, but I swallowed the urge to bite back at her as I joined her in the kitchen.

I'd tried it once, in the early days of being here, and she'd almost cracked enamel, gritting her teeth at me like a caged animal.

If there was one thing Sabrina Delacorte-Rowe did not tolerate, it was a lack of respect.

If you asked me, she needed to remove the giant stick from up her ass. But when you had more money than sense, it gave you license to treat people like objects apparently. Although I was pretty sure she treated most of her expensive vases and favorite sculptures far more delicately than she did her own children.

"Good morning," I said flatly.

"Were you out on the roof terrace again last night?"

"I didn't know it was a problem with me going up there."

"It isn't. But you really should tidy up after yourself."

"I didn't—"

"Harleigh." She let out an indignant sigh, scowling at me. "You need to try to fit in here. I know things haven't been... easy, but you are a part of this family now and I expect you to cooperate."

Cooperate.

I detested that word.

A word the staff at Albany Hills loved to band around.

We need you to cooperate, Harleigh.

Do you feel like cooperating today, Miss Maguire?

You know, Harleigh, this would go an awful lot easier if you just cooperated.

I shook off *those* memories: the voices, the intrusive dark thoughts, and centered myself with a therapeutic breath. Inhale slow and deep through my nose, hold, and exhale slowly through my mouth.

In through the nose, out through the mouth.

In through the nose, out through the—

"Harleigh?" Sabrina clicked her fingers and I blinked.

"S-sorry, I'm a little tired." I yawned for effect.

"So... will you?" She glowered at me.

"Will I what?"

"Cooperate. Will you try to fit in here and cooperate, Harleigh? Really," she muttered, "it's like talking to a brick wall."

Brick wall. Nice.

Although she had a point. But I couldn't help it.

Sabrina wasn't interested in my diagnosis. In her eyes, it was a cry for attention.

I could see myself, staring at her, gawking. Wondering what made her so... so cold. Was it something that happened in her past? Were her parents as absent as mine had been? Did she grow up desperate for attention? Craving affection? Did she—

"Harleigh." She slammed her hand down on the counter, making the fruit in the crystal bowl clatter.

Flinching, I forced out, "Cooperate, right. Got it." I ran a hand through my lifeless brown hair.

Her lips pursed, but Max's arrival saved me from yet another one of his mom's tirades. "Mom," he said, turning his attention to me. "Weirdo."

He made a beeline for the refrigerator, and I flipped him off behind Sabrina's back.

"Maximilian, I hope you're going to refrain from using the pool as your own personal hangout today."

"I had three friends over, Mom. Three. You need to relax a little."

"Yes, well." She cleared her throat as if the idea was too ridiculous to comprehend. "You left quite the mess. Mrs. Beaker was out there for hours cleaning up after you."

"I'm sixteen, Mom. A kid, remember. It's what we do." He shot me a knowing smirk, and I scowled back.

'Weirdo,' Max mouthed.

'Douchebag,' I countered.

Sabrina's head whipped around to me, her perfectly

made up face barely cracking. "Did you say something, Harleigh?"

"Who me? Nope." I grabbed a banana from the fruit bowl. "I'll pass on breakfast. If anyone needs me, I'll be on the roof."

"Do us all a favor and jump," Max called after me.

"Bite me." I flipped him off over my shoulder, only part hoping Sabrina wasn't watching.

Her silence suggested she wasn't.

By the time I reached the roof terrace, exhaustion had settled heavy in my bones. Verbal sparring with Sabrina and Max usually did that to me. But no one would bother me up here.

I sat in the swinging egg chair and inhaled a deep, calming breath. It was one of the first things I'd learned in therapy. To breathe. To ground myself in the moment. To feel the steady beat of my heart as I inhaled and exhaled. Because if my heart was still beating, if I was still breathing, I was still here. Alive.

And fighting.

The fingers of my left hand ran over the wrist of my right. Circular soothing motions, feeling the jagged scar there. The permanent reminder. My 'battle scar' as Celeste liked to call it. But it didn't feel like a trophy. Not to me.

A dark cloud swarmed into my head, blotting out the slither of light. *Breathe,* I silently demanded. *Breathe, Harleigh.* I sucked in a sharp breath, too fast, too greedy, and almost choked on the air caught in my throat.

Dropping my head back against the cushion lining the

rattan egg, I closed my eyes. This didn't feel much like living. I hated it here, hated it with every fiber of my being. Celeste and this roof terrace were the only good things about living in this house. If it wasn't for her, I wouldn't be here.

I wouldn't be trying to keep a promise I should never have made.

Chapter Two

Nix

"HEY BABY." Cherri ran her chipped pink nails up my chest and fisted my t-shirt. "I missed you last night." She pouted, flashing me puppy dog eyes. But they barely touched the ice around my heart.

Cherri was a means to an end. An itch I liked to scratch sometimes. Nothing more. But from the longing in her eyes, it was becoming increasingly fucking obvious she hadn't got the memo.

"Yo, Cherri," my best friend Zane called. Cherri glanced over her shoulder at him, arching a thin brow. "How about letting my boy breathe, yeah?"

"How about you go fuck yourself, Zane?"

"Ouch, she has claws."

"She bites too." Cherri snapped her teeth together, and I smothered a laugh. She was something else.

But Zane had a point.

She was growing clingy. Trying to put her claim on me. But I wasn't looking to go steady. With her or anyone else.

Girls were a distraction. A fucking headache I didn't want or need.

"Back up, Cher," I said, nudging her off me. "I've got shit to do."

"Come on, Nix, don't be like that. I came tonight for you." There was that pout again.

Jesus, she sure knew how to lay it on thick.

"Go find another dick to bounce on tonight, yeah?"

Anger flared in her overdone smoky eyes. I never understood why girls felt the need to smear that shit all over their faces so much.

"You bastard," she fumed. "I thought we were—"

"Run along, Cher." Zane could barely contain his laughter. Motherfucker was colder than me.

She stormed off, shouldering the other girls circling us out of her way.

"No pussy is worth all that aggro," Zane said, draining his beer. He threw it in the trash can and grabbed another from the cooler.

"I thought she knew the deal."

He gave me a pointed look. "They all say that, Nix. Until they catch feelings and think they can tame you into more, or even worse, trap you."

"Where's Kye?" I asked, changing the subject.

"Some drama with Chloe."

"Again?"

Kye Carter was the other third to our trio, and Chloe was his sister. He sure had his hands full with her. The two of them fought like cat and dog. But she was his family. His blood. And sometimes, when you grew up in a place like The Row, it was all you had.

Not that I knew a damn thing about that. My family was Zane and Kye. My brothers not by blood but choice. We'd had each other's back since we were in diapers. They were my guys, my ride or die. They were the only two people in the world I could depend on.

"You've got that look again," he said, kicking my boot.

I flipped him off, running my eyes over the party. Saturday night down at the reservoir was always the same: full of kids from The Row looking to cut loose and forget their shitty existences. Drugs, alcohol, sex... it was a fucking free-for-all down here, in a place long forgotten by the rest of Darling Hill.

"Yo, assholes."

The sound of Kye's voice loosened something inside of me.

"Everything good with Clo?" I asked.

"As good as it can be. She drives me in-fucking-sane. I wouldn't be surprised if she turns up later, drunk off her ass. What'd I miss?"

"Cherri tried to lock Nix down for the night."

"She's not someone you want to mess with, Wilder." Kye lifted a brow. "That girl is a different breed."

"Relax. I can handle the likes of Cherri."

"If you say so, man." He chuckled, grabbing a beer. "So, school Monday. You ready?"

"Ready as I'll ever be."

"Seniors." Kye whistled between his teeth as he

uncapped his beer. "Part of me didn't think we'd ever make it here."

"Yeah." I stared off into the distance.

The final year of high school. When you attended a school like Darling Hill High, that was an achievement in itself. By senior year, half the class was usually knocked up, hooked on meth, or too hungover to show up for class.

"Did you call Coach back?"

"Nah. Do I look like the type of guy who goes to college on a full ride?"

"Come on, Nix. You're good enough, you got to know that. You could go all the way, and—"

"Leave it, Carter. I came here to drown my sorrows, not fucking analyze the shit out of them."

"And I came here to get laid." He clapped me on the shoulder. "So I'll be seeing you two later."

"Horndog," Zane grumbled, watching as Kye slipped into the crowd with ease.

He was different to me and Zane. Lighter. More approachable. Like a chameleon, he could adapt to his surroundings and make himself blend in. Sometimes I envied him; his ability to walk into a room and have people gravitate to him. But not because they wanted something from him... because they wanted to be around him.

I'd long forgotten what it felt like to have people genuinely interested in me. They were interested in my game stats, or my dick, or the fact I could hook them up with a keg or smoke.

Wilder was a name that meant something in The Row,

and ninety-nine percent of the people I knew wanted to exploit that.

"Senior year, Nix." Zane let out a heavy sigh, scrubbing his jaw. "That's some fucked up shit right there. We're at the top of the food chain now." A feral grin tugged at his mouth.

But I didn't share his enthusiasm. Because the problem with being at the top—it was a fucking long way down.

And the fall was inevitable.

"After last year's success with the Hawks, you know Coach is gonna be riding you hard this season."

"I'm ready."

"And if the call does come for college?"

I snorted. "Seriously, drop that fucking shit." Guys like me didn't get out of a place like The Row.

"It could happen, Nix. Coach said Albany U were interested."

I accepted the blunt off Zane, and took a deep hit, letting the smoke roll through my lungs. His premium weed was about the only thing that calmed me down these days. Until school was back and I could take out my aggression on the field.

Summer practice had barely taken the edge off. I needed to be in the gym daily, running drills, and burning off some of the pent-up energy inside me. I needed the distraction. The tether to something real.

"Yeah, well, I'm not," I grumbled, taking another hit before handing it back to Zane. I didn't want to talk about senior year, about what came after we graduated. Not tonight. Not ever.

I had enough to deal with.

"How're things at home?" he asked, and I shot him a hard look. "Yeah, yeah. You don't want to talk about it. But last time he—"

"Drop it."

"We're worried, bro."

"I can handle it."

"That's what we're worried about."

"Yeah, well quit it," I grumbled.

"Come on, Nix, it's—"

"FIGHT!" someone yelled, and the air shifted as kids rushed toward the commotion.

But we stayed put. It wasn't anything we hadn't seen a hundred times already.

"You know DA will be gunning for blood this season," Kye said, referring to the private school on the other side of town. We had a long-standing rivalry with their football team, the Devils.

Last season, we'd kicked their asses on and off the field. Rumor was Marc Denby was their captain this year and there was no love lost between the two of us.

"He can bring it." I shrugged, staring toward the tree line. Beyond it lay Old Darling Hill.

One town separated by the reservoir and a mass of trees. Although they might as well have been two separate continents for the differences between them.

Old Darling Hill was rich. Filthy fucking rich. A

neighborhood of gated houses and perfectly tended lawns. Huge fucking estates with acres of land and housekeepers. Their kids attended Darling Academy and only ever wandered over to our side of town when they were looking for a fight or to live on the wild side.

They hated us and we fucking loathed them. After the fights and revenge pranks, it was a surprise that the school board hadn't already forced our teams into different divisions. We knew Coach Farringdon had repeatedly petitioned for it over the years.

"Shit," Kye appeared, a murderous expression on his face. "Why can't she ever fucking listen?" He stormed off toward Chloe who was weaving through the crowd.

"I'm so fucking relieved I don't have to deal with that," Zane said.

The two of them started arguing, Chloe's hands waving wildly in front of her while Kye glowered.

"Yep. Rather him than me." But as I said the words, an unwanted feeling rose inside me.

I didn't know what it was like to have a brother or sister to protect and watch over. But there had been a girl once.

My best friend.

Ex-best friend now.

Harleigh Wren Maguire.

Jesus. I didn't let myself think about her often. Didn't let myself think about her at all.

She was gone. Had been for a while.

And she wasn't ever coming back.

But it didn't stop me from dreaming, imagining what it

would be like to see her again. To stare down into her bewitching green eyes.

Nine months had passed since I saw her last.

Nine fucking months.

Some days, I didn't know how I'd survived without her. But I was a fighter. A survivor. I didn't need Harleigh or Cherri or anyone else except my best friends and my plans to make it through senior year.

"Yo, Nix, where'd you go just now?" Zane asked.

"Nowhere."

"Don't do it to yourself, man. It isn't worth it."

I didn't need to tell him what I'd been thinking because he knew.

He always fucking knew.

"Yeah, I know." I sighed, running a hand over my head and down the back of my neck. "Sometimes, it hits me."

Even after nine fucking months, it didn't hurt any less.

"Are you going to intervene in that, or should I?" Zane tipped his head toward Kye and an irate Chloe.

Muttering a curse under my breath, I headed in their direction. "Clo," I said.

"Oh, hey, Nix. Can we—"

"No, Chloe." Kye leveled her with a death stare. "I said let me handle it."

"Handle what?"

"Nothing, man. Come on, let's get another drink and chill. It's not important."

"He'd want to know, asshole."

"Chloe Mirabelle Carter, I swear to God—"

"Want to know what?" My brows pinched as I glanced between them. "What aren't you telling me?"

"He deserves to know." Pity glinted in Chloe's eyes.

My heart kicked up a gear, crashing against my rib cage, and I knew... fucking knew whatever she was about to say would change everything.

I hadn't realized how much five little words would rock me to the core until I heard them.

"She's back, Nix. Harleigh's back."

Harleigh

THE BLUE AND gray plaid skirt barely kissed my thighs.

"Are you sure this is standard school issue?" I asked Celeste.

"Right? I complained to Principal Diego twice last year. It's so misogynistic to expect us to wear these miniskirts while the guys get to walk around in slacks. Hello," she sang. "So much for equal rights."

"I think I'm going to put a pair of shorts on underneath." I went to my dresser and pulled out some plain black bootie shorts.

"I'm not sure Principal D will like that."

"Principal D can kiss my ass. Pun intended."

Celeste snorted. "Who are you and what have you done with the Harleigh I know and love?"

I smiled, barely meeting her eyes. If she didn't look too closely maybe she wouldn't see that this was a front. Smile. Laugh. Throw out a sassy comment or two. Give off the impression that I wasn't on the verge of puking my breakfast up over my pristine new uniform.

The skirt was too short, the blouse too form fitting, and the knee-high socks were... Well, I didn't have words to describe the navy-blue socks with gray trim. If Principal Diego had set out to make the female pupils of DA look like porn stars dressed up as high school teenagers, he'd succeeded.

The whole thing bordered on indecent.

But as I followed Celeste downstairs, none of the adults —my father, Sabrina, or Mrs. Beaker, the housekeeper— batted an eye.

"My, my," Michael said, folding his morning newspaper and locking eyes with me. "Now there's a sight I thought I'd never see." He winced at his choice of words, but I didn't let him see my own surprise. "Sorry, that was—"

"It's fine. We should probably go," I said, not wanting to drag things out any longer than necessary. "We don't want to be late."

"Celeste, watch out for Harleigh please."

"I will, Dad."

Dad.

I bristled.

"Aren't you waiting for Max?" Sabrina asked.

"Nope. He can ride with the Vaughns next door."

"Celeste, you know—"

"Bye, Mom. See you later. 'Come on,'" Celeste mouthed at me, and we took off down the hall. She grabbed the keys off the sideboard, and we slipped outside.

"We can wait for Max," I said.

"Are you kidding? It's your first morning. There's no way in hell I'm letting him ride with us."

"Thank you."

She smirked, yanking open the door to her car. "Come on, let's go."

I climbed inside, smoothing out the hem of my skirt, or lack thereof. There had been no uniform at Darling Hill High so this was new. Although, I figured it was a damn sight better than having to play the designer label game with my classmates.

At least in a uniform, I would blend in. With any luck, I would blend in so well I quickly became invisible.

"Are you nervous?" Celeste asked as she turned on the ignition and started backing out of the driveway.

It blew my mind that her car was worth more than anything I'd ever owned or lived in. It had been a seventeenth birthday present a few weeks ago. I didn't know much about cars, but from the sleek lines and leather trim I could tell it was expensive, so I'd googled it.

The custom Range Rover Evoque had cost a cool fifty thousand dollars.

Fifty. Thousand. Freaking. Dollars.

But it was a drop in the ocean for people like my father and Sabrina. During my time in Albany Hills, I'd learned a lot about my new family. Michael Rowe, only son to Thomas and Geraldine Rowe, was the CEO of Rowe Real Estate, a company dating back to the early nineteen hundreds. His grandfather and great-grandfather practically built Darling

Hill and the surrounding townships. The Delacortes were as equally wealthy, Sabrina's father a successful investor. Together, they were a local power couple.

"Harleigh?"

"Huh?"

"I asked if you were nervous."

Nervous didn't really begin to cover how I felt about starting senior year at Darling Academy. I'd grown up despising the kids across the reservoir. It wasn't a silly little rivalry between Darling Hill High and Darling Academy, it was a deep-seated hatred. A history steeped in inequality, injustice, and prejudice.

The families living in The Row were long forgotten by their richer counterparts on the other side of the reservoir. Over the years, Old Darling Hill had flourished. Thrived. It had received constant investment and renewal. While The Row had been left to rot.

And now I was one of *them*. Plucked from my life of poverty and strife and planted into this... this rich man's paradise.

It made my skin fucking crawl, shame constantly coiled around my heart like a barbed wire. I didn't belong here. I wasn't one of them. I wasn't like Celeste or Max or their obscenely rich friends.

I was from The Row. I knew struggle and hardship. I knew what it was like to starve because there was no food in the cupboards, or to sleep cold because your mom couldn't afford to have the hole repaired in the trailer roof.

So no, nervous didn't begin to describe how I felt about being stuffed into this pristine uniform, riding in Celeste's fifty-thousand-dollar car to one of the most expensive private schools in the state.

But I didn't say any of that.

Not a word.

Because although I didn't belong here... I didn't belong in The Row anymore either.

"I'm fine," I said, rubbing my hands down my skirt again. Repetitive actions... the feel of the soft filaments under my fingers grounded me. Held me in the moment.

"If anyone says anything—"

"Celeste, I said I'm fine." I snapped.

She let out a soft sigh. "I'm sorry, I'm only trying to help. I know this can't be easy."

Glancing over at her, I forced my lips into a smile. "No, I'm sorry. You're right, I am a little nervous. But I'll be okay." I'd survived worse. Far worse.

But Darling Academy came into view, like a hidden castle bursting out of the swathe of chestnut oaks.

I'd been here once before. To watch the Darling Hill Hawks football team play the Darling Academy Devils. But the school bus had driven in through the separate entrance for the football stadium, so I hadn't really gotten a good look at the school buildings.

"It's beautiful, right?" Celeste said, and I nodded, still gawking at the scene before me.

Darling Academy was a collection of pristinely restored

old buildings surrounded by oak trees. It reminded me of Harvard or Princeton.

"It's not so bad, I promise. Strip away the Prada handbags, sports cars, and trust funds, and you're left with a high school full of kids just trying to figure out who they are and what they want to do with their lives."

I wasn't so sure about that, but I didn't voice my disagreement. This was an entirely different world to the one I'd grown up in.

Celeste followed the stream of expensive cars into the parking lot and found an empty spot. "Okay." She cut the engine and looked over at me. "Ready?"

No. "Yes."

"You've got a meeting with Principal Diego first, right?" I nodded and she went on, "So I'll walk you to the administrative building and then Mrs. Farrell will show you to your first class."

"Got it." I clenched a fist, willing my hand to stop trembling.

It was just school.

Senior year.

Nine months before I could walk out of here and never look back.

I could do it.

I could.

Besides, what was the worst that could happen?

I had nothing left to lose.

"Ah, Miss Rowe, come in."

The word clanged through me like the slam of a door or the shatter of glass.

Rowe.

Rowe.

Rowe.

He'd called me Miss Rowe.

"It's Maguire. Miss Maguire."

Something akin to surprise flashed over his expression, but he quickly forced his mouth into a smile. "Yes, of course. My apologies, Miss Maguire. Please, take a seat."

Principal Diego was exactly as Celeste had described him. An older man with bushy gray eyebrows, a thick neck, and a leering gaze that seemed to run over my body like a hundred tiny spiders crawling over my skin.

A shudder rolled through me as I pressed my hands over my knees in an attempt to better cover myself.

"How are you feeling? Any first day jitters?"

"I'm fine."

"Good, that's very good." He steepled his fingers and sat a little taller. All the better to see me with, no doubt.

"I understand from your father that you are much better now and ready to embark on your senior year with what I hope will be a smile on your face and a spring in your step."

Was this guy for real?

I suppressed the urge to roll my eyes, instead counting the circles on the geometrical print hanging on the wall behind him. So many circles looped together, in and around each other.

One... two... three... four—

"Miss Maguire?" He cleared his throat, those bushy brows drawn tightly.

"Sorry, yes. Absolutely. Smile and spring."

His voice was a nasally drawl as if he had something stuck in the back of his throat. "Yes, well, I'm sure you're going to fit right in here at DA. We're one of the best schools in the state and our extracurricular program is quite impressive. Do you play any sports, Miss Maguire? Or perhaps you're more of a creative? Art? Drama? Maybe even the debate team? If you're anything like your father, I'm sure you'd be an—"

"I'm not. I mean, I'm sure I'll find something."

"I have no doubts." He smiled but it did little to ease the tangled knot in my stomach.

"If you have any problems settling in, you can come directly to me or visit our guidance teacher Miss Hanley. She's down the hall."

"Got it, thanks." I stood, carefully backing up in a way that didn't give him a front row seat view to my ass.

Maybe I would have to consider running for class president so I could overhaul this god-awful uniform. Now there was a thought.

A slight smile curled at my lips.

My main therapist at Albany Hills would be so proud.

She'd constantly said I needed to 'Look for the positives and find purpose in my life.'

"Thanks, Principal Diego," I said, grabbing the door handle and pulling.

"One last thing, Harleigh. Can I call you Harleigh?" His eyes narrowed. "We pride ourselves here at DA on our impeccable reputation. I expect, given your recent change of... living situation, you'll fit right in."

My cheeks burned, indignation heating my blood. "What is that supposed to mean?" My voice shook as I tightened my grip on the doorknob.

"Consider it a friendly reminder. Now get to class, Miss Maguire. You wouldn't want to be late on your first day." He gave me an easy breezy smile as if he hadn't just threatened me.

Because I wasn't from here.

I didn't belong.

And if Principal Diego knew, so would everyone else here.

Storming out of his office, I slammed the door a little too hard, instantly regretting it when the secretary glowered at me.

"Sorry," I said.

"First day jitters, sweetie?"

Dear God. I was going to need something to get through the day at this rate. Something to take off the edge at least.

But it wasn't like I could ask Celeste who could hook me up.

"Can you point me in the direction of..." I dug out my schedule. "AP English?"

"Of course, dear." She smiled. A genuine warm smile that reminded me a lot of Celeste.

"Would you like directions, or I can show you?"

I was almost eighteen years old. I was pretty certain I could find my way to class. But she was the first person outside of Celeste to put me at ease. And it cut me deep.

With a weak smile, as my façade cracked a little more, I said, "I'd really appreciate it if you could show me."

Nix

THUD.

My body hit the ground hard, the air sucking clean from my lungs. I rolled onto my back and stared up at the crisp morning sky. That fucking hurt.

"Wilder, what the hell was that?" Coach Farringdon boomed across the field.

"You went down like a fucking pussy." Darius Hench, our best defensive lineman snorted.

"Go fuck yourself, asshole," I spat, even though he had a point.

I was off my game.

Hench knew it. Coach knew it. We all fucking knew it.

It was only the first practice of the semester, but the guys were looking to me to lead them all the way to the playoffs this season. They weren't expecting to see their quarterback get his ass handed to him all morning.

But I couldn't get Chloe's words from Saturday night out of my fucking head.

She's back.

Kye leaned down and offered me his hand, pulling me up. "You good?"

"I'll live."

"Listen, about what Clo said. We don't even know—"

"Wilder, get the fuck over here, son. Now."

"Jesus, he's gunning for you today." Kye shot me a concerned look.

"Nah, it's nothing I can't handle." I tore my helmet off and jogged over to Coach and assistant coach Jameson.

"Talk to me, Wilder. What the hell is going on out there?"

"It's taking me a while to find my flow, Coach." The lie sounded convincing enough.

"Flow... it's like watching Bambi drunk off his ass trying to play ball. Your aim is off. You're dragging your ass around the field like you didn't break two state records last year. Talk to me, son."

"It's nothing, Coach. I promise." I scratched the back of my head. "Just need a little time to settle back in."

His eyes narrowed, cool and assessing. Coach Farringdon was a good man. A strong leader who didn't only demand respect from his players, he earned it. He'd been one of the few positive role models I'd had in my life.

But sometimes, I didn't know why he pushed me so hard. This was it for me—high school football. It didn't get any better than this, and I'd made peace with that a long fucking time ago.

"If there's something I need to know—"

"There's not," I snapped, immediately reining myself in. "I swear, Coach, I'm good. It's just first practice back jitters."

"Jitters, my ass." He grumbled, wafting his clipboard at me. "Get back out there and make the damn pass. We're not leaving here until you do. Even if I have to explain to Principal Marston why his football players weren't in second period."

"You got it, Coach." I pulled on my helmet and jogged back toward center field, giving the signal to my teammates. "Run it again."

"Again?" Hench chuckled. "Haven't you hit the ground enough already?"

"Just run the damn play," I barked.

Hench was good. Real fucking good. But he had a big mouth and a tendency to push my buttons. Usually, I let it slide.

Today though, today I was itching for a fight.

The scrimmage line moved into position, and my center got ready to snap me the ball. Inhaling a deep breath, I readied myself. "Hut," I called, and he released the ball. I caught it, pulling tall as I jogged backwards to scan the field for my wide receiver.

Once he was in my line of sight, I wound my arm back and made the throw. The ball sailed on a near perfect trajectory, cutting through the air like a bullet. Kye was tracking it, moving into position ready to—

He leaped off the ground and swiped the ball into the

palm of his hand, cradling it to his body as he took off down the field.

"Better," Coach yelled. "Much better. Good work, Wilder. Hit the showers. I don't want to see your ugly faces again until tomorrow."

"I let you have that one, Wilder." Hench smirked at me as he headed for the locker room, and I shoved down the urge to rush him and wipe that smug fucking smirk right off his face.

"I don't know how he's still standing," Zane said, jogging over to me.

"You know I can't get into any trouble."

Not on the first day, at least.

"Yeah, but an illegal jab or two wouldn't have hurt. He's such a smug bastard. I'd love to wipe—"

"Relax." I slung my arm over Zane's shoulder. "He's one of the best defensive players we have, and I'm man enough to overlook the fact he's a complete asshole."

"Yeah, but come on, Nix. Tell me you didn't imagine grinding his face into the ground every time he sacked you."

"Whose face we grinding?" Kye joined us as we reached the doors to the locker room.

"Didn't you hear? Nix has turned over a new leaf." Zane smirked, and I flipped him off.

"I can always make exceptions for you, Washington."

"Bring it, Wilder." He flashed me a wolfish grin. "I know you're itching for a fight." Tipping his chin in invitation, I glanced around, realizing we'd drawn an audience.

"Not here," I said, refusing to give our teammates a show.

I needed to burn off some steam, but it would have to wait until later.

"You shouldn't have." Chloe dropped down next to Kye and snagged a handful of his fries.

"You know, you could get your own lunch instead of stealing mine."

"Stealing? I was always led to believe that what's yours is mine, brother."

"And what about what's yours?"

"Simple. What's yours is mine, and what's mine is mine." She shrugged, fighting a smile.

"Seriously though, Clo. Do you mind? We're in the middle of something."

"The something of what exactly? Eating lunch? Rating girls on their racks? Uh, let's see, plotting world domination, no, you're not intelligent enough for that. So that leaves... ah, yes... nothing." Chloe grinned.

"She has a point, man." Zane mumbled.

"Don't tell her that. We'll never get rid of her."

"Hello, sitting right here. Seriously, Nix, I don't know how you put up with these two clowns."

"Always a pleasure, Clo."

"Actually, I thought you might want to know I found out something else... about Harleigh, I mean."

I froze, her words lashing my insides. Deep visceral cuts, splaying me open. But I schooled my expression and said with indifference, "I don't."

"Okay." She frowned. "So I'll just go." Her blue eyes bore into mine. Daring me to say it. To give in. But I didn't want to give *her* any power over me.

It was bad enough I'd barely gotten any sleep last night. I didn't need to drag this out any longer than it needed to be.

So Harleigh was back. It wasn't like there was anything left to salvage between us.

She was one of *them* now.

Her life was across the reservoir.

Everything we'd ever shared, everything we'd ever done...

It didn't fucking matter.

"You might as well say what you came to say."

Chloe inclined her head slightly. "She started DA today."

Kye sucked in a sharp breath. "You're sure?"

"How'd you even find out this shit?" Zane voiced my concerns. Well, the concerns I would be having if I could think straight for longer than a second.

My mind was a blur of questions. Things you tell yourself, things you tell each other to try to make sense of something.

Harleigh Wren was back. She was in Old Darling Hill, attending Darling Academy.

I never thought I'd see the day... but I could see it

clearly now. She was right where she was always supposed
to be.

Harleigh had always been too good for The Row. Too
pure and innocent, she had never truly fit in here. It's one
of the reasons I'd taken her under my wing. Because I was
made for a place like The Row. Born from it. Dredged up
from the bottom of its soulless depths and spat out.

Not Harleigh Wren though.

Over the years, when her gaze would linger a little too
long, or the lust in her eyes would burn too brightly, I'd
tried to tell myself that maybe our stories were the same.
That maybe we had a future... together. Outside of Zane
and Kye, she was my best friend. My ride or die. The only
girl in the world I could ever imagine sharing my life with.

But deep down, I knew we were too different.

She would make it out of The Row one day, and she
would fucking flourish. Spread her wings and fly. While I
would stay here and rot.

"Nix?" Zane nudged my shoulder. "You okay?"

"What?" I ran a hand down my face. "Yeah, I'm good."

The three of them watched me with a mix of doubt and
concern in their eyes. When Harleigh had left last year, I
hadn't handled things well.

"Do you want me to see what else I can find out?"
Chloe asked.

"Why?" I snapped, my voice as cold as ice.

"I-I guess I thought... It doesn't matter."

"Seriously, Clo," Kye jumped in, and I inhaled a sharp
breath, forcing air into my lungs. "Do I even want to know

how you know all of this? Don't tell me you're hanging out with someone across—"

"Relax, big brother." She smirked. "I'm not committing an act of treachery. Brianne got a job working at Crêpe-a-licious. It's popular with the DA crew. She heard some kids talking, and well, I asked her to listen out and... I can see that was a bad idea."

Their gazes shifted to me again and I scowled. "What? I said I'm fine."

"Oh, you look fine, man. You look totally fine." Kye snorted.

"Fuck you, asshole." I flipped him off.

"Crazy bitch alert," he muttered under his breath, his eyes going over my shoulder.

"Hey, baby." Cherri's voice made the hairs along my neck stand to attention, and not in a good way. She ran her hands up my arms and leaned down to whisper, "I missed you Saturday night."

"Cherri," I said, twisting slightly, forcing her to back up.

"How was practice?" she asked. "Did you miss me?"

Someone—Kye most likely—snickered. Cherri's head whipped around and she pinned my friends with her trademark death stare. "Why don't you three run along and give me and Nix some alone time. He looks a little stressed out and I can help with that."

"Here, really?" Chloe balked. "Classy, Cher, really damn classy." She turned her attention to me. "Please tell me you're not actually going to let her—"

"Okay, little bit." Kye clapped a hand over her mouth. "Time for you to go." He wrestled her out of her seat and threw me an apologetic glance. I tipped my chin, grateful he was getting Chloe out of here before Cherri's claws came out.

"Chloe Carter needs to learn to keep her mouth shut."

"She's family. Don't even think about it," I said coolly.

Cherri straddled the bench and walked her hands up my thighs. "Still needs to learn to keep her mouth shut. Don't you have places to be?" she asked Zane, not bothering to look at him.

"Actually, I think I'm good here." His eyes narrowed to deadly slits.

"Nix, tell your guard dog to go bark somewhere else."

"Listen Cher." I cleared my throat, really wanting to avoid one of her outbursts in the middle of the school cafeteria.

She slid closer, pressing her finger to my lips. Hooking one arm around my neck, she dipped her head and ran her tongue up the side of my neck, biting down on my ear. "We're good together, Nix. You know we are. I can be what you need." Her hand slipped between our bodies, palming my dick through my jeans. Heat flashed inside of me because, well, I was a guy, and she knew how the fuck to touch me.

Zane grumbled something and said, "I'm outta here."

I went to tell him not to leave me, but Cherri grabbed my face and slammed her lips down on mine.

Kissing the shit out of me.

Chapter Five

Harleigh

"WELL, well, if it isn't Wilder's pet."

My spine stiffened, my skin vibrating with an overwhelming mix of anger and sadness.

Wilder's pet.

Wilder's pet.

Wilder's pet.

The words were caught on loop in my mind.

His pet.

His pet.

Nix's pet.

His—

"Don't be an ass, Marc," Celeste said, shooting me an apologetic smile.

It was lunch. I'd survived three periods, kept my head down, and ignored the constant stares and muffled whispers. But I couldn't ignore this.

Discarding my half-eaten salad, I twisted around and looked up at Marc Denby, one of DA's biggest douchebags.

My stomach curled, every inch of me vibrating, but I tamped it down and focused on the guy looming over me.

"Sorry," I said flatly. "Did you say something?"

"Harleigh," Celeste hissed under her breath, but if she thought I was going to cower just because a bully like Marc Denby was standing before me with a wicked glint in his eye, she was sorely mistaken.

Even if the gnawing pit in my stomach threatened to consume me.

"You heard me, bitch." He snarled. "You think just because daddy decided to pull you out of The Row and—"

"Hey," Celeste's best friend Miles appeared. "What's going on?"

"Marc was welcoming Harleigh to DA," Celeste said in a saccharine tone laced with warning.

"Yeah, relax, Mulligan. I was offering Harleigh a warm welcome. Isn't that right?" His eyes drilled into mine, daring me to speak up and out him. But I wasn't looking to play games—with Marc or anyone else.

"Yeah," I said. "Marc was doing his good deed of the day."

His jaw clenched, and I suppressed a smug smile. Miles sat down at our table, keeping one eye on Marc, who eventually left mumbling something about practice.

"He is such a douchebag," Celeste said.

"What did he really say?" Miles asked.

"It doesn't matter." I glanced back, and sure enough, Marc was glaring right at me. His eyes seemed to say, 'Watch your back, bitch.' But his icy reception didn't surprise me. In fact, there was something oddly comforting about the fact that he remembered who I was and where I came from.

I didn't want special treatment because I was Michael Rowe's daughter. Even if he was one of the largest donors to DA. *Especially* because he was.

What I really wanted was to blend in and be left alone, but I guess that was never going to happen. My arrival at The Rowe-Delacorte household was the hot topic on everyone's lips. After all, it wasn't every day a kid got plucked from The Row and thrown into DA even if she had spent the last six months in a facility on the outskirts of Albany. Of course, *that* wasn't common knowledge. It would be most unbecoming for Michael Rowe's daughter to be an emotionally unstable nut job. So to the outside world, I'd spent the remainder of my junior year in Albany with my grandparents, Thomas and Geraldine, coming to terms with my grief from losing my mother in such dire circumstances.

Michael and Sabrina had spun a web of lies around me so tightly that people believed them. They didn't question why, until recently, I'd never appeared at family functions or why I never left the estate.

It was hardly any surprise that all morning I'd been greeted with a mix of expressions ranging from curiosity to pity to downright hostility.

I hated it. Hated their attention and interest and the way they looked at me like I was a science project they hadn't quite figured out. But if I was going to ever escape from Darling Hill, if I was ever going to forge my own path, I had to stick to the plan.

"So what are we doing later?"

"Sorry, what?" I frowned at Miles.

He reminded me of a puppy with his big brown eyes, mop of dark wild curls, and toothy grin. The Mulligans were good friends with my father and Sabrina so I'd seen Miles at the house a few times since I'd returned. He was always polite and friendly. But I wasn't looking to make friends. My heart was already shattered enough.

"After school, what are we doing? I thought we could head to Samphire and check out their fall menu."

"And Samphire would be..."

Celeste chuckled. "It's a little bistro downtown. It does the most amazing stone-baked pizza. So freaking good."

"Right."

"Sorry." Miles dipped his head. "I forget that you don't—"

"Miles," Celeste said quietly.

"Guys, it's okay. You don't have to do that. We all know I'm not... used to this."

I wasn't sure I was ever going to be used to it. But it was my life now, at least for the next ten months.

"Okay, I have a better idea." Celeste smiled. "What about if we get ice cream from Banana Splits and head down to the park? We might be able to get a table and it's such a nice day."

"I was going to head back to the house and study."

"But you have to come. It's our Monday afternoon ritual. We always do something."

"Celeste is right." Miles nodded. "Besides, you need the tour."

"The tour..." My brow quirked.

"Yeah. I know you haven't ventured out much, so we could give you the behind-the-scenes tour."

"You're not going to take no for an answer, are you?"

"Nope." Miles grinned, stealing a bunch of grapes off Celeste's plate. "I need to head to the library, but I'll see the two of you later."

As he walked away, I murmured, "He's very..."

"Cute?"

"I was going to say peppy."

"Don't be deceived by his good looks and charm. Miles Mulligan rocks a mean left hook."

"Good looks, huh?" I teased. "Sounds an awful lot like someone has a crush."

"On Miles? Please." Celeste scoffed. "He's like a brother to me."

"Hmm."

"Harleigh, I mean it. I don't like Miles like that. Besides, he wasn't gazing longingly at me."

I almost choked on my juice. "Don't be ridiculous. He doesn't even know me."

"Exactly. You have that mysterious new girl appeal."

"Yeah, well, I'm not looking to get involved with anyone. Good looks and charm or not."

"Miles is good people. He's—"

"Celeste, I said leave it." Appetite gone. I stood, threw my bag over my shoulder and grabbed my tray. "I'm going to go to the bathroom before I head to next period. I'll see you later."

Regret washed over her, but the damage was done. I needed to get the hell out of there.

Before I said something I couldn't take back.

No expense had been spared restoring and maintaining Darling Academy's original buildings and that extended to the ground floor girls' bathroom. It reminded me of a nineteen-twenties powder room, the kind you saw in old black and white movies. The hex floor tile and backsplash, and the art deco mirrors seemed far too elegant for a high school bathroom. But when money was no issue, I guess only the best would do for the girls of Old Darling Hill.

I ducked into the end stall and closed the toilet lid so I could sit. I knew it wouldn't be easy being here, pretending, keeping up the façade, but I had underestimated how much it would take out of me. I felt drained. Especially after my run in with Marc.

Avoiding him was impossible, but I hadn't expected him to remember me. Or maybe I'd foolishly hoped he wouldn't.

He and Nix were bitter rivals on the football field, and even worse off it. Marc and his friends had wandered into our territory once and things hadn't ended well for him. It was the same night when everything changed. When my life as I knew it went up in flames.

It was also the same night Nix had kissed me.

Kissed me, then ripped out my heart.

Because that's what the people around me did. They hurt me. Abandoned me.

My father.

My mother.

Nix.

Dropping my head, I inhaled a ragged breath, pressing my palms against the stall partition, needing to touch something to ground me. To remind me that I was in control of my emotions.

They didn't control me.

I wouldn't let them control me. Never again.

Never again.

My father.

My mother.

Nix.

None of that mattered anymore. They had broken me. Each in their own way. And I would never—

The bathroom door opened and laughter filled the room, sending my heart into a tailspin.

Relax, breathe. No one knows you're in here.

"You saw her right, the new girl?" a girl's voice said in a gossipy tone.

"Yeah, she's in my AP English class. Total loner. Sat huddled to herself the entire time, staring at nothing."

"Yeah, rumor has it, she found her mom dead.

Overdose. I mean, that's got to leave emotional scars. No wonder her dad sent her away last year."

"He's probably worried she's going to follow in mommy's footsteps."

"Ange, that is cold. So cold." They chuckled. Three, maybe four of them. Their dulcet tones blended together over the roar of blood in my ears.

I pressed my hands to my head, trying to block it out, block them out. I didn't care about what they were saying.

I didn't.

They were no one to me. Nothing.

Liar. It hurts and you know it.

My heart was a wild beating thing in my chest, making my palms sweat and my head pound. Slipping a hand down my body, I dipped it under my skirt and pinched the fleshy part of my thigh, digging my nails in until the pain blotted out everything else. Hand closed over my mouth, I smothered the yelp as I drew blood. Some of the tension seeped away like a balloon popping, and I sagged against the wall, desperately trying to remain silent.

The girls continued talking, waiting on their friend to pee. But I was too spaced out to focus on the details of their conversation.

When they left, the gentle click of the door behind them echoing through me, I grabbed a wad of tissue paper and wiped the blood away. It wasn't much. Just a few droplets. But they quickly absorbed into a fading smudge on the tissue. Funny how something so small could spread into something so gruesome.

I balled up the paper and shoved it in the small trash can down the side of the toilet. Slipping out of the stall, I washed my hands and inspected my appearance in the mirror. My lashes were damp, the color drained from my cheeks, my eyes shadowed and haunted. I barely recognized the girl staring back at me.

And it was only the first day.

The first of many.

I inhaled a thin breath. I could do this. I didn't have any other choice.

I wasn't my mother. She was weak. She let my father's betrayal destroy her. Her pain, her heartbreak drove to her breaking point and nothing—not even the daughter she'd sacrificed everything for—could save her.

I wouldn't become her.

Even on the hardest days, when it felt like my heart was breaking apart all over again, I wouldn't lose myself to the darkness again. I would live in it, bathe in it, and become one with it.

But I would never succumb to it.

Not again.

That was my promise to myself and Celeste and my therapist at Albany Hills.

People had the power to break you, to hurt and betray you. But in the end, nobody put a gun to your head and told you how to react.

We had to own our response mechanisms and we wouldn't always get it right.

God knows, I hadn't.

But I was still here. I was still fighting every day to do better.

To *be* better.

And I was determined to walk out of here—the town that had chewed me up and spat me out—with my head held high one day.

One day.

Nix

"YOU WANNA HIT BUSTER'S TONIGHT?" Zane asked as we headed out of school for the day.

"No can do."

"No." He frowned. "Why?"

"Got some shit to take care of."

"And by shit you mean..."

"Don't ask questions you won't like the answer to." My expression tightened.

We reached my car and I yanked open the door, climbing inside. Zane followed, giving me a concerned look. "Do I need to tell you this is a bad fucking idea."

"No. But I gotta see it with my own eyes, man."

"Yeah." He released a steady breath, running a hand over his jaw. "I get it; it's Birdie. She's—"

"Nothing, she's nothing," I said, hating how deep the words cut. "But I gotta know."

"Want me to come with? Watch your back? If Denby catches you on their side of the res—"

"I can handle the likes of Marc Denby." I jammed the key in the ignition and fired her up.

Zane snorted. "Still, a little back up wouldn't hurt."

"I appreciate it, Z. I do. But this is something I need to do alone."

"Okay. But if anyone sees you... get the hell out of there, and fast."

"I will." He lifted a brow and I added, "I promise."

"You know, I always thought the two of you..." He trailed off, tension making the air so fucking thick in the car, I couldn't breathe. "How's Jessa?" He changed the subject.

"She's... Jessa. Still convinced she can change him." Him being my piece of shit father. "I've given up trying to tell her to get out while she can."

"You know, you don't have to stay there. You could come stay with me and my gran. She wouldn't mind."

"I know." Mrs. Washington was the best, but I couldn't upend her life like that. Besides, I couldn't leave. Not yet at least. Jessa needed me; she didn't have anyone else.

"You're a good friend, Z. The best. But I've got this, I promise."

He gave me a clipped nod and I started backing out of the parking space. Most kids rode the bus or their bicycle to Darling Hill High. A handful of kids like me were lucky enough to have a hand-me-down ride. She was my pride and joy. The car my grandfather had restored with his own two hands. He'd left it to me in his will when he'd died a few years back, and I'd made good on my promise to look after her.

He was a good man. Nothing like his son. The fact he'd liked me while he was alive, was just another reason for my father to despise me.

It was only a ten-minute drive to The Row but with every mile closer, the pit in my stomach carved wider.

I hated this fucking place.

It was home, sure, and it held some of my best memories. Goofing around with Zane and Kye, causing mischief, hanging out with Harleigh...

Harleigh, fuck. My grip on the wheel tightened until I white-knuckled the damn thing. I was supposed to be over this shit. The guilt. The crippling hopelessness I felt. The simmering rage that burned inside me. Obviously it had only slumbered though, and now she was back, the monster was slowly awakening.

"You good?" Zane asked, and I flicked my eyes to his.

"I'm good."

When you were born in a place like The Row, it became a part of who you were. Part of the very fabric of your soul. The scent of weed in the air, stale liquor and bad decisions, clung to you like a second skin. There was no escaping that shit. No outrunning it. But when you were Joe Wilder's kid, his only flesh and blood, that stain was only amplified. There wasn't a single person in Darling Row who didn't know his name. If they didn't use him for his connections, they feared him because of them. He was a mean sonofabitch who doled out favors and always collected with interest.

"I'll come with you," Zane said.

"Nah, man." I shifted in my seat, feeling like a thousand fucking spiders were crawling under my skin as my trailer came into view. "I'll be in and out."

And if my luck was in, Joe would be out.

The car rolled to a stop, and we climbed out. Zane hesitated and I knew he wanted to say something else. But I beat him to it. "I'll text you later. See what you're up to."

"You'd better." He tsked. "Catch you later."

I tipped my chin and watched him disappear around the side of my trailer. Joe's beat up car wasn't parked out front but that didn't mean much. Sometimes, if he was too wasted to drive home from The Tap, Lyle, the owner, confiscated his keys and made him walk his sorry ass back here.

Trudging up the steps, I grabbed the door handle and yanked it open. "Jessa?"

"In here, sweetie."

The smell of freshly baked cookies hit me like a warm blanket. "Hey," I said, popping my head around the door leading to the open plan living space. Jessa was at the breakfast counter, adding cookies to the cooling rack.

"Where's Joe?" I frowned when she didn't look up at me.

"Out. He... uh..."

"Look at me," I said, clenching my hand into a tight fist

as anger rose inside me like a tidal wave hurtling toward shore.

"It's nothing, Nix. Honestly, it looks worse than it is."

Closing the distance between us, I gently gripped her chin and forced her to look at me. "Shit, Jessa." My stomach dropped at the ugly black-and-blue bruise that mottled her eye socket.

"He didn't mean it." She batted my hand away, giving the cookies her full attention again.

"Jessa, come on. That's some bullshit and—"

"I'm not having this conversation, Phoenix. He's stressed, under a lot of pressure. Sometimes he struggles to control himself."

She didn't need to tell me that. I had enough scars littering my body as evidence of Joe Wilder's regular lack of *self-control*.

"Fine," I snapped, barely reining in the anger vibrating inside me. "But I can't help you if you won't help yourself."

She glanced up and gave me a sad smile. "Sometimes it's harder to walk away than it is to stay, Nix."

"Yeah, I know."

And I fucking hated it.

Jessa wasn't my mom. But she was the closest thing I'd ever had to one. I was supposed to protect her. I had protected her more than once over the years. And it always ended up the same, with us both taking a beating.

We both knew to pick our battles now. When to stand our ground and when to stand down. But when I saw her like this, her fake smile and haunted eyes, I wanted to take the steak knife from the block and gut my father like a fish. It was the least he deserved.

Sometimes, I wondered how much of him I had inside me. How far it would take to push me before I snapped.

Rubbing my temples, I let out a steady breath, forcing some of the rage out of me. "I'm going out."

"Oh, I thought we could—"

Dejection washed over her, and I felt like an asshole. But I didn't trust myself enough to stay.

"I can't be here, not when he... I'm sorry."

"I understand. Please... don't make a thing out of this. He already apologized."

My teeth ground together so hard my jaw hurt. "Yeah, whatever. I'll see you later." I stalked down the hall to my room at the back of the trailer. The same room I'd grown up in. Same peeling gray walls and mildew encrusted window. The view at least was better than some trailers, overlooking the edge of the trees leading down to the reservoir.

I grabbed a black hoodie off the back of my chair and a packet of gum off the desk and got the fuck out of there before Joe returned.

And I did something really fucking stupid.

Maybe even more stupid than what I was about to do.

If The Row made my chest constrict as if I was being crushed under a concrete block, being in Old Darling Hill made my skin feel stretched too tightly over my bones. My car, even though I tried to keep her clean and tidy, stood out against the pristine vehicles lining the streets and parked in big sweeping driveways.

I felt like an exhibit in a zoo as I cruised toward the other side of the neighborhood, the strange glances and pursed lips brushing up against me like shards of glass. People knew I didn't belong here. Whether it was my car, my black hoodie, or inked skin, they took one look at me and branded me an outsider.

It bothered me more than it should, and the reason for that was one I didn't want to admit to myself. One that was looming ahead as I drove toward the gated estate, taking a left turn down a dirt road that ran perpendicular to the fenced perimeter.

I'd been here before. More times than I was proud of. I knew if I drove a little further, there was a hole in the privet that gave me a clear view of the house and the driveway.

The house *she* lived in now.

I parked and ran my hands around my steering wheel, trying to ground myself. The first time I'd come here, I'd almost puked over myself. Not my finest moment but realizing I had lost Birdie to... to *this* was like a punch to the gut. Of course she'd chosen this place over The Row.

What normal person wouldn't?

Except I never ever considered her as normal. She was... Fuck, it didn't matter.

It was done.

We were done.

I needed to get that through my thick skull.

And yet—

Movement caught my eye through the privet and a flashy sports car rolled to a stop outside the house, followed by a Range Rover. A girl climbed out, the daughter if my research was correct. There was a son too. He was sixteen and his sister was a junior. And then there was Birdie.

Harleigh Wren Maguire.

The girl I'd always imagined would be by my side one way or another.

The guy climbing out of the sports car; him, I didn't recognize. There was something about the way his eyes followed Harleigh, tracking her as she walked up to the house. My fingers went white as I clutched the steering wheel tightly as if it were the dude's neck. She looked good despite the fucking awful blue and gray uniform they made the kids at Darling Academy wear. But seeing her like that, dressed up as one of *them*, standing on the steps of the huge fucking mansion, I wanted to roar at the world.

Harleigh wasn't one of them. She wasn't. But my eyes weren't deceiving me. She was standing right fucking there. The same girl I'd always known and yet different somehow. I needed to get closer, to see her eyes. Her expressions. To hear her voice. It wasn't something I *wanted* to do. It was something I *needed* to do. Like breathing air or drinking water.

Without it, I wouldn't be able to rest.

To survive.

I wouldn't be able to move the fuck on.

But I couldn't exactly scale the fence and stroll up to

them and ask for five minutes of her time. If she saw me. If they saw me...

No, I'd have to be patient. Bide my time and wait for the right moment.

They disappeared into the house and disappointment curled in my stomach, my mind running wild with scenarios about the guy. Who was he? How did he know Birdie? How well did he know her?

Anger bubbled in my chest, burning me up on the inside. I'd always thought of her as mine. Even when I hadn't been old enough to realize what that word meant, the connotations it held.

Mine.

Mine. Mine. Mine.

Except she wasn't mine now.

Maybe she never had been.

Nix

"WHAT YA CRYING FOR?" I asked the dark-haired girl with the big green eyes. I'd been heading to my friend Zane's trailer when I saw her, sitting on her porch steps, crying into her hands.

She went to my school, but I hadn't talked to her before now. She was always on her own, doing a whole lot of nothing as she hung outside her double-wide, quiet and uncertain.

Like right now. She rubbed her eyes, blinking up at me. "I-I... nothing." Her throat bobbed as she swallowed a sob.

"Is it your dad? My dad makes me cry sometimes." He was a mean sonofabitch, always grumbling about something.

I knew he blamed me for my mom leaving. Not that it made any sense to me. It wasn't like I wanted her to leave. If anything, we should have been a team, hating on her together. After all, she'd left us both. But no, he preferred to blame me. As if I chased her away.

I would never understand it, or him. But it was what it was. Joe Wilder was as stubborn as they came.

"I don't got a dad," the girl said through her tears. "It's just me and my mom but she's... it doesn't matter." She wiped her face with the back of hand.

"I'm Phoenix but my friends call me Nix."

"I'm Harleigh Wren Maguire. But you can call me Harleigh."

"Wren like the bird?"

She shrugged. "I guess."

"Cool. Did you eat dinner yet? I'm going over to my friend's house and his grandma makes the best hot wings in the whole of The Row."

"Oh, I'm not supposed to leave the porch alone."

The corner of my mouth tipped into a smirk. "Good thing you won't be alone, Wren like the bird. I'll protect you." I puffed out my chest. "What do you say? Wanna come eat hot wings with me and Zane?"

She chewed on the end of her thumb, big eyes darting up and down the dirt road outside her trailer. "I don't know, she might wake up."

"Wake up?"

Her eyes widened with fear. "I-I mean... forget I said anything."

"Why don't we go ask her, your mom, I mean." I stepped closer to her. "I'll tell her I'll look out for you and we can—"

"N-no." She leaped up. "That's okay. She's sick, we

probably shouldn't disturb her. I'll come with you. But only if you're sure."

"Wouldn't have asked if I wasn't. Come on Wren like the bird, I'm starving."

Harleigh Wren was quiet as we walked the short distance to Zane's place. I watched her out of the corner of my eye. She was small for seven. A fragile little thing. Seemed right that she was called Wren, she reminded me of a bird. Tiny and helpless. Me, Zane, and our other friend Kye camped out once in Kye's backyard and spent all night listening to the birds. I liked listening to them, watching them too.

Kye was lucky, his family had one of the modular prefabs. It was on a bigger plot on the other side of The Row. They had a driveway and a small yard. It was one of nicest homes in the whole of the trailer park.

"You okay over there?" I asked her.

She glanced up at me and nodded.

"You don't talk much, do you?"

"Not unless I have something important to say."

"I'll have to remember that." I chuckled, relieved that we'd reached Zane's trailer. "So don't worry about Zane, he... uh—"

"Who's your new friend?" He appeared, eyes narrowed right at Harleigh Wren.

"This is Birdie." The words tumbled out, but it

sounded right. Harleigh Wren like the bird. "She lives in the trailer across from mine."

"Okay." He frowned. "But why is she here?"

"Because she needed a friend, and she looked sad and lonely on her porch."

Birdie sucked in a sharp breath, flicking her eyes to mine as she hovered behind me. Zane's eyes narrowed again. Zane didn't like outsiders; he didn't really like people. Sure, he liked me and Kye and his gran. But Birdie wasn't a threat. She was too small and fragile for that. He only had to look at her, with those big green eyes and the way she stood huddled in on herself to see that she was scared.

And if she was scared, that meant she needed someone to protect her.

"I don't know, Nix. You know my gran doesn't like strangers."

Code for: I don't like strangers.

"Yeah, but I couldn't leave her there, Z. She was so... sad."

"Uh, fine. But remember she's a girl, Nix. And my gran says you can't never trust a girl."

My dad said something similar.

I glanced back at Birdie, and she flashed me a small smile. Surely, she couldn't cause that much trouble.

I decided right there and then. Birdie was sad and lonely, and something told me she didn't have many friends.

But I could be her friend.
I could protect her.

Chapter Seven

Harleigh

"THIS WAS A GOOD CALL," Miles said as we headed toward the bench, ice cream cones in hand.

I'd gone for something classic. A simple mint choc chip. It reminded me of better days. Of being a kid and playing over at Mrs. Feeley's house while my mom slept off another hangover. She always kept a pint of ice cream on hand for the days when I was sad about my mom. Me and Nix would easily get through half the tub before she pried it off us and made us eat something nutritional.

"Harleigh, you going to stand there all afternoon?"

"W-what?" I blinked and realized my mistake.

Miles and Celeste were already seated at the picnic bench. I'd obviously zoned out again.

"Sorry." I slid in next to Miles and he grinned at me.

"Have you been here before?"

"No. It's pretty."

"Wait until the season changes, the leaves turn these

amazing gold and red colors. It's really something." His eyes twinkled with excitement.

"You're really into the trees, huh?" I said, fighting a smile.

"I-I... uh, I guess." He stuttered out, rubbing the back of his neck, and Celeste smothered a laugh.

"Relax, Miles," I added. "I'm teasing you." My lips pulled into a thin smile.

"So how was your first day?"

"I survived. Guess that's the best I could hope for." Taking a bite of ice cream, I tried to ignore their heavy stares. "Nate tried to talk to me in fourth period, it was weird."

"Ugh," Celeste grumbled around her ice cream. "He is such an ass."

"Miller's pretty harmless. But if Marc Denby says anything again, Harleigh, I want you to tell me."

"Why would I do that?"

Miles gave a small shrug. "So I can beat his ass, obviously."

"I don't want you to fight over me," I said.

"It wouldn't be fighting over you," he corrected. "It would be helping you."

"I'm not so sure about that. Marc has it in for me..."

"Because of Phoenix Wilder, right?"

Wow. Miles went straight for the jugular.

I threw him an incredulous look and he rolled his eyes. "Come on, Harleigh. People talk. The kids at school talk.

And no one talks louder than Marc Denby and his guys. Rumor has it you and Wilder were—"

"Don't," I snapped, my appetite recoiling as much as my heart.

"Shit, sorry. It's a sore subject, got it. I won't mention him again."

"Good, don't." I leaned over and dropped the remainder of my ice cream cone into the trash can.

Pulling my legs up onto the bench, I folded my arms around my knees and dropped my chin onto them. Miles was right, it was beautiful out here. The big idyllic oak trees gave it an ethereal atmosphere. The chime of a child's laughter and the gentle whir of the generator from the ice cream stand only added to the ambience.

I focused on the sounds, losing myself in the caw of the birds; the rush of water as kids played at the small water table in the park, shrieking with delight every time it overflowed, soaking their bare little toes. The gentle ripple of the breeze whistling through the trees. That was the sound I loved the most. I could get lost in it, especially when I felt it brush the back of my neck.

Miles and Celeste chatted beside me, giving me space to just be in the moment. Miles probably thought I was meditating or something, but I didn't care. It was hard work always being present. Always staying engaged and active. Sometimes it was like having a parasite living inside me, and at any moment, it could take my body hostage, forcing it with its will. Sometimes, like right now, that meant crashing, retreating into myself to the point of silence. Other times, it meant lashing out. Screaming and yelling and crying and destroying things. Hurting things.

Usually myself.

Although my medication controlled that side of things much more effectively than it did this side.

"Hey, Harleigh." A hand touched my shoulder and I almost jumped out of my skin. "Shit, sorry," Miles said.

"No, it's okay. I was just..."

Celeste gave me a sympathetic smile. She was used to me checking out.

"It's peaceful out here," I added. "I like it."

"That's good, really good." Miles rubbed his jaw. He looked so clean cut and well put together, so different to the boys I was used to. His smile was easy, warm and inviting.

I liked Miles, I did. But he also scared me. The way his eyes lingered a little too long, searching for my secrets. The things I didn't want to share or confess.

"Have you thought about any extracurriculars this year?"

"Who, me?" I glanced at them both.

"Well, yeah. It's senior year. College applications are looming."

"Oh, I haven't really thought about it."

"But it's college? Your future. Surely you have some plans for—"

"Miles." Celeste shook her head again.

"Nope," I said. "I'm taking each day as it comes.

Focusing on the little things. The rest will be there when I'm ready to—"

Raucous laughter filled the air and we glanced over to find a group of kids from school goofing around with a football. One of the guys tackled one of the girls and she shrieked, trying to escape his clutches.

"I really hate those guys," Miles muttered.

"Who are— Oh." Marc Denby appeared, arm slung over a pretty blonde girl I'd seen around at school.

"Come on, let's get out of here before they notice us."

"Yeah, okay." I didn't want to deal with Marc again. Not here. Not with his friends in tow.

We slipped out of the park unnoticed. At least, I thought we had until a trickle of awareness went through me. Discreetly glancing back, I scanned the park, expecting Marc to be watching me. Glaring at me. But he wasn't even looking this way, too busy feeling up the blonde.

My brows furrowed as I did another sweep of the surrounding areas. I'd felt it, a zap of trepidation that went through you when you knew you were being watched.

But there was nothing.

With a frustrated breath, I hurried after Miles and Celeste, shaking off the sensation.

Maybe you really are losing your mind, Harleigh.

After giving me a drive-by tour of the town, Celeste and Miles decided to introduce me to Strike One, Old Darling

Hill's bowling alley. Everything was bigger and better and sleeker than any bowling alley I'd ever seen. It was an old industrial unit that had been renovated and turned into a boutique establishment. Dark brown leather booths serviced each lane, giving an air of privacy. The balls weren't the usual neon colors but muted tones of brown, black, gold, and gray. Even the pins didn't have the usual twin rings of red around their necks but instead a thick gold and black band. A bar made from industrial grating and steel pipes lined the far wall, complete with brown leather stools that looked almost as comfortable as the Chesterfield sofas dotted around the place.

"Neat, huh?" Celeste said as I followed them toward the back of the room. Past the bowling lanes and the couches to an archway that led to another space that housed a number of retro video games, foosball, air hockey, and a couple of pool tables.

"Could be worse," I said with a dismissive shrug.

The truth was, it was kind of cool, and maybe in another life, I would have appreciated its industrial, edgy appeal. But I was exhausted. Emotionally spent from my first day at school, of constantly keeping myself in check.

"Want to play?" Miles asked, flicking his head to the games.

"I'll watch."

"Suit yourself." He handed the other cue to Celeste who grinned.

"Prepare to go down, Mulligan."

"Oh, it's like that, huh?"

The two of them were so freaking cute, but I wasn't sure either of them realized what they had. People often didn't until it was too late.

I shut down that line of thought. Going back there—to The Row, to my life *before*—it did me no good. Dredged up a whole lot of heartache and pain for no damn reason.

Pulling out my cell phone, I opened up a social media app and hovered over the search bar. It was a dangerous game I liked to play sometimes, toeing the line of curiosity and self-torment. I hadn't crossed the line, not yet. But it was growing increasingly hard to resist the urge to have one little peek.

I typed his name.

PHOENIX WILDER

... and quickly deleted it.

Then I typed another name.

ZANE WASHINGTON

Biting my bottom lip, my finger hovered over the search icon. If I did this, if I opened that door, there would be no going back.

It's just once, I tried to tell myself. But it wouldn't be once. I didn't need my therapist to tell me that. It would be twice a week. Once a day. Every time I picked up my cell phone. Until it became part of my routine.

My new obsession.

A dangerous addiction.

Delete.

Delete.

Delete.

I clutched my cell phone and inhaled a ragged breath.

It was only a window into their lives, their world. It wasn't a door. I couldn't walk through it.

"Harleigh, you want a slushie?"

I glanced up at Miles and frowned. "You're done already?" It only felt like I'd sat down five minutes ago.

"Yeah, we've been playing for like twenty minutes. You were busy on your phone."

Twenty minutes?

My stomach dipped.

"Sorry, it was a really interesting... article."

"And here I thought you were reading one of those dirty romance books Celeste thinks I don't know she loves so much." A smirk traced his mouth.

"I-I do not read those types of books." Celeste's cheeks flamed but Miles only shrugged.

"Hey, whatever floats your boat. You know, I caught my gran reading Fifty Shades of Grey once. That was... interesting."

"Oh my God," Celeste breathed, fighting a grin. "That is... wow."

"Anyway, slushies." He clicked his fingers. "Harleigh?"

"I'm good, thanks."

"Water? Soda? They do a mean green tea if that's more your thing."

"I guess I could go for a bottle of water. Thanks."

"Celeste, the usual?"

"Of course," she murmured, unable to look him in the eye. He disappeared and Celeste joined me on the couch.

"You know, I didn't have you down as a smut reader." She scowled at me, and laughter bubbled in my chest. "Relax, I'm joking. People should read whatever they like."

"Hmm. What article were you reading?" One of her brows lifted.

"Touché."

"Sorry, if we ambushed you into coming here."

"It's fine. I think I've gotten too used to being at the house."

"You're safe with us, Harleigh. I hope you know that."

"I do. Where are the restrooms?" I asked, needing to escape the tension swirling around us.

"Back through the main room and down the entrance hall where we came in. They're on the left. I can show you?"

"No, it's okay. I'm sure I can handle it."

I excused myself and backtracked through the building, passing Miles on the way. Finding the women's restroom was easy enough, but the second I stepped back out into the hall, that tingling sensation trickled through me again.

I quickly scanned the hall, but it was empty. Some inner sense pulled me toward the window wall that fronted the building. It overlooked the small parking lot and the road beyond that. Celeste's Range Rover was parked in between two cars probably belonging to the other people bowling.

But it wasn't their car that caught my attention.

Because there, hidden under an overhanging tree was a car that was all too familiar.

Before I could think about the consequences, I rushed over to the door and ripped it open, storming outside. It was *his* car.

He was here.

Nix was here.

I couldn't breathe.

My heart was stuck in my chest, my lungs tightening with every step.

He was here.

He's here.

But when I reached his car, it was empty.

Was this some cruel joke? I reached out to touch it, to run my finger along the hood and make sure it wasn't my mind playing tricks. That I wasn't hallucinating. But the paintwork was cool to the touch, smooth and slick beneath my palm.

Real.

It was real.

Which meant, he was here somewhere. Nix was here.

He was—

"Hello, Birdie."

Two little words.

So soft and innocent.

Yet they hit me like bullets, tearing through skin and muscle, embedding themselves in my soul, shattering something vital.

I turned slowly and fast all at the same time. My eyes landed on him and I breathed, "Nix."

He was here.

Standing in front of me.

Real. Alive. Here.

And I didn't know what the hell to do with that.

Nix

"WHAT ARE YOU DOING HERE?" She sounded the same, yet something was different.

"I... I had to know," I said, stepping forward, my heart beating wildly in my chest.

She instantly retreated, her eyes darting around me, flicking beyond me. Looking for a way out. "You shouldn't be here."

Ouch. That hurt.

It fucking stung.

"After all this time, that's what you say to me?"

She let out a bitter laugh. "What did you expect?"

My brows drew together as I tried to find my balance. Because seeing her, hearing her voice, it did things to me. Dark, dangerous things. She'd always been my kryptonite, but this was different.

We were different.

"So it's true. You're one of them now?"

"Nix." She sighed. A soft, exasperated sound that cut

me down. As if I was an annoyance. Nothing more than dirt under her shoe.

Fuck.

Zane was right. It was a mistake coming here. I should have been content with watching her at the park from a safe distance.

"What are you doing here?" she asked again, fiddling with her sleeve. No, not fiddling with it I realized, but more like stroking it.

"It's a free country, Birdie." I shrugged, my lip curling. "Just because I don't drive a brand-new car or have a fat wallet doesn't mean I can't be here."

"I didn't..." She stopped herself, inhaling a deep breath and whispering something to herself. When she refocused her attention back on me, there was something cold in her gaze. "You should go. I have to get back to my friends." Harleigh moved around me, keeping a wide berth, and headed back toward the building.

"So that's it, huh?" I called after her, frustration bleeding from every word. "That's all you've got to say to me?"

Drawing to a sharp stop, she spun around and narrowed her eyes at me. "Nothing," she said. "I have *nothing* to say to you. Go back to The Row, Nix. And never come back here."

"Fuck that," I snapped. "We aren't done—"

"Harleigh?" The half-sister appeared. "What's going on?"

"N-nothing." Harleigh didn't meet my heavy stare. Instead she grabbed the girl's arm and led her to the door.

"Who was that?" she asked, but Harleigh ignored her and yanked her back inside.

Fuck.

That could have gone better. But I'd fucked up the second I followed them here. I should have stayed in the car, should have listened to the little voice telling me it a was huge fucking mistake. But it wasn't enough. I needed more.

I needed to see her.

No one had batted an eyelid at the hooded guy hanging out, watching the three kids in the back. Harleigh hadn't joined in with her friends. She'd sat alone, engrossed with something on her cell phone.

I'd planned to skip out unnoticed when she disappeared into the restroom. But I couldn't do it, I couldn't walk away.

I hadn't expected her to spot my car, to storm outside and... what? Confront me?

It had hardly been a confrontation. She'd barely said ten words to me. But every single one of them had cut me open.

I needed to go—needed to get the fuck out of here before things really went to shit.

So I got in my car and left.

I met Zane and Kye at Buster's after all. They were busy with the free weights as I blew through the place, heading straight for Bryson, the owner.

"Wilder, didn't expect to see you here tonight. The guys said—"

"I need to get in the ring," I said.

Pushing my body to its limits in the gym wasn't going to cut it. I needed more. I needed it to hurt.

"Come on, Nix. Last time I let you go at it, you almost killed my guy."

"Always did have a flair for the dramatic." I rolled my eyes. "He was fine."

"You shattered his jaw."

"I'd had a bad day." I'd had a lot of those in junior year. "Guys know what they're signing up for when they train here."

Busters wasn't your average gym. It was hardcore. You only got in Bryson's ring if you were comfortable sparring without gloves or head gear.

"I don't know, Nix. I don't need you scaring off—"

"I'll spar with him." Some meathead tipped his head at me. I'd seen him around but didn't know him to talk to, preferring to keep to myself. Outside of Zane and Kye, I didn't have many friends, and I liked it that way.

"You're on," I said, cutting Bryson out of the conversation. He threw his hands up and grumbled, "Fine. But don't expect me to peel you off the canvas when Sy beats your ass."

"This is a bad idea," Zane called over to me as I started to wrap my knuckles.

I ignored him and pulled off my hoodie and t-shirt. Meathead ran a cool, assessing gaze over me, giving a small unimpressed huff as he climbed up into the ring. Asshole would pay for that. For underestimating me.

Not that I really gave a shit.

"Come on, Nix." Kye walked over, keeping his expression casual even if his smile was tight. "Coach will be pissed if you show up at practice tomorrow with a broken rib or two."

"Your confidence in me is astounding." Sarcasm clung to my voice as I flexed my hands testing the wraps. They felt good, tight, but with enough movement.

Grabbing the ropes, I started hoisting myself up, but Kye stopped me with a hand to my shoulder. "What happened?"

"Nothing I didn't already know," I said, shrugging him off, refusing to remember how she'd looked standing there, glaring at me. Spewing those traitorous words at me.

"Don't do this, man. I'm begging you."

"I've got it, don't worry." I hooked the ropes and climbed inside, banging my fists together as I sized up Meathead. He was big. Bigger than most of the guys I fought. But where he was big, I was angrier.

And he was about to feel a whole world of hurt.

"Motherfucker," I grunted, the air *whooshing* from my lungs as he landed another hard jab to my stomach.

That was going to hurt tomorrow. But the pain was a good thing. The pain numbed all the other shit.

Doubled over, I tried to catch my breath, inhaling a ragged breath. It burned, my muscles tired and weary. We'd been at it for a while. Dancing around each other, testing each other's strength and weeding out the weak spots. I'd given Meathead an impressive split lip and he'd returned it with a cut right above my cheek. My eye was already swelling, but I'd ice it later. When this thick-necked asshole ate dust.

"End it, Nix," one of the guys shouted; a couple of the other guys who had stopped training to watch, cheering along.

"What do you think? Ready to call it a night?" I smirked, baiting Meathead. Adrenaline surged through my bloodstream like a drug, making me feel invincible. Making me feel like a motherfucking god. Nothing could touch me here. Not Joe or Jessa or school or Coach...

Or *her*.

Inside these ropes, darkness reigned. I gave over to the beast living inside me, the bitter disappointment and lingering stain of shame.

I wasn't good enough. I never had been and never would be, and that had never been clearer than tonight when I came face to face with the girl who had always held my heart in the palm of her hands.

Harleigh had always made me want to be better, so much better.

Without her, where did that leave me?

The memories came thick and fast. Too fast. I couldn't shut them out, couldn't switch them off and force them back into their little box.

Meathead used my distracted state to his advantage, coming at me like a bull out of a gate. His fists rained down on me. A jab to my jaw, two to my ribs. Someone yelled my name. Yelled at me to pull my head out my fucking ass and focus, but it was too late.

I staggered back against the ropes, the coppery tang of blood pooling in my mouth.

Everything hurt.

Hurt so fucking good.

I gave Meathead a feral grin. "Do it," I spat, spraying blood into the air. "End it."

He grinned back, letting out a dark chuckle as he said, "It would be my pleasure."

Pain exploded along the side of my face as he made the hit that knocked my feet from under me.

Down I went...

Down.

Down.

Down.

Reveling in the pain, the blistering agony radiated through parts of my body. I knew it would pass though. The pain would end, and the numbness would fade.

And in the end, it would hurt far less than my dirty ravaged heart.

"I could kick your fucking ass," Zane grumbled as he and Kye helped me to my car.

There was no fucking way I could drive, so Kye climbed into the driver's seat, leaving Zane to deal with my broken ass.

And I was broken.

Meathead had done a real number on my face and ribs, but I was too high on Vicodin to care.

"I love you, Washington, man. You know that right." I tapped Zane's face, grinning like a fool.

Fuck, those pills Bryson had thrust at me were some good shit. I was flying. Soaring across the motherfucking sky.

"Get the fuck in the car." Zane shoved me inside and pain lanced through me.

"Whew, that is some crazy shit. I feel like I got my ass handed to me by The Hulk."

"You did." Kye added from up front. "What the hell are we going to do with him?"

"I'll take him with me. My gran will clean him up."

"You sure?"

"Yeah, just get us there."

"I can do that."

I opened my jaw, trying to work out the stiffness, but the Vicodin made everything numb.

Zane shook his head at me, running a hand down his serious face.

"You need to lighten up, Washington. I almost had him." Laughter spluttered out of me, a little raspy and wet.

"If you've cracked a rib, so help me fucking God, Nix..."

"It's only bruising." At least, I hoped it was.

"You're a dumb asshole sometimes. After everything, she's still—"

"Don't." Pain—a different kind of pain—shot through me. "Just... don't." I tipped my head back and closed my eyes.

"You can't let this happen again, not now. Not after all this time. It's senior year. We're so fucking close, Nix. So fucking close. Tell me you get that, man? Tell me you won't let—"

My eyes flew open right as my fist shot out, ramming into the back seat.

"She's fucking inside me, Z." Pain and frustration bled from every word. "Buried so fucking deep, I don't know how to cut her out." I reached over and grabbed his arm, despair rippling off me. "You have to help me, man. You have to make it stop."

"We'll figure it out, Nix. I promise."

"You mean that?" My swollen gaze met his and I smiled weakly. "Because it's been one day, and I already feel like I'm losing my fucking mind."

Birdie was back.

She was back, but it wasn't the same.

Nothing was anymore.

But what did I really expect?

They said you didn't really understand what you had until you lost it. Well, I knew firsthand how true that statement was. But no one told you that it was more than just words and heartache.

It was visceral.

A physical alteration inside you.

A hole that over time festered and grew and turned into something ugly and rotten.

It was something that changed you so much that you were never the same again.

Chapter Nine

Harleigh

"HARLEIGH, COME ON, OPEN UP." Celeste banged softly on the door again. Well, as softly as a bang on a door could be.

After I'd all but dragged her into Strike One, I'd demanded her and Miles take me back. She wanted to know what had happened, I hadn't wanted to talk about it.

I still didn't want to talk about it.

I couldn't.

Not without edging closer to that dangerous line.

It made no sense why he was there tonight. Watching me.

Stalking me.

I didn't understand... couldn't organize my thoughts into any kind of order that made sense.

Phoenix was my past. Not my present nor my future. So why the hell was he at the bowling alley earlier? As if he... Knew. Exactly. Where. To. Find. Me.

"Harl—"

L A COTTON

"Come in." I sighed.

She slipped into the room and pressed her back against the door, offering me a weak smile. "I promised myself not to push you, but I couldn't do it. I couldn't go to sleep without knowing you're okay."

"I'm not going to do anything stupid, if that's what you're asking."

Celeste flinched at my cold tone. "Harleigh, that's not..." She released a heavy sigh. "Look, I get it. You're not used to letting people in. And I know Mom and Dad haven't exactly made it easy for you, but I don't care about them. I care about you. You're my sister and I'm here. Whether you want to talk, sit in silence, or binge-watch cheesy horror movies and eat our body weight in candy. I'm here."

"You're a good person, Celeste. One of the best people I know."

"Is that your way of saying you love me too?" A smile tugged at the corner of her mouth.

I patted the bed and shuffled over to give her enough room. Celeste took a run and jump, flopping onto her back and stuffing a pillow behind her head.

"So which one are we doing? A, b, or c?"

"His name is Phoenix Wilder."

"I know who he is, Harleigh."

"You do? But you said—"

She lifted her shoulders in a small shrug. "I wanted you to come to me. I heard what Marc said to you. Everyone knows his beef with Darling Hill High's star quarterback

90

Phoenix Wilder. I've heard some of the stories. I didn't realize you two were... close."

"I'm not really sure there's a word to describe what Phoenix was to me." I ran my hand over one of the shaggy pillows, letting my finger sink into the soft fibers, the texture soothing the wild, erratic beat of my heart.

"You loved him." She didn't ask it as a question but stated it as something definitive.

Inevitable.

That's what I'd always assumed about me and Nix. That we were inevitable. That one day, he would look at me and realize he loved me the way I'd always loved him.

"I did. So much that I didn't ever imagine a time when I didn't love him."

"What happened?"

"He abandoned me. When I needed him most, he... abandoned me."

God, it hurt as much now as it did then. The day my life changed forever.

"I found her you know? My mom. Trina Maguire," I whispered her name as if it was forbidden. In a way, I supposed it was. Something I barely let myself think about. Because remembering that night, letting myself go there... it resurfaced too many feelings, too many memories. Feelings and memories that had almost destroyed me.

"I found her cold and dead in her room and the first person I screamed for was Nix. I think I was still screaming when the police arrived and wrestled me into the back of their cruiser while they wheeled my mom's lifeless body to the ambulance."

"Jesus, Harleigh... I'm sorry. I didn't know. I didn't—"

Of course she didn't know. Michael had made it clear the details of that night were to stay under wraps, even from his own family. I suspected Sabrina knew, but if she did, she'd never tried to talk to me about it.

"It's okay."

It wasn't something I'd ever talked about. Not with my father or Celeste. Definitely not with Max or Sabrina. My therapist had tried to broach the subject more than once, to encourage me to explore my feelings around my mom's ravaging alcohol dependency and her subsequent overdose. But every time I'd tried, it was like a switch inside me flipped and I shut down.

"It doesn't sound okay," Celeste whispered. "No wonder you were..." She trailed off.

"Messed up?" I glanced over at her, smiling.

"It's not funny," she said.

"No, it isn't. But sometimes smiling or laughing is the only way to deal with emotions so intense they paralyze you. Like if I don't smile or laugh or tell myself it's okay, everything will collapse and I'll—" I inhaled deeply, the shuddering breath rolling through me like thunder in the distance.

"What happened with Phoenix?"

"It was last Halloween. We'd been to some stupid party... He took me home and when I found my mom, I texted him right away. But he never replied. When

Michael showed up at the police station, I begged Nix to come and get me. But I never heard from him again."

"That doesn't sound right. Why wouldn't he reply? I mean, you were friends, right?"

"Best friends," I confirmed despite the pain it caused.

"What about his friends? Didn't you call them?"

"I did, at first. But when no one replied, I stopped... and well, you know what happened after that."

I'd been a mess.

As the days went by and I didn't hear from Nix or the guys, I withdrew until I wouldn't leave my room. I wasn't eating. I wasn't interacting with anyone in the house. My grief was a living, breathing thing inside of me, except I wasn't only grieving the death of my mom, I was grieving the death of my friendship with Nix.

Celeste was right. It didn't make sense. None of it did. But I'd been too numb and anguished to step back and be rational about things at the time. And the more time passed, the more my heart withered and died in my chest. Because Nix didn't come for me. The only person I'd ever trusted, left me. Whatever his reasons were, he'd abandoned me when I'd needed him most, and it was unforgivable.

It's why seeing him earlier had been such a shock.

Nine months.

Almost forty weeks had passed since I'd last seen him.

It might as well have been a lifetime.

I wasn't the same person anymore. And I very much doubted he was.

So why had he come?

Five little words that had haunted me since we left Strike One and I'd desperately searched the parking lot for any signs of his car.

"There must be more to it," Celeste said. "He wouldn't abandon you, only to turn up all these months later and—"

"It doesn't matter."

"Of course it does. You're in love with him—"

"Was. I *was* in love with him."

Now I wasn't sure I had the capacity to love. My heart was too damaged. Even though they had brought it back to life, it was still broken. And I wasn't sure it would ever fully heal.

Some cracks were simply too deep to repair.

My mom and Nix were the only two people I'd had in the world, and I'd lost them on the same night. You didn't walk away from that kind of trauma unscathed. No, it stayed with you. Intrinsically altered you.

"Yeah, but those feelings don't just go away, Harleigh," Celeste said, peeking over at me. "You know love and hate are two sides of the same coin. You can hate what he did to you but still love—"

"I don't."

"Okay, but—"

"It's late and I'm getting tired," I said, refusing to look at her. If she was going to push the Nix thing, I couldn't be around her.

"Sorry. I'm prying and it's not my place."

"No, it isn't."

With a heavy sigh, Celeste climbed off the bed. "I

didn't mean to upset you. But I think Nix showing up tonight must mean something, and I think you'll regret it one day if you don't try to find out what."

"You know. You're pretty annoying sometimes," I said.

"I can live with that so long as I know you're not in here hurting yourself."

"Celeste, I'm not—"

"Just promise me you won't let this derail your progress."

"I won't, *Dr. Rowe.*"

She poked her tongue out at me. "Get some sleep. Good night, Harleigh."

"Night, Celeste." She slipped out of my room, the sudden silence deafening.

I pulled the pillow onto my lap and buried my fingers in the soft fibers, scratching back and forth.

Back and forth.

Nix was out there somewhere.

Not right outside or anything. But he was out there, on the other side of the reservoir. In The Row.

Seeing him had ripped away every defense I had built the last few months. He was one of my biggest triggers. His betrayal, at least. I'd mourned losing him. Grieved him right alongside losing my mom. But now he was back. Resurrected from my nightmares.

And all that was left was my bleeding heart and weary soul.

"What the hell happened to you?" Max gawked as I padded into the kitchen.

I ignored him, barely awake after a fitful night of broken sleep and haunted dreams. Every time I closed my eyes, I saw him.

Phoenix.

Sometimes he was standing there, arms open, wearing an easy smile. I would run, throwing myself at him and taking the comfort he was offering. Soaking it up. Basking in it. But other times, he was laughing. Dark, wicked laughter that made my stomach clench and shivers run down my spine. That Nix chased me. Hunted me through endless shadowy surroundings until he caught me and choked the life right out of me.

To say I'd woken exhausted was an understatement.

"Hey, weirdo, I'm talking to you," Max sneered.

I met his eyes and quirked a brow. "Sorry, all I heard was an annoying squeak."

"Fucking crazy bitch," he mumbled into his cereal.

Before I could respond, Celeste appeared. "Morning." She headed straight for the refrigerator, grabbing a carton of juice. "You want?"

"No thanks," I said, hovering by the coffee maker.

"Rough night?"

"You could say that."

Max stood abruptly, the stool scraping across The

Rowe-Delacorte's expensive parquet flooring. "I'm outta here."

"Where are you going this early?" Celeste asked.

"Like I'd tell you."

"Max, come on. Mom won't—"

"Mom can eat shit." He stalked out of the room, taking the air with him.

Celeste let out a heavy sigh. "He's so angry. I don't know how to reach him anymore."

"He's an entitled brat." Her eyes flashed to mine, and I shrugged. "What? It's true. Your mom demands respect and decorum, but it isn't a substitute for actual parenting. He has too much money and freedom and he thinks no one cares."

"I care."

"Yeah, but you're his sister. It's not the same."

"You know, sometimes I think you were sent to us on purpose."

I bristled, my fingers curling around the edge of the counter.

"I don't mean..." She let out a soft sigh. "That came out wrong. I just meant that you have a unique perspective because you didn't grow up here."

"It's fine," I said.

It wasn't, but whatever.

For as much as Celeste tried to pull me into their lives, their family, the truth was, I would never fit. Because you couldn't fit somewhere where there had never been space for you.

Michael Rowe had gotten my mother pregnant—a young woman seven years his junior—and made her choose. Her life in Old Darling Hill or the baby he would never recognize as his own.

She chose me.

And in the end, it killed her.

Nix

"WILDER, MY OFFICE. NOW," Coach boomed down the hallway.

"I told you to stay at home today," Kye murmured.

"Yeah, well, couldn't fucking do that." I gritted my teeth trying to swallow the pain radiating through me. "I'll figure it out."

"Don't think Coach will fall for the old 'I ran into a door' story. You look like shit." Kye reached for me, and I swatted his hand away.

"Fuck off. I'll see you later."

"Yeah," he called after me. "If Coach doesn't kill you first."

People gave me a wide berth as I shuffled down the hall. Kye had a point. I probably should have stayed at home, or in Zane's trailer at least. But his gran would have fussed over me like a child, and for as much as I loved the old woman, she was sick. She didn't need my sorry ass making her life any harder than it already was. And going back home wasn't an option.

So here I was, at school, trying my best not to seek out Paul Odell, school's resident dealer, and beg him to give me some hardcore pills to make the pain go away.

By the time I got to Coach's office, I was in agony. My ribs were an ugly patchwork of bruises, and my face was a gruesome mess despite Mrs. Washington's attempts at cleaning me up last night.

"Sit," Coach Farringdon said the second I entered. He leaned back in his chair, crossing one leg over the other and resting his hand on his ankle. "Is the other kid alive? Or do I need to prepare to bail my star player out of jail because he couldn't keep himself in fucking check?"

"It's not what you think, Coach." My leg jostled with nervous energy. "I wasn't fighting. I mean, I was... at the gym."

"At the gym? You're telling me that piece of shit Bryson let you step in the ring after I explicitly—"

"I messed up."

"Damn right you did, son. Damn fucking right." He blew out a thin breath. "Look, Nix, let me level with you. You're my best player. You have what it takes to use your talent and get the fuck out of this place. But you have to want it, son. You have to *believe* it. After last season, I'd hoped this year would be different. I'd hoped—"

"I saw her."

The words pierced the air like the crack of gunfire.

"You saw... Harleigh Wren?"

I nodded. "She's back. At her father's house, I mean. She started DA yesterday."

"I see." He leaned forward, steepling his fingers and looked me dead in the eye. "I know you don't want to hear this, Phoenix. But maybe it's for the best. She got out of The Row. She made it out and maybe she's where she belongs now."

Did he think I didn't know that?

Did he think I didn't spend weeks, months even, obsessing over the fact she was gone, swinging between hating her for leaving me and being so fucking relieved that she got out?

In those early days, when she'd first left, it had messed with my head. I couldn't think. Couldn't focus or get my head in the game. I'd gotten into more fights last season than my entire high school football career.

All because of her.

She left and it was like she took some vital part of me with her leaving a gaping hole that had only festered over time.

I clenched my fist against my thigh, trying to rein myself in. Breathing in long and slow, forcing my heart to calm the fuck down.

"Nix," Coach sighed. "This life is hard, kid. The Row, it's brutal. If you're lucky it'll chew you up and spit you out with enough wits to survive. But if you're really lucky, if you have the talent you have... you can escape this place, son. Put it behind you and never look back.

"Now this is what's going to happen." He opened his

hands and pressed his palms flat against the desk. "You're going to head straight to medical and get checked out. You better pray to God nothing is broken. Assuming it isn't, you're going to sit out of practice for the rest of the week—"

"Coach, I—"

"Shut it. When and only when I say you can start practicing again will it happen. Until then, stay out of trouble. Think about what you want, Nix. And I mean really think long and hard about it, and put Miss Maguire out of your goddamn head, son. She got out. You could too one day. But it won't happen unless you show up, do the work, and stop being so goddamn reckless."

"Yes, sir," I muttered, in too much pain to argue.

"What was that?" He cocked his head, a faint smile tracing his mouth. "I didn't hear you."

"Yes, sir."

"Better. Now get out of my sight and go straight to medical. Tell them I sent you. I want to know exactly what we're dealing with."

Feeling like a scolded child, I shuffled out of there, and headed for medical.

Praying to a God I didn't believe in that nothing was broken.

"So, what's the verdict?" Zane asked me the second he sat down at our usual table in the cafeteria.

"Nothing's broken. Doc says the bruising will take a

little time to heal, but ice should help bring down the swelling."

"And Coach...?" He cocked a brow.

"He's pissed. Wants me to sit out of practice for the rest of the week. He's worried about my state of mind." I air quoted the words.

"We're worried about your state of mind," he snorted, and I flipped him off with a half-hearted middle finger.

"I saw her, it's done."

"You're more deluded than I thought. You two will never be done, Nix. You're like night and day or some shit. One can't exist without the other."

"You're wrong," I said, sounding a lot more confident than I felt.

Because that's how it had always felt to me too; like we were two opposite halves of the same coin. The same fucking soul.

Birdie had been the quiet to my loud. The calm to my storm. The voice of reason when I was reckless, a flicker of light in the endless dark.

But things had always been more complicated than that between us.

"Oh my God, Nix, baby. What happened?" Cherri arrived at our table with an over-dramatic gasp.

"Relax, Cher, your boy will live."

I kicked Zane under the table. The last thing I needed was Cherri misreading his tone.

"Jesus." She leaned down and gently cupped my face. "Does it hurt?"

"What do you think?" I said, wincing as she smoothed her thumb over my jaw.

"Need me to kiss it better?"

"I bet he has something you can kiss."

I shot Zane a hard look and he chuckled. "I'm out of here. Mrs. Kyrie wants to discuss my future, like we don't know my options are pretty fucking limited. Text me later."

"Yeah, thanks a lot, *friend*."

His dark laughter followed him out of the cafeteria.

Asshole.

Cherri continued checking over my injuries as if she was a qualified nurse. "You need me to—" She reached for me, but I snagged her wrist.

"Just leave it, yeah, Cher. I'm not in the mood."

"You're never in the mood lately, Nix. Is it because of her? You know, I've heard the rumors. We all have."

"What rumors?"

"That she started DA. Prancing around with her new rich friends, acting like she didn't grow up in The Row like the rest of us. I heard she's been seen with Miles Mulligan. You know his father is the town planner, right? I bet her daddy is hoping they'll get together and have little rich babies and Trevor Mulligan will have no choice but to give Michael Rowe whatever he wants because they'll be fam—"

"Cher." I slammed my fist down on the table. "Stop. Talking."

"You're so miserable lately." She yanked her hand free of mine and trailed it up my neck, leaning in close until our breaths mingled. "But I can help with that. You just have to—"

"Mr. Wilder, Miss Jardin, keep it PG-13 in my cafeteria please," Principal Marston boomed across the room.

Cherri rolled her eyes, sliding off my lap.

"Better, thank you. This is a high school cafeteria, people, not a club."

"Don't we know it," she murmured. "How about I come over tonight and nurse you better?" Hunger blazed in her eyes as she let her finger hover over the waistband of my sweats.

"I can't."

"So come to mine? We can—"

"I can't."

"Can't?" Her brows narrowed, and her expression turned icy. "Or you don't want to?"

"Don't start with this shit, Cher. You know the deal. We're not—"

"Not what? Together? So that's why I was the only girl you were fucking all summer?" She sneered.

"You said it yourself..."

"You're a bastard, Phoenix Wilder. I'm yours. I've been here. I've been the one you've come to for the past six months whenever you need..." She steeled herself. "Do you know what, forget it. This summer I thought that maybe you were ready to move on. But it'll always be her, won't it?"

She stared at me expectantly, as if I had answers to give her.

I didn't.

I had nothing.

Not a damn thing.

Cherri's expression morphed into a deadly calm, but I saw the jealousy and anger in her eyes. Felt it rippling off her.

"You think she'll really want you now she's living it up with her rich daddy? Now she can have anyone or anything her heart desires? Little Harleigh Wren might have been born and raised here but she never had what it took to survive The Row. She never had what it took to be the kind of girl who—"

"Word of advice," I said in a low growl. "Jealousy isn't a good look on you, Cher. I suggest you run along before I remind everyone in here why you don't ever cross a Wilder."

Hurt flickered in her gaze, but she quickly masked it with pure rage.

"You'll come crawling back eventually, Nix. And when you do," Cherri stood, looming over me as if she held power over me. "I'll enjoy telling you to go fuck yourself."

She sauntered off, a sight that was becoming too regular where the two of us were concerned.

She had a point—many valid points—but I was too weary to acknowledge them and too fucking stubborn to ever admit them. Besides, I'd never promised her anything.

She knew the deal. She knew that I wasn't looking for more than the occasional hookup.

From the shit that had spewed from her mouth, Cherri knew too much about everything.

She made it her business to know. Because knowledge was power and leverage, and Cherri Jardin liked to have a hold over people.

It had never bothered me before because I had nothing left to lose.

I still didn't...

So why did her words feel like a threat?

And why did I want to drive straight to Old Darling Hill and tell Harleigh to watch her back?

Chapter Eleven

Harleigh

I SURVIVED the rest of the week.

It wasn't easy, but I made it.

Celeste refused to let me wallow. And I both loved and hated her for it. If I went up on the roof, she followed me. If I shut myself in my room—the locks had been removed on my bedroom and bathroom door before I returned from Albany Hills—she knocked until I answered. She was an obstinate presence in my life.

The anchor I hadn't even realized I'd needed.

School was harder. We only had one class together, and I had another with Miles, which left a lot of time without either of them by my side.

My least favorite class was math because Marc Denby and his douchebag friends liked to write me notes and get their all too willing minions to deliver them to my desk. After the first one, I didn't bother to read them, stuffing them in my bag before Mr. Jefferies spotted them and had me read them aloud for the whole class to hear.

It was Friday afternoon, and I only had another thirty minutes before school got out for the weekend when it happened.

Mrs. Paulsen, the AP English teacher, asked me to read my poem to the class.

"I'd rather not," I said, hoping she would move on to the next poor unsuspecting kid.

Didn't she know my history?

Apparently not if the disapproving scowl she gave was anything to go on.

"Miss Rowe, I don't—"

"Maguire," I muttered under my breath. "It's Maguire."

She gave me a dismissive sigh. "We can either hear your poem now or we can hear it after school in detention. But this is a participatory class, Harleigh. Therefore, I expect participation. It's your choice."

Obviously it wasn't.

The entire class looked at me, the weight of their expectant stares like a concrete slab crushing me. "Maybe I can hand it in instead. I would—"

"Just read the fucking poem," someone grumbled from behind me.

"Really, Harleigh, I'm not sure how they do things over at Darling Hill High, but here we expect our students to participate."

"I'll read it, Mrs. Paulsen," someone called. "If she can't do it, I'll—"

"No," I rushed out, the idea of some... some stranger taking my words and making them their own was almost worse than the idea of standing in front of the class and reading them myself.

It was just a poem. A string of words and sentences about the prompt she'd given us. I could read it and move on with my life.

I could—

"Harleigh Wren, today please," she snapped, growing impatient. A couple of kids snickered, whispering a little too loudly what they thought about my stalling tactics.

"O-okay," I said.

"Up front, let's go." She beckoned me forward.

My skin tingled like a thousand ants were under the surface, dancing in my veins.

"What the fuck is her problem?" someone else mumbled.

On shaky legs, I got up and slowly moved to the front of the room. It grew small, the walls pressing in around me until my vision grew hazy.

"Anytime now, Miss Maguire."

I'd never noticed before, but Mrs. Paulsen was kind of a bitch.

I glanced down at my notebook, trying to discern the words.

Breathe, Harleigh. Just breathe.

"Let's go."

"Okay, okay..." I gave her an exasperated sigh, my heart crashing violently against my chest. "This is called These Dirty Lies."

Forever.
The only word my heart knew to be true.
You and me. Me and you.
Two halves of a whole, soul mates entwined.
I felt it there, like strands of silk that bind.

Love me today, tomorrow more.
Leave me never and not before.
These dirty lies that shatter and break.
Bring the darkness, but don't forsake.
All we have, so deep and true.
The only thing I ask of you.

Forever.
The only word my heart knew to be true.
You and me. Me and you.
Two halves of a whole, soul mates for evermore.
Set me free, and I will soar.

Silence.

Complete and utter silence hung in the air. Not even the sound of a pencil tapping against a desk or a student shuffling in their seat.

Even Mrs. Paulsen was too stunned to speak. After what felt like eternity, she cleared her throat and gave me a strange look. "Yes, well, very good. Thank you, Harleigh, for sharing that... enlightening piece."

Enlightening piece?

It felt like I'd cut out a piece of my broken bloody heart and held it up for all to see. But it was too late now. As I moved back to my desk, everyone watched me. But there was a little more wariness in their eyes now.

I wasn't only the new girl from The Row. I was the strange new girl from The Row who wrote maudlin poems about love and loss and darkness.

Thankfully, Mrs. Paulsen moved on to someone else who gave a much less sobering performance of their poem. It even got a laugh or two. But she'd told us to write from the heart.

From inside of us.

I just hadn't ever anticipated that I'd have to share my intimate thoughts with the entire class.

Folding my arms on the desk, I dropped my chin down and focused on my breathing. In for four. Hold for seven. Out for eight. In for four. Hold for seven. Out for eight.

At least, I hadn't written about hurting myself. About the darkness that resided inside me, constantly fighting for a way out. That would have landed me a one way trip to the guidance counselor's office.

And a whole heap of attention I didn't want or need.

"What happened?" Celeste asked the second I met her outside of class.

"Nothing." I shook my head, hoping she would leave it. But some guy said, "Nice poem, Maguire."

"What—"

"It doesn't matter." I grabbed her arm and pulled her down the hall.

"Okay, are you going to tell me what that was about?"

"Mrs. Paulsen made me read my poem to the class."

"So?"

"I didn't realize she would do that when I wrote it. It was personal."

"Personal how?" She frowned, stopping by her locker to trade some books.

"Doesn't matter. At least it's the weekend and I can lock myself away with a good book and not worry about school for forty-eight blissful hours."

Celeste's disappointed expression threw me off my conversation, and I asked, "What?"

"You really don't remember, do you?"

"Uh..."

"Harleigh! You promised me and Miles you'd come to the fair tonight."

Crap. Now that she mentioned it, I had vague memories of a conversation. But that happened a lot around Celeste and Miles. They made plans and I usually half-heartedly mumbled a reply.

But the fair?

That didn't sound like my idea of fun.

"Mom and Dad have the mixer tonight, remember?"

"That's tonight?" I really needed to pay more attention.

But the truth was, since seeing Nix I was finding it hard to concentrate, to stay grounded and in the moment.

I couldn't help but search for him, half-expecting to see him watching from afar.

But I never did.

"Yeah, I didn't think you'd want to be home for it so I suggested we could go to the fair with Miles, and you said—"

"Yeah, that's fine."

"For real?"

I nodded. It sounded a damn sight better than being forced to play nice with my father and Sabrina's fancy rich friends.

"It'll be fun," she added with a smile.

Fun.

It had been so long since I'd had fun, I'd forgotten what it felt like. And since all my memories were deeply entwined with Nix, I wasn't sure I wanted to remember.

But maybe I could make new memories with Celeste and Miles.

Maybe I could pretend long enough to let myself have fun again.

Maybe.

The Darling Hill end of summer fair was an annual event held on the edge of the reservoir on a small patch of land. Technically, it was beyond the reach of Darling Row *and*

Old Darling Hill and since the fair was only temporary, it was considered to be neutral ground.

At least, that's what Miles told Celeste and me as he drove us to the fair.

"So you're saying anyone can come this weekend and there isn't a thing the other side can do?" Celeste clarified.

"The fair has always been neutral. I heard the unspoken rule is there's a truce for the duration of the weekend."

"A truce? Sounds like a bunch of crap if you ask me." Celeste rolled her eyes.

"You never came before?" He caught my eye in the rearview mirror and I shrugged, looking off to the distance.

"Once, with my mom." But what a disaster that had been.

Nix, Zane, and Kye had gone in ninth grade. Nix had begged me to go but I didn't want to go and watch him flirt his way around the place. The next day, I'd found out he'd made out on the Ferris Wheel with Hope Gryffin.

How many times had that happened?

How many times had he begged me to go along with him and the guys to something only for me to find out the next day that he was with Hope or Cherri or Sarah or Neve?

Nix had constantly acted like I was his best friend, that he couldn't live without me... yet it was never me starring in those rumors and stories the next day. It was always him and someone else. Some other girl. A prettier, bolder, sexier girl.

I was so sure about him back then, about my feelings for him. I thought he needed to figure things out; that when the time was right we would find our way to each other. But time didn't reward us, it ruined us.

It ripped us apart so severely that when he'd stood in front of me at the bowling alley the other night, I'd felt nothing but the bitter sting of anger and regret.

I'd waited for him for years, and the second he was able to escape from me, he had.

As I stared out of the window, watching the town roll by, my lip curled with disgust. I'd gotten it wrong; so very wrong.

But I'd been a girl then. A meek, innocent, naïve girl.

I wasn't that girl anymore.

I wouldn't be so easily led astray again.

"We're here," Miles said. He found a parking spot, the field already packed full of cars and people. Up in the distance, I could see the Ferris Wheel, and the flashing lights of the other rides.

My stomach roiled.

"Harleigh?" Celeste glanced back at me, concern creeping into her expression. "We don't have to—"

"No, I'm fine. I'm not used to so much stimulus."

The lights.

The noise.

The people.

So. Many. People.

"We can take it easy, stick to the perimeter and get a

feel for the place first. You don't have to do anything you're not ready for."

I nodded, worrying my bottom lip as I studied the sight before me.

I only had one memory of the fair. I was about eight and my mom brought me. I'd begged her for days and days to let me ride the Ferris Wheel. We rode the bus to the nearest stop and walked the rest of the way. I was so excited I couldn't stop talking about it. But the second she'd spotted the beer stand, I knew I'd lost her attention. She gave me five dollars and told me not to spend it all at once while she spent the night chatting up guys in hopes they would keep her glass topped up and her ego full.

Determined to ride on the Ferris Wheel, I'd bought myself a ticket and stood in the line for twenty minutes. When I'd finally got to the front, the attendant said I was too short to ride alone and no one in the line took pity on me.

I'd never been to the fair since.

Until this moment.

I'd always imagined if I ever did return, it would be with Nix. That I'd let him help me replace that traumatic memory with new ones. Nice ones.

But maybe that was my problem. Maybe I was always waiting for someone to make things better for me. When really, the only person I needed was myself.

Chapter Twelve

Nix

"WHOSE IDEA WAS THIS AGAIN?" I mumbled as we cut across the field toward the hustle and bustle of the fair.

"You can thank Chloe," Kye said. "Mom said she couldn't go unless I went... and I wasn't coming without you two."

"So now you owe us, asshole." Zane smirked.

"Don't look at me like that, Washington. You always loved the fair."

"Yeah, when we were twelve," he scoffed. "If I remember rightly, it was always Nix's favorite place. All those girls juiced up on fear and adrenaline, looking for a guy to—"

"Leave it, Z." I raked a hand through my hair and down the back of my head, rubbing my neck.

I wanted to be here as much as he did. But this morning was the first day I hadn't woken up as stiff as a board, my body crying out in agony. Which was a good fucking thing because I needed to be back at practice. It was killing me sitting on the sidelines, watching my team run plays without me.

But when Kye had asked us to go with him tonight, yes seemed like a better answer than no.

"Let's hope Cherri isn't going to be here."

There went my mood.

She'd been quiet all week, but every time I'd seen her around school, she'd cut me with an icy glare that would send fear into the heart of most guys.

Luckily for me, my heart was already a withered, dead thing inside my chest. Even so she wasn't exactly giving me the warm and fuzzies.

"Okay, let's get this over with." Chloe appeared out of thin air with a guy I didn't recognize in tow.

"Big brother, this is Daniel. Dan, this is my brother Kye and his friends... you don't need to know their names. Now can we go?"

"Hold up," Kye stiffened. "You're on a date? What the fuck, Clo?"

"Uh, I'm gonna... go get a hot dog," Dan said, his eyes dodging Kye's murderous stare. "Meet you over there, Chloe."

"Sure." She pursed her lips at Kye, then me and Zane.

"Don't look at us," I said. "We're only along for the ride."

"Jesus, Clo. You told Mom you were meeting a friend."

"Dan is a friend.... of the male variety. Please don't make a big deal out of this. He's a good guy and I really like him."

"Looks like a pussy to me." Zane shrugged.

"No one asked you, asshole."

"Who is he? I don't know anyone in your class called Daniel. Guys, do you know any—

"He's from Dartmouth."

"No shit," I said, impressed. Chloe Carter was nothing if not resourceful.

"I don't like this, Clo. Mom will kick my ass if she knows you're on a date. You know how she gets."

"That's why we won't tell her, right?" She switched on the puppy dog eyes, and I chuckled.

Kye was useless against those fucking eyes.

"Fine. But Daniel better keep his hands to himself. Meet us back here at eleven and we'll give you a ride home."

"Thank you, thank you, thank you." She hugged him. "Oh, and Nix, little word of warning. I saw Cherri earlier and she's on the warpath."

Fuck my life.

I inhaled a thin breath. "Thanks for the heads up."

"Okay, I'm going. Bye." Chloe hurried after her friend, and Kye let out an exasperated breath.

"She's a fucking nightmare. A date. She's on a motherfucking date."

"Little bit is all grown up." I smirked. "Regretting telling Maddox to stay the fuck away?"

Maddox West was a guy in Chloe's class. He and Chloe had always been tight, but their friendship had never crossed the line. Probably because Kye told Maddox exactly what he would do to him if he ever laid a hand on her.

"West isn't right for her," Kye grumbled.

"And Ken Doll from Dartmouth is?" Zane arched a brow.

"He does kinda resemble a Ken Doll, doesn't he? Fuck. Maybe we should follow them."

"No way, no fucking way. I came for back up, but I draw the line at stalking your sister around the fair."

"Yeah, you're right. I don't want to do that either. But I swear to God, if he tries anything—"

"Relax, big bro." I slung my arm around his neck. "The night is young and there's too much pussy in the fairground to worry about little bit and her date. Come on. Let's go find you a distraction."

And who knew, maybe I'd find one too.

I heard her before I saw her.

We were hanging out near the concession stand, eating hot dogs and chatting to some guys from the team when a tingle of awareness ran down my spine.

"No, no way." Her voice was like a punch to the stomach. "I can't ride that, I'll puke."

"But you have to ride with us."

It was the guy from theother day, at the park and bowling alley. I discreetly watched them, positioning myself so that the rest of my friends shielded me from sight.

Zane noticed, his expression turning grim, but I shook my head.

I've got this, I silently conveyed.

Like hell you do, he shot back.

So maybe he was right, maybe I didn't have this. But I wasn't about to do anything stupid like go over there and make myself known. Instead, I watched. Eavesdropped on their conversation as they stood on the other side of the concession stand, watching the Tilt-A-Whirl in action.

"I'll wait here," Harleigh said. "You two go."

"There's a line. It could take a while."

"I'm sure I'll manage." There was a tightness to her words as if she knew she wouldn't manage but didn't want to ruin their fun.

I was hardly surprised. She always had been self-sacrificing, putting the needs of others before her own.

Me included.

Guilt snaked through me, coiling around my chest, squeezing the air from lungs, my dead fucking heart.

Her friends joined the line and Harleigh moved over to one of the keg tables, looking all kinds of awkward.

It would have been so easy to go to her, to corner her into talking to me. But what the fuck would I say? Besides, the place was swarming with kids from school and DA.

If Harleigh felt their curious stares, their lingering glances as they recognized her standing there, alone, she didn't react. In fact, she was unnaturally still, staring off into the distance as if something had her full and undivided attention.

"Crazy bitch alert, two o'clock," one of the guys said, and I swung around just in time to see Cherri arrive at our group.

Shit.

If she saw Harleigh...

It wouldn't end well for anyone.

"Nix," she clipped out, and I flashed her one of my trademark smirks.

"Looking good, Cher."

She arched a thin brow, folding her arms over her chest. "You've changed your tune."

"Come on, don't be like that." I moved around her, dragging her attention with me, and away from the direction Harleigh was standing.

Zane cast me a strange look and I shook my head slightly, hoping he would realize my plan.

"Let me guess, your precious little birdie decided you weren't good enough after all." The words were full of venom and fire.

"It's not like that between us," I said, my chest tightening at the truth of the words.

Cherri made a derisive sound in her throat and glanced away, dismissing me.

"Look, I was an asshole—"

"Major asshole." She pinned me with a hard look. "But maybe I'll let you make it up to me later. If you're lucky." Reaching for my t-shirt, she trailed a finger up my chest.

Jesus, she made it too fucking easy.

Zane's heavy stare burned into my back, but when I looked over it wasn't Zane watching me at all.

Time seemed to stop as my eyes collided with Harleigh. Her lips parted as she inhaled a sharp breath, one I felt down to the pit of my stomach. Hurt flashed in her green eyes for a second but she quickly masked it with anger.

"What are—"

I stepped closer to Cherri, breaking the connection with Harleigh, the loss like a physical pain inside me. "Ride the Ferris Wheel with me?" The words were forced but she didn't notice.

"Come on, Nix, you know I don't like that one."

"Scared?" I challenged, knowing she would take the bait. I needed to get her away from Harleigh, as far away as possible.

"Fine. But I get to choose the next ride and you can't bail out."

"Fine." Another smirk. Another false promise.

But I'd do it. I'd do it if it kept Harleigh out of Cherri's warpath.

"Come on then." She grabbed my hand in a gross display of ownership. But I shoved my disgust down to that place I reserved for all the bullshit in my life.

I was hardly surprised when my cell phone vibrated. Digging it out of my pocket, I read my text from Zane.

Zane: What the fuck are you doing?

I texted him back, careful not to let Cherri see.

Me: Get Harleigh out of here before Cherri spots her.

Zane: Me?

Me: Who else?

Zane: I knew coming here was a bad fucking idea.

Me: Yeah, well, it's too late for that. Just... get rid of Harleigh.

Zane: Fine. But you owe me.

"Problem?" Cherri glanced down at my cell phone. I shoved it in my pocket and slung my arm around her shoulder.

"Just the guys giving me shit."

We joined the line for the Ferris Wheel and Cherri droned on about her assessment of the first week of senior year. Who was hooking up with who, who had gotten fat or dropped a few pounds over summer, who had gotten hot. She was almost as superficial as the girls across the reservoir at DA. Same shallow judgments, just a different set of measures.

"Are you listening?" She nudged me as I searched the fair for Zane... and Harleigh. But I couldn't see them from all the way over here, the crowd was too dense.

"Uh, yeah."

"So you'll... to Homecoming with me?"

"Homecoming?" I balked. I wasn't going to fucking Homecoming, with Cherri or anyone else.

"Yeah. You know you'll be crowned King, right? And chances are, me or Hope will be Queen. We have to go."

"School dances aren't really my thing, Cher," I said, relieved as fuck that we were next in line.

The attendant took our tickets and pointed at the car he wanted us to sit in.

"Come on." I strode over to it and climbed in, leaving Cherri to fend for herself.

"Nice, asshole." She glowered, tucking herself into my side. She even went as far as to lift my arm over her shoulder.

The music pierced the air, drowning out her words, her fucking plans for the dance. But it wasn't until the ride started and the balmy air whooshed past me as we climbed higher and higher that all the bullshit eddied out of my head.

Coach.

Joe.

Cherri.

Harleigh.

For those few precious minutes, I was free.

But Cherri's shrieks of trepidation rose higher, bursting my bubble of silence as she buried her face into my chest. I looked down at her and frowned.

It wasn't supposed to be like this.

Me and her.

I'd ridden this ride with a handful of different girls over the years. Let my hands wander and my lips swallow their cries of exhilaration. But every single time, I'd wished it was Harleigh.

Every single time, I'd imagined it was her.

And I guessed some things never changed because when Cherri lifted her face and dropped her eyes to my mouth, leaning in to brush her lips against mine...

I was still thinking of little Harleigh Wren Maguire.

And wishing like hell she was the one here beside me.

Chapter Thirteen

Harleigh

IT TOOK Celeste and Miles forever to ride the Tilt-A-Whirl. I stood at the table, watching the world go by as they boarded a car, desperately trying to ignore the stares of my classmates, old and new.

At least it was busy. The noise and lights and din of the crowd helped.

I would have preferred not to be here, but it was better than the alternative—playing happy family back at the house, watching my father and Sabrina schmooze with their richer than rich friends, imagining all the ways I could cause a scene.

The hatred I felt toward Michael Rowe wasn't superficial, like the way most teenagers hated their parents at one time or another. It was intrinsic, burrowed deep inside me. It was the result of years of abandonment and neglect and feeling unworthy.

He had so much wealth, enough that money would never be an issue for him and Sabrina, or Celeste and Max and probably their kids too. Yet, he'd happily stood by and watched my mom leave her home, her life in Old Darling Hill and settle in The Row.

She gave up everything and he let her.

I didn't want his money, his life, or any part of it, but I couldn't get over the fact he just... let it happen. He went on to marry the perfect wife and have two perfect children and live his perfect life, in his perfect fucking neighborhood while every day in The Row was a struggle for me and Mom.

Every day was like wading through quicksand, sinking further and further under, suffocating slowly, slowly, slowly until the pressure was so dense, so heavy that just taking a small breath seemed impossible.

But I'd persevered. I'd kept on pushing, keeping my head barely above the surface while Mom drowned. It didn't happen all at once; it was a slow, festering process. Until she was so far under nothing could keep her afloat.

Nothing except a bottle of vodka. It became her life raft, her anchor. But in the end, even that wasn't enough.

Or maybe it was too much.

I squeezed my eyes closed and forced myself to inhale a deep breath. When I opened them, I was certain I must be hallucinating. "Zane," I whispered.

"Birdie." His lips curled but I felt no warmth from his words.

"Hey, it's been a while."

"You need to go." His expression was cold, devoid of emotion.

"E-excuse me?" My stomach sank.

"You can't be here, Harleigh. Not tonight."

"Last time I checked, it's a free country." A tremor coated my voice. How dare he. "I can go wherever I want."

He blew out an exasperated breath, narrowing his eyes.

Zane Washington was an enigma. If Nix was a closed book, Zane was an impenetrable high security safe. But he'd always been patient with me.

Until now.

"Look, B... Harleigh." He corrected himself, and it stung. I'd never been Harleigh to Nix, Zane, and Kye. But things were different now. "You need to stay away from Nix."

"I need to..." I trailed off, trying to make sense of what he was saying. "Did he say something?"

"Nix tells me everything, you know that. But this thing between the two of you, it isn't healthy. And it's a distraction he doesn't need, not again. So go back to your new life and forget about—"

"Harleigh?" Celeste appeared, glancing at Zane and then me. "Is everything okay?"

"Yeah, fine." My lips pursed, my heart hammering against my chest so hard I felt sure they must be able to hear it. "This is Zane. We... we went to Darling Hill High together."

"Hi, I'm Celeste, Harleigh's sis—"

"Don't care," he said flatly.

"Wow, rude much?"

"Come on, we should go," I said, reaching for Celeste, but she shrugged me off, stepping toward Zane.

"What did you say to her?"

He inclined his head, glaring at her with icy intent. But Celeste didn't flinch. Not even a little bit.

"Harleigh has been through a lot, she doesn't need you." She jabbed her finger at his chest. "Upsetting her."

"I suggest you get your finger out of my face, little girl." His voice was low, deadly, and I stepped up to Celeste, gently tugging her arm.

"Or what?" she seethed, the air crackling.

"Ladies, what are we— Celeste?" Miles drew to a stop, gawking at the scene before him. "You're Zane Washington," he said.

"If you know what's good for you, you'll take Harleigh and Celina home."

"It's Celeste, asshole."

A smug smirk tugged at Zane's mouth as he pinned me with a final warning look and took off, melting back into the crowd.

"Okay is someone going to tell me what the fuck I just walked into?" Miles looked between us, confusion clouding his eyes.

"Nothing," I whispered, wrapping an arm around myself.

"Do you want to go?" Celeste asked, and I loved her even more for it.

And maybe I should have heeded Zane's words, maybe I should have told Celeste yes.

But I didn't.

Because hearing Zane talk to me like that, it steeled something inside of me.

"No, let's go check out the stalls," I said. "Didn't you say something about Miles winning us a stuffed toy each?"

A slow, knowing smile tugged at her mouth. "Why yes, yes I did." Celeste moved beside me, lacing her arm through mine. "Feeling up to the challenge, Mulligan?"

He returned her smile and I saw a flicker of desire there. "I was born ready."

Their laughter enveloped me like a warm blanket as we took off toward the stalls. But I couldn't stop myself from glancing over my shoulder.

There was no sign of Zane among the crowd, as if he'd been a mirage, a ghost. But his words lingered, coiling around my heart like barbed wire. The way he'd warned me to stay away from Nix, as if I was the danger. As if I was the one who had held the power in our friendship.

It was laughable really, when I'd spent years, *years* under his thrall. Years begging for any scraps of his attention I could get.

I'd never held the power where Nix was concerned. So for Zane to stand there and suggest otherwise was, quite frankly, insulting.

Shaking the whole conversation out of my head, I focused on Celeste and Miles.

Screw Zane Washington.

But most of all, screw Phoenix Wilder.

I felt good. Maybe it was the couple of beers Miles managed to score us from the cute girl at the concession stand, or maybe it was the fact he'd won me a giant stuffed toy. But I felt so freaking good.

Not the kind of good that lasted, but the temporary kind. A fleeting high that buzzed in my veins and made my skin tingle. It hovered around me like a warm breeze, and I basked in it.

"What?" I asked Celeste as she watched me grinning at Miles as he tried his luck on the strong man game.

"Are you okay? You look... I don't know..."

"Happy?"

"Yeah, it's weird."

"Bitch." I poked my tongue out at her. It felt weird, tingly and numb.

"Oh, it's a good look. But I guess I'm surprised after earlier. With Zane."

"Nope. Not listening. La la la la la." Clutching the stuffed bear to my chest, I spun around, refusing to give Zane Washington even one iota of space in my mind.

"Is she okay?" Miles asked.

"I'm fine, you guys."

It was a good night. Everything felt easy and breezy and the balmy air felt so good kissing my skin. I tipped my face to the night sky, sucking in a deep breath, letting it roll through me.

"Maybe we should go," Celeste said.

"Go? But it's early."

She studied me. "How much did you have to drink?"

"Like two beers."

"Just two?"

"Yeah. You were right there."

"And you didn't take anything else?"

"Like what?" I balked, not liking the accusatory tone in her voice.

"Pills?"

"Just my usual meds..."

"Maybe you're having a reaction."

"Would you relax? I'm not having a reaction to anything. I'm fine. Fine." I flung my arms out and the stuffed bear fell to the ground. "Oops." I giggled, bending down to scoop it up. But the world spun and I swayed, almost falling on my ass.

Come to think of it, I did feel a little tired. Maybe I could lay on the ground and stare up at the stars and—

"Okay, we're taking you home." Celeste grabbed my hand, steadying me.

"Don't be such a spoilsport, *Mom*," I slurred a little.

"Miles, some help."

He bent down to pick the bear up. "Come on, Harleigh, let's get you home."

I laced my arm through his and rested my head on his shoulder. "You're a good guy, Miles Mulligan."

"Uh, thanks, I think."

"The two of you would make a cute couple. You should ask Celeste out. I bet she'd say yes."

"I... uh, maybe we can talk about this another time?" he said, flicking his eyes past me.

"Oh crap. Did I say that out loud? Did Celeste hear me?" I glanced around and grimaced, mouthing, 'Sorry.'

She shook her head gently. "Just... come on."

They led me through the thinning crowd toward the parking lot, which was really just part of the field that had been cordoned off with temporary fences.

"I'm just going to..." Miles pointed toward the line of porta-potties.

"Me too actually. Harleigh, do you need to go?"

"Not me," I said. "I'll wait here."

"Miles can go first and then I'll—"

"Seriously? I'll wait riiight here." I dropped down on the bench just down from the line. "Go."

"Promise you won't move?"

"Scouts honor." I lifted two fingers in the air but my arm felt all heavy.

Weird.

"Go." I shooed them off.

"We'll be as quick as we can."

Miles handed me the oversized stuffed bear and I waved them off, swaying from side to side as I watched people come and go. Sweat beaded along the back of my neck, my skin clammy. Maybe Celeste was right, maybe I was having a reaction. It would explain the goofy smile I couldn't wipe off my face.

There was probably a good reason you shouldn't drink alcohol on benzodiazepines.

But it was only two beers.

Although I hadn't been thinking about the risks at the time, desperate to escape the gnawing pit inside me. The way Zane's words had clung to me like a bad smell despite my attempts to brush them off.

You need to stay away from Nix.

Because I was the problem.

Me.

My fingers curled around the edge of the bench, pressing into the rough wood. No, my high was slipping. My adrenaline levels plummeting into my toes. Down, down, down. I wanted to sleep. To close my eyes and fall into oblivion.

Then I saw them, standing near Nix's car.

Nix and Cherri Jardin.

She had him pressed up against the hood, running her hand up his chest in a bold display of ownership.

I sucked in a sharp breath, trying to force air into my lungs.

Of course he was with her. They had always had a thing—or at least, she'd always had a thing for Nix.

She leaned in, nuzzling his neck. Nix slid a hand into her bottle-blonde hair. I'd imagined so many times what it would feel like to have his undivided attention like that. What it would feel like to have him touch me so possessively. How it would—

His eyes snapped to mine, and everything went quiet.

The air turned as taut as a bowstring as she continued to kiss his neck, teasing him, touching him. All while he watched me.

I began to tremble; my breaths coming in short, sharp bursts. But I couldn't look away. I couldn't tear my eyes away even though it felt like my heart was being ripped out of my chest.

My stomach roiled, churning with acid. Those imaginary walls closing in around me, the air thinning.

God, please no. Not here. Not now.

I shot up, staggering toward the rows and rows of trailers and RVs.

Breathe, Harleigh. Just fucking breathe.

But I couldn't. My lungs wouldn't work right as I started gasping for air, my body trembling. I collapsed against the side of an RV, my vision blurring around the edges. My heart was beating too fast, working too hard inside my chest as I drowned in the erratic sensations slamming into me from all directions.

Breathe.

Just breathe.

BREATHE, HARLEIGH.

Tears stung my eyes as I warred with myself, pressing my palms flat against the cool, smooth surface of the RV, trying to anchor myself.

Trying to stop the darkness swallowing me whole.

Chapter Fourteen

Nix

I WATCHED Harleigh stumble into the shadows, disappearing between the trailers and RVs.

What the fuck was she doing?

She'd looked ready to puke or faint. The blood had drained from her face, leaving her skin ashen. Her big green eyes wide with horror as she watched Cherri kiss me.

Fuck.

Fucking motherfucker.

I pushed Cherri off me and ran a hand through my hair. "I need to piss."

"Now?" She frowned. "But I thought—"

"I'll be back."

"What the hell, Nix?" she called after me, but I didn't look back, focused on one thing.

Finding Harleigh.

I pretended to join the line for the porta-potties but veered off between the two trailers, melting into the shadows. They ran in a neat grid formation but there was no sign of her.

Fuck. Where the hell was she?

The sound of gentle sobs filled the air and I ducked between another row of trailers and found her on the ground, her head hanging between her knees.

The sight of her, sitting there crying, was like a fist to my heart. It punched right through me, taking hold, and squeezing like a fucking vice.

"Harleigh," I said, inching closer. But she didn't respond, her body visibly shaking. "Harleigh Wren, look at me."

That got her attention. She sniffled, lifting her face slowly, her eyes narrowing before widening with surprise. "You shouldn't be here," she said, her voice off, silent tears rolling down her cheeks.

"What's wrong with you?"

Because this wasn't normal. The way she'd stumbled away from the bench and darted between the trailers. Sitting here, in a trembling heap, sobbing her heart out.

Guilt pricked my insides. She'd seen me with Cherri and I'd taunted her with it. But I'd only wanted to get under her skin the way she'd burrowed under mine at the bowling alley. No, even before that. Ever since I'd heard she was back.

"Just go, please," she cried, burying her face in her hands.

Anger and frustration bled together inside me and before I could stop myself, I stalked over to her and crouched down. "I asked you a question." I peeled her hands away. "What the fuck is wrong with you?"

"And I told you to go." She snarled, yanking out of my hold.

The air crackled. Thick and heavy around us.

"Harleigh, I—"

"What are you even doing back here, Nix?" Her head rolled back against the side of the RV as if sitting upright was a struggle. "Shouldn't you be with Cherri? I bet she's getting lonely."

A red mist descended over me. "Jealous?" I spat the word with a smirk. I didn't intend on coming back here and verbally sparring with her, but she drove me in-fucking-sane.

Clearly spending time across the border had done something to her because the girl I used to know would never have spoken to me this way. But maybe that was the problem back then. She had been too meek, too shy and quiet and unsure of herself. Acknowledging her crush on me had felt like taking advantage of that somehow.

So I'd fought it. I'd denied the evolving connection between us. Pretended that she wasn't changing right in front of my eyes. That I didn't notice her curves, her unassuming beauty.

I'd lied to myself every second of every day, telling myself that crossing that line would ruin us. Ruin me. She was my friend. My best fucking friend. Anything more could jeopardize what we had.

It was a risk I hadn't been prepared to take.

L A COTTON

Because I'd needed her. More than she ever knew.

"Of Cherri?" Harleigh spat her name. "Never."

She sounded tired, so weary and exhausted and sad.

But it didn't stop me from saying, "Did you forget I know when you're lying, Birdie?" I reached out, toying with the ends of her hair. "You flush." My finger brushed her jaw, dipping along the side of her throat. "Right here."

She swallowed. An audible, choked swallow as if she was forcing air past something in her throat.

"Stop touching me." Her hand swatted mine.

"Why were you freaking out?"

"It's none of your business. But I can assure you it had nothing to do with the fact you were watching me while you were kissing Cherri."

Actually Cherri had been kissing me, not the other way around. But I didn't bother to correct her. Because maybe a little part of me wanted her to hurt. To feel the sting of jealousy.

"Can you get out of my way?" Harleigh leveled me with a hard look, her eyes conveying nothing but hatred.

I stood and backed up, my thoughts running a mile a minute. I shouldn't have followed her back here, and I definitely shouldn't have gotten all up in her face about why she was hiding out here in the first place.

But I couldn't stop myself.

I just couldn't fucking do it.

Clambering to her feet, Harleigh brushed off her jeans, swaying on her feet. Her hand shot out and she steadied herself against the RV.

What the fuck was wrong with her?

She inhaled a shaky breath, glaring at me. "You can go now," she said with fake arrogance. Because her eyes... fuck her eyes were like two glittering pools of uncertainty. No, it was more than that... her eyes didn't look *right*.

"And if I don't want to?" I inched forward. Pushing myself into her space. Harleigh stumbled back, pressing herself against the trailer.

"W-what are you doing?"

"Proving a point."

"And what exactly would that be?"

I leaned in, ghosting my lips over the corner of her mouth. A mouth I'd only ever allowed myself to kiss twice before. Because she'd always been off-limits to me.

Too good.

Too fucking pure for the dirt on my soul.

The corner of my mouth kicked up as I said, "That you were so jealous of watching me with Cherri that you couldn't think straight."

Her body trembled, but she didn't cower, glaring at me with the heat of a thousand suns.

Silence enveloped us as we stood locked in a brutal stare. I refused to look away. Refused to give her even one more ounce of control over me. I'd been a fucking mess ever since Chloe had said those five little words.

She's back, Nix. Harleigh's back.

But it was the words that rolled off Harleigh's lips that shattered my thoughts.

"I hate you."

Barely a whisper, the words clanged through me. "What—"

"I hate you. I hate you. I hate you." She started chanting the words over and over, each syllable more frantic than the one before.

I staggered back, so fucking confused and concerned.

"I hate you. I hate you. I hate—"

"Oh my God, Harleigh." The sister rushed over to us, practically shoving me away. "What did you do?"

"D-do? I didn't do fuck all. She just started freaking out like this."

"Shh, Harleigh, it's okay." She stroked Harleigh's brow. "Let's get you out of here."

Harleigh slumped against her, and she draped her arm around Harleigh's shoulder as she began leading her away.

"Wait," I called after them. "What's wrong with her?"

She shot me a terse glare over her shoulder before hugging Harleigh closer and guiding her away from me.

Leaving me standing there, wondering what the fuck had just happened.

"You spent all night trying to keep Cherri off Harleigh's scent and then end up pulling that shit. What the fuck were you thinking?"

"I wasn't, okay?" The car rolled to a stop as I parked outside my trailer. "That's the problem. I can't fucking think straight. Ever since I found out she's back, it's like... fuck." I exhaled a long, steady breath, but it did nothing to abate the anger inside me. The powerlessness and utter despair I felt.

Harleigh had been a mess. But I was fucking wrecked inside. Seeing her like that... it had fucked with my head.

Zane ran a hand over his buzzed hair and down the back of his neck. "I told her to leave."

"Yeah, well, she didn't fucking listen."

"Seems that makes two of you."

"Asshole," I grumbled, even though he wasn't wrong.

"So what's the plan?" he asked. "I mean, I assume there is a plan?"

"Avoid her for as long as possible?" I shrugged. "Fucked if I know."

I didn't want to avoid her, I wanted to drive straight over to that fucking house and demand answers. But I couldn't.

"What about Cherri? She was pissed you left her waiting so long."

"Cherri is inconsequential."

"Try telling her that when she's sucking on your neck like a fucking vampire. You've got a nice hickey, bro. Right... there." He leaned forward and pressed his finger to my neck.

"Fuck off."

The atmosphere turned somber as he asked, "What do you think was wrong with her? Harleigh, I mean?"

"Shit, I don't know, Z. But the way she bolted up off the

bench and stumbled between the trailers, it was as weird as fuck."

"Maybe she had a panic attack or something?"

Or something.

"She's different," I said quietly.

"Yeah, she is. But does it matter?"

I glanced at him. My best friend. The guy who knew me better than I knew myself at times. Most people thought Zane was cold and cruel, but I knew him as a guy steadfast and unwavering in his friendship. Sure, he didn't take any shit and he always told it like it was, but I appreciated that about him. He kept me grounded.

And when things had gone to shit last year, he'd been there. Right by my side, holding me up.

"No, I guess not."

There was no going back for me and Harleigh. I knew that. I fucking knew it, and yet, it was like my heart was singing for closure. Demanding it.

I stared up at my trailer, dread slithering through my gut.

"You can stay at my place again."

"Thanks for the offer, but I need to show my face. You know how it is."

Zane nodded before climbing out. "I'll see you tomorrow," he said.

"Yeah, see you."

He disappeared, but I made no move to get out of my car. Anything to reduce the amount of time I had to spend breathing the same air as my father.

The soft flicker of the television reflected off my windshield. A warning beacon that he was awake, or hopefully ass over elbow drunk, passed out in his threadbare armchair.

With a heavy sigh, I climbed out of the car and trudged up the stairs to the door, slipping inside. Except for the low din of voices coming from the television it was quiet, a thick haze of smoke lingering in the air. Sometimes, I wondered how he hadn't already burned this place to the ground. Cigarettes, and a penchant for drinking liquor until he passed out weren't exactly a good combination.

I kicked off my sneakers and went straight to the refrigerator, grabbing a beer. Something to take the edge off and maybe help me sleep after my weird as fuck conversation with Harleigh.

Her broken expression and hateful words were burned into my fucking skull like a brand. I don't know what I'd expected to find when I followed her tonight, but it wasn't that. She was so broken. So fucking sad. At the time, I couldn't see past my own anger and frustration but she wasn't okay.

Harleigh wasn't okay.

And I didn't know what the fuck to do about it.

Leaning back against the counter, I closed my eyes and took a long pull on my beer, letting the cold liquid douse some of the fire burning inside of me.

A rustle and heavy thud made my eyes snap open.

"Where the fuck have you been?" my father slurred, running a hand down his off-white wifebeater. Faded ink covered most of his arms, wrapping around his shoulders and creeping up his neck like dark vines.

"Out." I held his stare, as much hatred radiating in my eyes as he reflected back at me.

"Don't fucking speak to me like that, boy."

Great. He was in one of *those* moods.

"It's late. You're drunk. We can do this tomorrow." I went to move around him, but he grabbed my arm. Hard enough that I flinched, my spine going rigid.

"Don't fucking touch me," I said with simmering fury. It exploded inside me, angry flames licking my stomach, my chest, burning my goddamn throat.

His grip only tightened, pure rage shining in his eyes. "Or what, kid? What the fuck are you going to do about it?"

Kid.

I hadn't been a kid in a really long time. But he knew the word grated on me. And Joe Wilder was a master at knowing which buttons to push.

"Get the fuck off me," I said, yanking my arm free. My wrist smarted but I bit down the yelp of pain. Just what I didn't need—another fucking injury.

"You've always been a pain in my ass," he spewed the words as I walked away, heading toward the back of the trailer, toward the sanctuary of my bedroom.

"I'll never forgive her for leaving you here. Stupid fucking bitch," he mumbled. "Always knew she was a good for nothing whore. Just didn't realize you'd been the same. A—"

I slammed my door shut, drowning out his cruel, vicious words.

We had little in common, me and my father. But the one thing we could agree on...

I hated her too.

My mother.

The one woman who was supposed to love me unconditionally. The woman who had abandoned me, left me here at his mercy.

The woman who had thrown me to the fucking wolves with no thought as to whether I'd survive.

Nix

"HEY," I said to Zane at break. "Have you seen Wren? She was supposed to meet me after third period."

"Nope. Came straight here though." He tore into the end of his sandwich. "Want some?"

"No, thanks. I need to find her."

"Seriously, Nix," he said around a mouthful of food. "You need to lighten up where Birdie is concerned. We start high school next year, bro. High. School. Do you really want her trailing around after you, ruining your street cred?"

"Wren's cool," I said, scanning the schoolyard for her. Harleigh didn't ever break a promise, and she'd promised to meet me after third period. My stomach twisted. What if something had happened to her mom Trina? She was barely sober these days. Or what if Harleigh had gotten sick? What if someone had—

"What's up, douchebags?" Kye swaggered over to us.

"Nix is worried about Birdie again."

"Again," he grumbled. "What happened now?"

"She said she'd meet me but she didn't show."

"Maybe she ran off with Peter Fairn. You know he likes—"

"Shut up." A heavy weight pressed down on my chest. I didn't like thinking about Harleigh running off with anyone. Let alone a douchebag like Peter Fairn.

"If you're so bothered about who she likes, why don't you ask her out?" Kye gave me a pointed look.

"Ew. Gross, Carter. She's like a sister to me."

My best friend. She was my best friend.

Kye and Zane were my best friends too, but it was different with Harleigh. She got me in a way they didn't. Maybe it was because her mom was as checked out as my dad.

He was getting worse lately. Just the other day, I'd accidentally broken the coffee maker and he'd been so pissed he'd almost knocked my teeth out. I had a wicked bruise around my jaw and a swollen lip. Everyone thought I'd fallen off my bike and hit the sidewalk face first, but Harleigh had taken one look at me, wrapped her arms around me and whispered how much she hated him.

She settled something inside me, and I liked to think it was mutual.

But it wasn't like *that* between us.

Harleigh was too innocent. Too soft and shy. She wasn't like Cherri Jardin and her friends who had already started wearing pushup bras and talking about sex.

"I'm going to look for her," I said, feeling unsettled that she hadn't showed.

"I'm telling you, Nix, she's probably with Peter Fairn under the bleachers."

I flipped Kye off and took off across the courtyard. Some of the guys on the team called after me, but I waved them off. I needed to find Harleigh. Wouldn't be able to settle until I knew she was okay.

But as I rounded the building to check out the football field, a figure stepped into my path. "Hey, Nix," Cherri smiled up at me. "I was hoping to catch you."

"Have you seen Harleigh Wren?"

"Harleigh... no, why?"

"I need to find her." I went to move around her, but she grabbed my arm, demanding my attention.

"I'm sure she's fine. At least she will be once Peter Fairn—"

"What?"

"Yeah." She grinned. "I heard he's going to ask her out. Personally, I don't know what the hell he sees in her, but whatever."

"He's going..." Crap. "Do you know where he planned to do it?"

"By the library, I think. He knows she hangs out there a lot. She is such a loser. Anyway, I didn't find you so we could talk about—"

"I gotta go." I shoved past her and started jogging toward the library.

Harleigh couldn't go out with Peter Fairn. He was too... too tall, and boring, and he... he smelled funny.

She deserved someone far better than Peter Fairn.

By the time I reached the library, my heart was crashing against my chest. But it instantly calmed down when I spotted her.

"Wren—" I swallowed my words, watching as Peter appeared, smiling at her. He got closer—too close for my liking—but Harleigh stumbled back, keeping a safe distance between them.

Atta girl.

I couldn't watch any longer, so I marched over to them and said, "There you are."

"Nix." She flashed me a nervous smile, her gaze flicking between me and Peter and back again. She nibbled the pad of her thumb as she asked, "W-what are you doing here?"

"We were supposed to meet after third period, remember?"

"I'm sorry. Mrs. Diver gave us this homework and I needed to check a book out. But I was going to come and find you afterward."

"Um, Wilder." Peter said. "We're actually in the middle of something."

"You are?" I kept my eyes on Harleigh.

"It's fine. Peter was uh, he was just asking if I wanted to hang out after school, but I told him we already have plans."

Damn right we did. It was Wednesday and we always went over to Mrs. Feeley's house for cookies and ice cream.

She was like a grandma to Harleigh and me. She let us watch silly cartoons on cable and eat candy until we were on the verge of puking. It was the one place we didn't have to worry about our parents.

It was our thing.

"We could do tomorrow," Peter said, and I glared at him, a low growl rumbling in my chest.

Back off, asshole, I silently said to him.

He was brave enough to stare right back. "Didn't I see you making out with Holly Mansfield on the weekend?"

"So?" My spine went rigid.

He let out a bitter laugh. "Forget it. I'll see you around, Harleigh." He stalked off and I felt like I could breathe again.

"He's such a dork."

"Nix..." Harleigh sighed, and I frowned.

"What? Don't tell me you actually wanted to go out with the guy?"

"No, but he's the first person to ever... it doesn't matter." She walked over to the bench outside the library and sat down.

"Why do I feel like I screwed up?" I said, sitting next to her, a strange weight settling in my chest.

"It's easy for you," she whispered, looking at her feet instead of me. "You're popular and funny and gorgeous..."

"You say that like it's a bad thing," I teased, nudging her shoulder with mine.

"Maybe I should have said yes to Peter."

"What the hell, Birdie? You just said you didn't want to go out with him."

"I don't. But I don't want to go to high school and..." She stopped herself.

"And what?" My brows scrunched tighter.

"Nothing."

"Come on, B. This is me. We don't keep secrets."

She peeked up at me and let out a breathy sigh. "I don't want to start high school and be the only girl who hasn't ever kissed a guy, okay?" Her cheeks flushed and it was so damn cute.

"You want to kiss someone, B?"

The thought of Harleigh kissing someone made me feel all weird inside. Because she was like a sister to me, yeah that must have been it.

What else could it be?

I blinked the strange thoughts away and scoffed. "You can do better than Peter Fairn."

"Thanks, but we both know that's not true."

Silence hung between us. This was weird. We didn't talk about kissing. Even when Harleigh had seen me kissing girls—and there had been a few already—she didn't say anything.

Unable to stand the silence for a second longer, I nudged her shoulder again, capturing her attention. When she lifted those green eyes to me, I said, "I wish you could see yourself like I see you, Birdie. You're special."

Too special for the likes of Peter Fairn.

And definitely too special for the likes of me.

Chapter Fifteen

Harleigh

"HEY, HOW DO YOU FEEL?" Celeste slipped into my room the next morning and tiptoed over to the bed, climbing in beside me.

"Like I've been hit by a truck."

I'd slept like the dead, my head barely hitting the pillow before I crashed.

"No more mixing alcohol and pills for you."

"It was two beers. I didn't know..."

But I should have known. It was the first talk they gave you at Albany Hills—the dangers and side effects of mixing medication with alcohol and recreational drugs.

I'd just wanted to be normal though. For one night, I'd wanted to say screw it and be a regular teenage girl out having fun with her friends. And maybe, just maybe, part of me had wanted to say a giant fuck you to Zane Washington.

But I shoved *those* thoughts down. Right down beside

the hazy memories I had of Nix finding me by that trailer, freaking out.

Ugh.

Darling Hill was a big enough town, big enough for the both of us. Especially with him being in The Row and me being stuck on this side of the reservoir now. But time and time again, like magnets unable to fight their natural attraction to one another, we found our way back together.

I guess we'd always been like that. Or I'd always gravitated to him. He was the flame and I was the moth who couldn't stay away. No matter how much it burned.

And burn it had.

"Do you want to talk about it?" I stared at her blankly, and she added, "What happened with that asshole Zane and Nix, I mean?"

"No." My bottom lip trembled. "But thank you."

"I think we should lay low today. Hang out by the pool and soak up the last few days of the sunshine. Mrs. B said the weather is set to turn soon."

"Actually, that sounds kind of perfect."

This place might have felt like a prison, but the one good thing about the gated perimeter, it didn't only keep me in, it kept unwanted visitors out.

Zane and Nix couldn't reach me here, not that I ever imagined them wandering into Old Darling Hill territory.

At least of all for me.

Not after everything.

"What?" I whispered, noticing the distant look in Celeste's eyes.

"Nothing."

"Spit it out..."

Heat bled into her cheeks. "Do all guys like look that at Darling Hill High?"

"Like what?"

"Nix... and Zane."

"Oh my God, Celeste. Whatever you're thinking, unthink it, right now."

"What? A girl can look."

"Zane Washington isn't someone you want to get tangled up with," I said with warning.

She clicked her tongue. "Please. The guy is a Grade-A asshole. But you can't deny he's a hottie."

I shrugged. "I've never really thought about it."

I hadn't. Because Nix eclipsed everyone else.

Always had.

Probably always would.

Only back then, I'd thought we stood a chance. That *I'd* stood a chance. Until I'd realized that everything we'd ever shared had been a lie.

I'd loved him. Desperately... hopelessly... irrevocably. He had been my friend, my protector, and I would have given him my heart if he'd have taken it.

I inhaled a shaky breath, closing the door on the old, painful, pointless thoughts.

We weren't the same people anymore. I had to move on.

"Nix isn't so bad either."

"Will you stop?" I implored, despite the smile tugging

at my mouth.

Nix wasn't a hottie; he was the most beautiful guy I'd ever laid eyes on. All that dark hair and those piercing gunmetal gray eyes. The muscles and tattoos. The fact he towered over me and made me feel safe and protected. That hadn't changed. Not even when he was spewing cruel hateful things at me.

The face of an angel, the voice of the devil.

Pain rolled through me. An unrelenting wave that threatened to pull me under. To swallow me whole. But a warm hand wrapped around mine, squeezing hard. "I'm sorry," Celeste whispered, a buoy in angry, angry seas.

My eyes flickered open, focusing on her. Her soft smile. The sympathy glittering in hers.

"I'm sorry for all of it."

The sun was good for my soul. I basked in it, letting the warm rays heat my skin, filling some of the icy cold cracks inside me.

I wasn't brave enough to lie in a swimsuit like Celeste—not even in the privacy of my father and Sabrina's yard—but I had agreed to wear a bikini top and some black cotton shorts, shoving a fluffy hair scrunchie over my wrist.

"Are you sure you won't come in?" she called from the pool, flicking some water in my general direction. A couple of drops landed on my foot, and I rolled my eyes.

"Do you ever stop?"

"But it's so refreshing."

With a murmur, I got up and moved to the edge of the pool, dipping my toes in.

"It's just the perfect temperature," Celeste added with a reassuring smile.

I carefully sat down, letting my legs dangle into the water. "Happy?"

"It'll do, I suppose." She shrugged. "It's a shame Miles had to babysit."

"I'm sure he'll be disappointed he missed you in your bikini," I teased, earning me another splash. This time the water soaked me through, making me shriek.

"What's going on?" Max wandered toward us with a group of his friends.

My precarious good mood instantly died.

"I thought you were out all day?" Celeste asked.

"We decided to come back here and hang out."

"Well, we were here first, so you can leave now."

"Last time I checked, Einstein, I lived here too. Which means, if me and the guys want to use the pool, we will." Max looked back at his friends, snickering. A couple of them high-fived, leering at us as if we would ever be interested in their barely pubescent teenage boy bodies.

"Go fuck yourself, Maximilian," Celeste drawled, mocking the name Max hated so much.

"Come on, guys, last one in has to pay for the pizza." Max ripped off his t-shirt and took a running jump, water spraying everywhere as he cannonballed into the pool.

Celeste shrieked, swimming to the far end away from her annoying brother.

She began climbing out when a figure loomed over me. I held up an arm to the sun, blocking it out so I could see whoever it was.

"Nate," I said dryly. "What a surprise."

"Don't sound so pleased to see me, baby."

"Baby, really?" I sneered.

Nate was just another entitled asshole who liked lording it over people, reminding them they were beneath him. Thankfully, I'd managed to avoid him all week at school despite his efforts at catching my attention in class, but my good luck had obviously run out.

"Always so salty, Maguire."

"How's the hand?" My mouth twisted into a smug smile.

He flexed his hand as if he felt the phantom pain of me stabbing him with the fork. But he'd deserved it, putting his hands on me after I'd repeatedly told him I wasn't interested.

Nate murmured something under his breath.

"Why are you even here? Isn't hanging out with your kid brother and his friends a little pathetic?"

"Maybe I wanted to see you?"

A derisive noise caught in my throat.

"You know, if you weren't such a bitch, we could have a lot of fun, Harleigh Wren." His brow lifted, a suggestive smile gracing his stupidly handsome face.

"I don't think so somehow."

"Because you're still hung up on Wilder?"

"How do you...?" I stopped myself. Of course he knew. People talked. In a place like Old Darling Hill all people did was talk. And he knew Marc Denby and his friends.

"I can see I hit a nerve. You know, Wilder's beneath you now, Maguire. Besides, I can give you something he can't on this side of the reservoir."

"What could you possibly give me?" I drawled with fake bravado.

"Protection. Just... think about it."

Protection?

What the hell was that supposed to mean?

I didn't ask though, watching him walk over to an empty lounger instead and pull his white t-shirt over his head. There was no denying Nate was gorgeous. Tall, lean body with a hint of muscle, dirty blond hair, and a smile that spelled trouble; but I knew all about bad apples wrapped up in pretty packages, and I wanted nothing to do with him.

Or whatever he was offering.

"What was that about?" Celeste flopped down beside me, kicking her foot through the water to cover Max and his friend Toby in a spray of water. They both flipped her off but didn't make a play for her.

"Just Nate being Nate." I shrugged, smoothing hands over the tiled edge of the pool.

"He's a creep," she hissed. "If he bothers you again, tell me and I'll—"

"I can handle the likes of Nate Miller, Celeste."

"Oh, I know you can. But maybe I want a shot at him too." Her brows waggled, and we shared a quiet chuckle. "So I guess our afternoon by the pool has been hijacked. Want to go inside, get dry, and watch reruns of *The Walking Dead*?"

"Sounds good to me." We stood and grabbed our towels.

Someone wolf-whistled and Celeste cut Toby with an icy glare. "In your dreams, asshole."

"Every damn night, baby." He dipped his hand beneath the water and cupped his junk. Or, at least, that's what I imagined he was doing.

"So gross," she whispered as we headed for the house.

"Call me," Nate shouted, and I lifted my hand up and flipped him off. His gaze narrowed, a strange expression passing over his face, but I broke our heated stare, unwilling to play his mind games.

Celeste gave me an impressed smirk. "Why are guys such assholes?"

"Miles isn't," I countered.

"No, but he's also too good, ya know? Like he doesn't have that..."

"Don't say it. Don't you dare say it."

"Oh, come on, Harleigh. It's the oldest cliché in the book. Girls are attracted to the bad boy."

"And we all know how that ends," I grumbled.

I had that t-shirt hanging in my closet.

"Miles is the type of guy you settle down with. He isn't the type of guy you fool around with in junior year."

"Ouch. Don't let him hear you say that." I grabbed the can of soda she offered me. "As someone who has plenty of experience with bad boys, trust me when I say, they're not worth it."

My heart rejected the idea, slamming against my chest violently as if to say *no, no, no*. Because Nix had been worth it. He'd been worth every damn thing.

Until he hadn't.

"Harleigh, Dad probably has my future husband already picked out. I need to make the next few years count before I'm married off to some stuffy lawyer or investment broker and bred like a prized mare."

"He wouldn't..."

"No, of course not." She chuckled, but the smile she wore didn't reach her eyes. "But I'm sure they'll have an opinion on every guy I ever bring home. Got to uphold the family reputation." I bristled and her eyes grew wide. "Crap, sorry... I didn't—"

"It's fine. We know I don't belong here. I never will."

"Honestly, I like that you're not one of them. You're real, Harleigh." She gave me a warm smile that eased some of the tension running through me. "That's more than ninety percent of the student population at DA can say."

"I like that I'm not one of them too." I grinned but it was forced. Turning into Daddy's little princess was the last thing I ever wanted. But part of me wondered how easy it would be to lose myself here. To don the blue and gray uniform and smile in all the right places and pray to the altar of daddy's trust fund.

Easy maybe, but never honest.

Because this life, the fact I was here in the first place, was built on nothing but secrets and lies. And the truth was, I wasn't here to assimilate. I was here to do my time and then get the hell out of Darling Hill and put the past where it deserved to stay.

Behind me.

Nix

"SERIOUSLY, Clo, I'm not your fucking personal taxicab. Couldn't you have called whatshisface, Dean?"

"It's Dan, asshole. And no, he has to work today. Besides, you said you were heading out."

"Yeah, but I didn't say I wanted to drive all the way out here."

"Carter, quit your bitchin'." I kicked the back of his chair, sinking further down the back seat. "My head feels like it's going to explode."

"What's up with that?" Zane asked.

"Just a headache."

I didn't want to tell them the truth. That I'd been kept up half the night listening to my father and Jessa go at it. Somewhere during round two it had turned nasty and Jessa's moans had become screams of rage until stuff started smashing and clattering against the wall.

In the end, I'd grabbed a pillow and my duvet cover and slept out in my car. She'd woken me up this morning by knocking on the window with an apology muffin and a mug of coffee, but it didn't replenish the decent night's sleep I'd missed out on.

The guys wanted to go for a drive so I'd said I would tag along. But Kye landed babysitting duty first.

We pulled up outside Crêpe-a-licious and Kye cut the engine.

"You're coming in?" Chloe balked. "Because you don't need to do that. Brianne is—"

"I'm hungry for crêpes." Kye glanced back at me and Zane, wearing a shit-eating grin. "Are you two hungry for crêpes?"

"I could eat." Zane shrugged, shouldering the door.

"Guys, come on. You can go. I don't need—" But her protests were drowned out as we climbed out of Kye's car and headed inside.

"Guys, seriously." Chloe grabbed my arm, and I dropped my eyes to where her fingers curled around my wrist.

She immediately let me go huffing out, "This is completely unnecessary."

"Naw, little bit." Zane ruffled her hair. "We're not embarrassing you, are we?"

Her friend Brianne smothered a laugh, watching the four of us from behind the counter. "You didn't say you were bringing Kye and the guys," she said.

"I didn't *bring* them." Chloe rolled her eyes.

"Hey, Bri," Kye said. "What's good?"

"Depends on what you're in the mood for. I'm all about

the savory options right now. The spinach and cheese is amazing."

"Sounds good to me. Load her up." He winked and Chloe's friend blushed right to the tips of her ears.

"You dog," I whispered, and he elbowed me in the ribs. "She's a junior, man. Behave."

"Like that's ever stopped you before," Zane scoffed.

"She's my sister's best friend."

"Again, like that's ever—"

"I can hear you, you know?" Chloe glowered at the three of us. "And I'll tell you two what I told Kye last year. Come anywhere near any of my friends and I will gut you like a fish."

"Ooh, little bit. I'm shaking in my boots." Zane smirked, and she flipped him off.

'She makes it so easy,' he mouthed at me, and I shook my head.

Chloe Carter was something else and part of me was almost disappointed we wouldn't be around next year to watch her kick senior year's ass.

"One spinach and cheese." Brianne slid a container toward Kye. "What about you guys?" she asked me and Zane.

"I'll have whatever he's having," he said, and she turned her full attention on me.

"Okay, I'll have a banana and hazelnut spread, please."

"Oooh, good choice."

Brianne set about making our crêpes. The doorbell chimed and I glanced back at the sound of laughter.

"Well, well, what do we have here?" Marc Denby stepped forward. "You know this is DA territory, right?"

"Don't be an asshole, Denby," Kye said. "This place has always been neutral."

"Bull. Shit. It's ours and everyone—"

"No fighting in the store," Brianne said. "Or you'll be banned."

"Says who?"

"Says me." An older man appeared from out back and leveled Denby with a hard look. "This is my store and I make the rules, son. Now you can either stay and eat, or you can leave. Choice is all yours."

Marc ran his eyes over the three of us, scowling. But surprisingly, he conceded. "We're not here to cause trouble."

"Good. If you need me, Brianne, I'll be in my office."

"Sure thing, Uncle Decker."

Uncle.

"Well shit," I whispered. "I never realized Brianne's uncle owned this place."

She handed me and Zane our desserts and Chloe ordered, the two of them chatting about Chloe's date last night.

"I'm going to sit. I don't want to listen to this shit." Kye headed for one of the empty booths.

"Here." I dug out my wallet and threw a twenty down on the counter. "For all four of us."

"You got it." Brianne smiled, but there was no heat there.

We slid into the booth, and I watched Denby and his friends goof around in the line.

"Who's the new guy?" I asked no one in particular.

"Nate Miller." Chloe joined us, sliding in next to her brother. "His dad is good friends with Michael Rowe."

I went rigid. A bolt of anger darting through me.

"I don't know whether to be impressed or freaked the fuck out that you know all of this."

"I spend a lot of time here with Brianne. I hear things." She went still, her eyes glazing over slightly.

"Clo?" Kye whispered.

But I heard him then. Denby running his big fucking mouth.

"A little birdie tells me you're making a play for Maguire?"

Nate's eyes flicked to mine as if he'd clocked me the moment he'd stepped inside. "Who, Harleigh?" He held my stare as he answered. "She's a pretty girl."

"Nix," someone hissed but I couldn't be sure who over the roar of blood between my ears.

"You're a brave fucker, Nate. Braver than me if you're willing to dip your end into that piece of trailer trash. Who knows where she's been."

I saw red.

One minute I was in the booth, the next I had my hand around Denby's throat, and his body pressed up against the wall. "Say that again," I growled.

"Easy, Nix. Easy..." Zane said, but I couldn't think.

Couldn't see past Denby running his mouth about Harleigh.

Fuck.

Fuck.

"I suggest you get your fucking hands off me," he smirked. "Before the cops show up and throw your sorry ass in jail."

I released him with a hard shove and stepped back, running a hand down my face.

"Yeah, that's what I thought." He chuckled darkly. "But good to know you still care. I'm sure Harleigh will be really—"

I lunged for him again, but strong arms yanked me backward. "Calm down," Kye hissed. "Calm the fuck down."

"What's going on out here?" Brianne's uncle appeared, clutching his cell phone. "You three," he said, pinning me, Kye, and Zane with a disdainful look. "Get out of here, all of you."

"Go," Chloe urged me. "Just go. I'll speak to him."

"Yeah, yeah." Shrugging Kye and Zane off me, I gave Denby a cold stare. "Stay the fuck away from her," I spat.

"Or what, Wilder? What the fuck are you going to do? She's one of us now. She—"

Zane shoved me out of the store. "Move, now."

"He's a fucking asshole."

"And you walked right into it. What the fuck, Nix?"

They herded me toward Kye's car and I climbed in the back seat, slamming the door behind me. But not before glancing toward the windows of the store. Denby glared back at me, a shit-eating grin on his face as he pointed two fingers at his eyes and then toward me as if to say, *I'm watching you.*

"I'm going to fucking destroy him," I muttered, clenching a fist.

"Is that before or after you get your ass thrown in jail?"

"I barely touched the guy."

"Come on, Nix, Z's right. It didn't look good. Brianne's uncle—"

"Yeah, yeah, I screwed up. Just fucking drive, Carter. The sooner I get out of here the better."

But before he could get the car into gear, Nate burst out of the store, jogging toward us.

"What the fuck does this asshole want?"

"Beats me," Kye murmured, cranking his window. "What?"

"You should be more careful, Wilder. Denby doesn't need any more reason to go after her," the guy said, hands tucked in his pockets with casual poise.

"Oh yeah, and who the fuck are you?" My throat bobbed, my heart sinking into my fucking toes.

"Consider me... a friend."

"Yeah, right." Kye chuckled but it was full of warning and distrust. "We literally saw you arrive with Denby and his group of douchebags."

He leaned down and rapped his fingers on the window frame. "Sometimes, you gotta know how to play the game.

I'll be seeing you." He gave me a curt nod and doubled back around toward the store.

"Okay, that wasn't weird at all."

I stared after him, watching as he slipped back into the store and Denby approached him. The conversation got heated, the two of them arguing about something.

Or someone.

Fuck my life.

How have things gotten so complicated in such a short period of time?

Whichever way I looked at it, Kye and Zane were right. It all came back to her.

Harleigh.

And I didn't know what the fuck to do about it.

Monday at practice was brutal. Every inch of me hurt but I reveled in it. Siphoning every ounce of pain, every *crash* and *thud* of my defense against my barely healed body, into a vicious unstoppable weapon.

"Go, go!" Coach yelled across the field as I dodged a player and faked left and then darted right, cutting around him and taking off toward the end zone.

I wasn't typically a rusher. My strength on the field lay in my passing, not speed. The precision with which I commanded my team. But sometimes, like right now, I needed to run. I needed to feel my cleats hitting the ground, the ping of exertion in my muscle as I pushed myself harder... faster. Pushed myself until my lungs burned and legs ached.

Hench grinned as he dropped back to block my route. "Your ass is mine, Wilder." The promise in his words only propelled me faster.

"Come get me, asshole," I taunted, switching directions and racing toward the end zone. Thirty yards. Twenty... Ten.

Out the corner of my eye, I saw a wall of magenta and black fly toward me. That fucker had timed his assault down to the second, and I knew... fucking knew he was going to take me down. But I wasn't going to go without a fight. Pushing down onto my knees, I leaped into the air, sailing as high and far as I could. His hand connected with my ankle, fingers grasping, clutching, but I shoved myself forward. Willed it from my very soul and landed out of his reach.

Hell yeah. I mentally high-fived myself as I cockily jogged into the end zone and slammed the ball down, glancing back at him.

Touchdown, motherfucker.

One hand pressed to the ground, he glared up at me, shaking his head. "I almost had you, asshole."

"Yeah, yeah, tell it to someone who cares."

The rest of the team descended on me, jostling me and clapping me on the back.

"Now that's what I'm talking about." Coach made his way toward us. "That right there is going to take us all the way to the playoffs. Nice work, son." He gave me a small nod.

Zane shot me an amused grin over Coach's shoulder, mouthing, '*Nice work, son.*'

I flipped him off discreetly. Sarcastic fucker.

"Okay, listen up. I had a call earlier and there's been a change to the schedule. Dartmouth will no longer be our first game. Instead, we'll be playing DA at their stadium."

Fuck.

A chorus of grumbles went up around me.

"Seriously, Coach. We've got to go to their place again?"

"It's out of my hands, ladies." He shrugged. "But look at it this way, when we beat their sorry asses it'll feel that much sweeter."

"Fuck yeah," Hench bellowed and everyone followed, cheering and clapping.

But I didn't share their excitement.

Going up against Denby and his pussy friends on their turf was going to be a dog fight. I wasn't worried about losing... but I was worried about the shit they might pull to throw us off our game or get us in trouble with the game officials.

"Okay, bring it in. Hawks on three." Coach said, shoving his hand into the crude circle. Hands fell on top as everyone closed ranks, pressing closer. "One... two... three. Go Hawks. Now hit the showers."

The circle broke apart, guys jogging toward the locker

rooms. But I lingered behind, hardly surprised when Zane and Kye joined me.

"Where's your head at?" Zane said, quietly out of earshot of the coaches.

"I don't like it."

"Me neither," Kye said. "First game of the season at their place. Denby will put a target on your back. And now that B goes there—"

I shot him a cold look and he dropped that line of thought. "I'm just saying, he'll be out for blood."

"Or maybe he'll lay the trap to let you hang yourself."

"What the fuck is that supposed to mean?" I narrowed my eyes at Zane, and he shrugged.

"It's means she's still your fucking kryptonite and she's in the hands of your worst fucking enemy."

Chapter Seventeen

Harleigh

"IGNORE HIM," Celeste said as I returned Marc Denby's hateful stare.

"What's his problem all of a sudden?" I asked through gritted teeth. "I've been here six days now."

It was Tuesday, and painfully apparent that my settling in period at DA was over. Yesterday, the whispers had been louder, the stares less curious and more hate-filled.

Marc Denby's crowd of followers had poked fun at me every time our paths crossed.

Wilder's pet.

Weirdo.

And my personal favorite *trailer trash.*

I'd let their taunts, their barbed words, and cruel snickers roll off my back. At least, for the most part. But by the end of the day, some of their poison had seeped into the tiny cracks of my heart.

Today... today I felt restless, walking a tightrope of emotion, like one wrong move could tip me over the edge. I resented being here. Resented my father and Sabrina and their stupid, rich, entitled lives. I hated Marc Denby and his friends and the way they looked at me as if I was less than dirt on the bottom of their shoes. But most of all, I hated myself.

I hated that I wasn't stronger. That I wasn't brave enough to storm up to Marc and dump my sloppy lunch all over his smug face. I hated that the first thing I'd thought of this morning when I'd woken up was slipping into my father and Sabrina's bathroom and raiding their medicine cabinet for something—*anything*—to take the edge off.

I hated that my thoughts kept veering to Nix. That I kept imagining him swooping in to save me. He wasn't my protector anymore, but my head and heart were having a real hard time sorting out the truth from the lies.

Once upon a time, Nix had been my best friend. Truth.

Once upon a time, he had made me feel special and cherished and had threatened anyone who dared hurt me. Truth.

Once upon a time, he had promised to always be there for me. Lie.

Big. Fat. Giant. Lie.

Because when I'd needed him the most, Nix had been nowhere to be seen. I could remember how it felt realizing he wasn't going to come and save me from my father's clutches. How it felt to realize that the boy I loved more than anything had abandoned me.

Yet, he'd stood there the other night, acting like something still existed between us. Like I was supposed to feel anything except pure hatred for the boy who broke me so permanently that I lost a part of myself.

"Harleigh?" Someone kicked me under the table, and I bolted back into the moment.

"Y-yeah?"

"Stop looking at him. You'll only make him worse," Celeste muttered.

Sure enough, Marc and his entire table were glaring in my direction.

"I'm not scared of him," I said with a defiant tip of my chin.

"He's not someone you want to cross, Harleigh. Is he an ass? Yes, yes, he is. But he's a relentless ass. Don't give him a reason to come after you." Bitter laughter spilled out of me, and she gawked at me. "Are you okay?"

I was so far beyond okay. But I simply nodded, shoveling a forkful of spaghetti into my mouth, barely tasting it.

"Maybe you need to talk to Dr. Katy," she said quietly.

"I'm fine." Calling Dr. Katy was for emergencies only. I'd done my time at Albany Hills, attended their outpatients therapy group in the weeks before starting DA.

"You look like you're about to go over there and flay him alive."

My brow lifted with wicked intent. "Now there's an idea."

She snickered and some of the tension between us dissipated. "It's the pep rally Friday..."

"No," I said flatly.

"I was assuming you would say that. So me and Miles thought we could hang out instead and have ourselves an anti-pep rally." She grinned but my chest constricted.

"You'd give up going to the pep rally for me?"

Even at Darling Hill High pep rallies were a big deal, so I knew a school like DA would go all out.

"Duh, of course. I never liked those things anyway. We can head downtown to the park again or hang out at Miles's house."

"Maybe," I said, bowing my head slightly.

It felt weird to have Celeste and Miles include me in their plans. Outside of Nix, I'd never really had friends before.

"Don't look so worried, Harleigh." She chuckled, her soft laughter like an unexpected balm to my racing heart. "You're one of us now, whether you like it or not."

She meant the two of them—her and Miles. But as I tried to ignore Marc's scowl, I wondered if her words held a bigger meaning. Because although I would never belong here, I was one of them now. A thorn among roses, an ugly duckling among a flock of swans. I was the piece that didn't fit right.

The piece that ruined the whole damn puzzle.

Some days it didn't bother me. Some days, I was barely aware of it. But today, today I couldn't think about anything else.

"Psst."

I glanced over my shoulder, frowning at Angelica Hatton, one of Marc Denby's inner circle. "Is it true?"

"Is what true?"

"That... you spent time in a nuthouse."

The ground slipped from under me, the world tilting on its axis.

"E-excuse me?"

Why wasn't the teacher demanding decorum? Why wasn't she intervening?

"You heard me, freak." She sneered despite her saccharine tone. Her friends all snickered, blatantly listening in. "My sister is in your brother's class, and he said you weren't at your grandparents at all, that you—"

Blood roared in my ears, drowning out her voice.

Max.

Max had told her sister.

He had told someone the truth.

I couldn't breathe. I couldn't open my mouth to take a breath, let alone answer.

I couldn't do anything.

"Oh my God, she's freaking out." Angelica snickered under her breath. "She's totally freaking out. Someone get the straitjacket ready."

"Ange," a deep voice from the back of the class said, and my eyes flew to Nate. He didn't so much as glance in my direction, but that had been him, warning her.

"Relax, Nate." She laughed it off, the sound like nails along a chalkboard. "We're just talking, right, Harleigh?"

L A COTTON

My body trembled as I clutched the lip of the table. She knew. Which meant they all knew. All because Max couldn't keep his goddamn mouth shut.

Tears stung the backs of my eyes, but I locked them down, refusing to let even a single tear fall. My teeth clenched behind my pursed lips. *Do not engage. Breathe. Be the bigger person. So what? They know. There's no shame in it. You got help... you healed... you—*

"Miss Maguire, is there a problem?"

"Uh, what?" My head whipped around and I blinked at Ms. Holland.

"Harleigh Maguire, you will not take that tone with me."

"Sorry, I didn't mean—"

"It's simply unacceptable young lady."

I sunk in my chair, trying to disappear. I wasn't purposefully being rude, but I couldn't organize my thoughts quickly enough. Not after the bomb Angelica had just dropped.

"Rude and a headcase. No wonder her mom offed herself."

Someone gasped. "So cold, Ange." Snickers rang out around me, echoing through my skull.

Without a second thought, I shoved all my things into my bag and stumbled over my chair.

"Miss Maguire, what—"

"Sorry, but I need to go."

"You will not just leave my class, young lady."

"Don't let the door hit you on the way out," Angelica called after me, driving the knife a little deeper.

She didn't owe me anything; none of them did. But what happened to basic human decency and compassion?

I burst into the empty hall and made a beeline for the girls' bathroom, relieved to find that also empty. My body crashed into one of the stall doors and I sank down onto the floor, tipping my head back against the partitioning wall.

Fuck her.

Fuck Angelica and her friends, and Max, and Ms. Holland. They didn't know. They had no fucking idea what I'd been through. How my life had been turned upside down that night and never quite turned back around.

The bathroom door creaked open, and I held my breath, hoping to God she hadn't followed me in here to finish the job.

"Maguire, you in here?" Nate's voice filled the room.

"Go away," I shouted.

"Afraid I can't do that." His footsteps grew closer.

"This is the girls' bathroom for a reason, asshole."

"Yeah, well, I'm not leaving until you show yourself."

"Creeper much," I murmured as I pressed my nails into my palms, willing the erratic beat of my heart to calm down.

There was a thud to the side of me and Nate appeared over the partitioning wall.

"Oh my God, what are you doing? I could have been peeing." I clambered to my feet.

"Good thing you weren't then. Want to get out of here?"

"With you?" I balked. "No thanks."

"Come on, don't be like that. I can make it worth your while."

"How can you possibly—"

He dangled a small baggie in his hand, and my world went quiet. It was a bad idea. The worst. But I couldn't go back in there.

"You're thinking about it, aren't you?"

"We'll get into trouble for skipping class."

He gave me a crooked smile and said, "That's half the fun."

"I can't feel my face," I said, closing my eyes and letting the weightlessness sink into me.

"It's some good shit, right?" Nate chuckled.

Slowly, I turned my head to look at him. "You look funny."

"That's the drugs talking."

It was a bad idea leaving school with Nate, letting him drive me across town to the edge of the reservoir and hotbox his car until we were both blissed out. But I couldn't find it in me to care.

I felt great.

So fucking good I wanted to stay here forever.

"Do you have any more?" I asked, every syllable

elongated as if it was an effort to make my lips form words.

Nate smirked, his eyes thin, expression goofy. "I think we had enough."

"Yeah," I let out a soft sigh, stroking his soft leather seats. "You're probably right. I like your car."

"I think it likes you too." He chuckled and then I was laughing until we were both hysterical with tears streaming down our faces.

"I-I can't breathe," I wheezed.

"For real? Do you need CPR? Or mouth to mouth? You know, I'm pretty good at that." He started smacking his lips together.

"Oh God, stop. Stop. I love your car, not you."

Never you, my stupid traitorous heart echoed.

He was a sleazy asshole.

A sleazy asshole with some damn good weed.

"Is it true?" he said when our laughter died down. "What Ange said?"

"What do you think?" I stared him dead in the eye.

"I think something inside you is broken." Sincerity coated his words, sobering me.

Rolling my eyes, I said, "Is this the part where you tell me you want to fix me? Be the one to piece me back together?"

He studied me, too closely considering how high we both were. "I'm not the good guy here," he said cryptically.

"No. What are you then? The villain? Because I've met plenty of those before and you don't scare me, Nate Miller."

"I'm..." He paused considering his answer for a second. "A friend."

"What if I don't need any more friends?"

His brow lifted. "Something tells me that you do."

"Is this a game? Did Marc Denby put you up to this? Should I expect him and his friends to appear any moment and—"

"Ever heard of keep your friends close and your enemies closer?"

"You know, being high aside, I can't get a read on you."

"Maybe that's the way I like it."

"I think you should take me home."

We'd been out here too long. School was over and Celeste had been blowing up my cell phone. I'd given her the CliffsNotes version of what happened, and she'd promised a) not to kill Max with her bare hands and b) to cover for me with Michael and Sabrina if they got home early from work.

I didn't think anyone would appreciate me turning up at the house as high as a kite.

"I'm gonna need time to sober up," he said, cranking his window down.

"Actually, before you take me home, can we get something to eat? I'm starving."

"The lady wants food, the lady shall get food." He swished a hand in the air. "But first, we must hydrate." Snagging the bottle of water out of the central console, Nate uncapped it and downed the thing in one.

"Why'd you really bring me out here today?" I blurted

out, the fresh air already counteracting the THC in my system.

"Because Maguire..." His eyes narrowed at me. "You looked like you could use a friend, and we all need one of those sometimes."

"I... really don't know what to say to that." I cranked my own window open and inhaled a deep breath of fresh air.

"Feeling okay?"

"This was a bad idea."

"Ouch."

"You tried to feel me up at that mixer in the summer... I stabbed you with a fork."

"I haven't forgotten. But listen, I was drunk. I'm an asshole when I'm drunk. Actually, I'm an asshole most of the time, it's easier that way," he said cryptically.

I studied him through glazed eyes. He was like all the other rich entitled pricks at DA, but there was something in his eyes I hadn't noticed before. Something that looked like sadness.

His cell phone started blaring and he cussed under his breath. "We need to go."

"But I thought you said you need to sober up first."

"I do. But I also need to be somewhere. We'll have to take a rain check on dinner."

"Oh, it wasn't... yeah, okay."

This was weird.

He was acting weird.

And it occurred to me that maybe there was more to Nate Miller than I first thought.

Nix

"IS YOUR OLD MAN AROUND?"

I glared at Vince Colombo, unable to hide my sheer contempt for the guy.

"He's not here."

He glanced over my shoulder, peering into the trailer. Yanking the door behind me, I stepped forward, forcing him to back up. "I said, he's not here."

A wolfish grin tugged his mouth, revealing three gold-plated teeth. They glinted in the moonlight making him look deadly. "You know, Nix, I always did like your balls, kid."

He shouldered me out of the way and entered the trailer uninvited. Anger rolled down my spine like lightning. Vince Colombo was a local dealer. A bad guy. The type of guy you didn't want sniffing around. Joe worked with him sometimes, but even Joe knew Vince was someone you kept at arm's length. So the fact he was here, in the trailer, was a huge fucking problem.

"Jessa's been good for this place," he said, running his fingers over the soft throw draped over the couch. "Where's she at?"

"At work." My spine stiffened.

Please God let her be at work.

"What can I do for you, Vince?" Leaning against the counter, I tried to keep my posture casual. Easy. Guys like Vince preyed on the weak. They devoured that shit for breakfast, chewing up and spitting out whatever was left. Which usually wasn't much after he'd finished.

"Now there's an idea." His eyes glinted. "What can you do for me?"

"Look, man, I'm not—"

The door handle rattled, Jessa's soft voice filtering inside. "Nix," she called. "I'm home."

Shit.

Vince rubbed his jaw, watching through hungry eyes as Jessa entered the trailer, a grocery bag tucked under her arm.

"I got din—Vince." The blood drained from her face.

"Looking good, Jessa."

"W-what are you doing here?"

"Came by to see Joe, but can't deny it's always good to see your face, dolcezza."

"Nix, a little help." She motioned to the bag, and I took it from her, setting it down on the counter. "We're about to eat, Vince, if you want to join us?"

"I wanted to talk to Joe about a few things." He raked his leering gaze down her body, and my fist clenched against my thigh. Jessa was beautiful. A good soul. Too fucking good for likes of my father and definitely too good for the likes of Vince Colombo. But the 9mm pistol tucked into the waistband of his jeans kept my mouth shut.

Vince didn't dick around. If you stepped out of line, he dealt with it. Consequences be damned.

I eyed my cell phone on the counter, contemplating trying to get a text to my old man. But Jessa caught my eye, shaking her head discreetly.

"Want me to call him?" Jessa said. "I'm sure he'll come back and—"

"Actually, I think we can come to another arrangement. Joe owes me a favor or two." He took a step toward her. "I'm sure he wouldn't mind me collecting."

"Come on, Vince," I said. "Let me call him. He wouldn't want—"

He turned his attention on me, and a chill ran through me. "Why don't you go play with your toys, kid, and leave the grown-up talk to me and Jessa?"

"What the—?"

"Vince is right, sweetie." She cut me off. "Why don't you see if Zane wants to hang out?"

Jessa gave me a pleading look. *Don't do anything stupid, please.* But I couldn't bear the thought of Vince putting his dirty fucking hands on her. It was bad enough that my father treated her like shit.

"He's busy," I said, pulling to my full height. I wasn't stacked like Vince, but I wasn't a pussy either.

"Phoenix." Jessa used her sharp voice, the one she

usually reserved for the nights my old man came home drunk and smelling like cheap perfume. "Vince is right, you should—"

"No. No fucking way." I stepped in front of her, shielding her. "I'm not about to leave you alone with—"

He whipped his pistol out, clicking off the safety and pointing it straight at my head. "You really don't want to fuck with me, kid. Now I suggest you get the hell out of here so me and Jessa can settle your old man's debt."

"Nix, please," Jessa clutched my back, her fingers trembling against my t-shirt. "It's okay, sweetie. I can handle it." Fear clung to her whispered words despite the conviction in them.

She would do this for my father. For me. And it fucking gutted me.

"What's it gonna be, kid?" Vince pressed the barrel of the gun closer until the cool steel touched my head. Fear and adrenaline coursed through me. I didn't want to leave her... to leave her like a lamb to the slaughter. But Vince Colombo wouldn't think twice about putting a bullet through my skull. And I wasn't any good to her dead.

Fuck.

Fuck!

My body trembled, blood roaring between my ears. I wanted to roar, to throw my fists into his smug fucking face and protect Jessa. She deserved more, so much more than being used like a fucking whore all because my old man ran in dodgy circles.

"Nix..." she whispered again, nudging me gently.

Me: I know you'll never see this, B. But I really need to talk to someone… need to… fuck, I don't even know what I'm saying. You got out. You got out and I'm so fucking relieved. This place is bad, B. It wears you down and poisons your soul until there's nothing left. How can I hate you for never looking back? I shouldn't… But I do. Part of me hates that you made it out and I'm fucking stuck here, in this life.

Inhaling a shuddering breath, I exited out of the chat thread and threw my cell phone on the dash. But I'd opened that window, letting her ghost creep inside. I felt her here with me. Could imagine her big green eyes watching me, full of sympathy and understanding.

I was so fucking messed up.

Light blazed from the trailer door and Vince appeared, one hand on the button of his jeans. Bile washed through me as I watched him yank the door shut and make his way down the steps. He didn't see me, sitting there in the darkness. If I had a gun, maybe I could have done it. Maybe I could have put a bullet through his skull. Fuck knows the world would have been a better place with one less person like Vince Colombo in it. But how could I abandon Jessa like that? After all she'd done for me.

The second Vince disappeared into his car, I headed

inside, my heart crashing violently against my rib cage. "Jessa?" I called.

At least the place wasn't trashed.

A trickle of unease went through me when she didn't reply. "Jessa?" My voice echoed through the silence.

Slowly, I approached their bedroom, my throat dry, blood roaring between my ears. I pushed the door open. "Jess—"

She lay curled up in a ball in the middle of the bed, the sheet pulled up around her body.

Glancing down at the floor, I inhaled a calming breath. "Jessa?"

"N-Nix." Her voice cracked.

"Are you okay?"

"Can you get me some Tylenol please and a hot water bottle." She clutched the sheet tighter, refusing to look at me.

"Maybe I should take you to the ER."

"N-no. I'll be fine, sweetie. I just need to rest."

"Yeah, okay." The words soured on my tongue as I backtracked to the kitchenette and found her some pain pills and filled the hot water bottle.

"Here you go." I went to the side of the bed, crouching down so she had no choice but to look at me.

Her face was free of bruises, but I didn't for a second doubt her body would be littered in them.

Another wave of bile churned in my stomach. "I can get you out. I could—"

"I think I want to rest now," she said, accepting the

water bottle and pain pills. I helped her sit up a little to wash them down.

"Jessa, this isn't—"

"You're a good boy, Nix." Her weak smile didn't reach her haunted eyes. "Promise me one day you'll get out of here."

"I..."

"Nix." She clutched my hand. "Promise me."

"Y-yeah." I blew out a steady breath, the word cracking something in my chest.

Relief washed over her, and she settled back against the pillows, closing her eyes.

"I'm sorry," I whispered, the words cutting me deep.

How much more could she take before she broke, before her body broke?

The thought gutted me.

Jessa didn't reply. She didn't say anything. I walked out of there and took up position on the couch, with a clear view of their room.

If my father came back drunk and horny there was no chance in hell I was letting him anywhere near her.

Not tonight.

I really fucking hoped he found somewhere else to sleep tonight.

Chapter Nineteen

Harleigh

"HARLEIGH," my father's voice was an unwelcome sound as I roused from a deep sleep. Everything ached; the lingering effects of my afternoon with Nate no doubt.

"Harl—"

"Yeah, yeah" I murmured. "I'm awake."

"Actually," he said, poking his head around the door, "I was hoping we could talk."

"Talk, right." My lips thinned as I tried to force myself upright against the headboard.

"May I come in?"

"Technically, you've already let yourself in, so..."

He gave me a disapproving look and slipped into my room. "How are you feeling?"

"Fine. Good... why?"

"Principal Diego emailed me. He's concerned you skipped out yesterday afternoon."

"Are you keeping tabs on me?" I bristled.

"I would like to think that Principal Diego would inform any parent if their child was cutting class."

Their child. As if I'd ever been his child.

"I had a stomachache."

"You were seen leaving the school grounds with Nate Miller."

Crap.

"He gave me a ride, yeah."

"I'd assumed from the altercation at the mixer at the end of the summer that you and Nate weren't compatible."

"Compatible? What the hell is that supposed to mean?"

He let out a strained chuckle and I hated it. Hated that he had the same cleft in his chin as I did. The same green eyes. I didn't want to look like him, to resemble the man who abandoned me.

"Excuse my poor choice of words," he said. "I merely meant I didn't see the two of you striking up a friendship."

"I wouldn't call us friends."

"But you let him give you a ride?" His brows knitted.

"Is there a point to this interrogation? It's too early for this."

"Principal Diego asked your teachers for some feedback..." He let the words hang, his insinuation heavy in the air.

"So you are monitoring me."

"Harleigh, be reasonable. Last year was... difficult. We all just want to make sure you're handling things okay."

"I don't know how many times I need to say this, but I'm fine."

"So what happened?"

"Ask Max."

I hadn't seen the little shit yet or figured out what the hell I was going to say to him.

"Do I even want to know?" He let out an exasperated sigh.

My fingers curled into the covers as I weighed up my options. I could try to handle Max myself, but risk Sabrina's wrath. Or I could own up to my father and hope he dealt with his treacherous loose-lipped son.

"He told some people... about Albany Hills."

Anger rippled across his features. Michael Rowe was an imposing man. Tall with broad shoulders and a good physique thanks to his regimented workout routine and Mrs. Beaker's healthy cooking. His hair was dark like mine, our eyes and dimple the same. But his expression was always one of cold composure. I guess you didn't become one of the richest men in Hudson Valley through smiles, charm, and a kind heart.

"He did what?"

"Yep." I popped the P. "So as you can imagine, my classmates loved grilling me about that. Me and a girl got into it and Ms. Holland called me out on it, so I bailed."

"I see." He ran a hand over his neatly trimmed whiskers. "Still, I can't have you skipping out on class, it doesn't give off the right impression. I pulled a lot of strings to get you into DA."

Like registering me as Harleigh Rowe instead of Maguire.

Incredulous laughter bubbled in my throat, but I smothered it. I should have known, of course he would care more about the optics of me cutting class than the fact people knew the truth.

"That's it?" I asked as calmly as possible.

"I'll talk to Max, but I suppose the truth would have come out eventually. Please just... don't do anything stupid."

"As opposed to what exactly?"

"We knew it was going to be hard, Harleigh." He pursed his lips. "But you can do this. You can assimilate into DA and have a productive senior year."

"I'll get right on that." I rolled my eyes in disgust, and he blew out a long, steady breath.

Did the man ever lose his cool?

"You're taking your medication?"

"What kind of question is that?" I snapped. "Of course I'm taking it."

I couldn't function without it.

"Sorry." He held up his hands. "That was an insensitive thing to say. I'm just..." A sigh rumbled through him. "This is still new, for all of us."

Still new?

It had been nine months, not that I was counting. But I supposed I had been exiled for most of them.

"Are we done here?" I said. "I need to get ready for school." And try to shake off my awful hangover.

"Yes, okay. I'll make sure Max is punished."

I almost snorted. Like Max was ever punished for anything. And even if he was, he didn't listen.

Michael went to leave, but paused at the door, glancing back at me. "Harleigh, I know I haven't always done right by you, but I really am trying."

He said the words, but all I heard was, 'she's gone and she isn't coming back.' Because if Mom was alive, I wouldn't be stuck in this hellish place. I'd still be in The Row. And yeah, maybe life was hard there. Maybe every day felt like trudging up a mountain with no peak in sight. But it was better than this... this world built on falsities and riches.

Michael lingered, waiting for an answer.

But the bitter truth was, I couldn't give him one.

"I can't believe you skipped class with Nate Miller," Celeste said as we pulled up at school. She cut the engine and turned to me. "I thought we'd decided he was bad news."

"He is bad news. But he was in the right place at the right time."

"You could have texted me." Dejection clung to her words.

"And ruin your squeaky-clean, star student reputation? I wouldn't ever do that."

"Okay, so I probably wouldn't have cut class with you, but I could have helped."

"I know. I just really needed to get out of there."

"Angelica is such a bitch." She scoffed. "Maybe you should tell Miss Hanley."

"No, it'll only make things worse. I can handle it, I promise. Yesterday was just... a blip."

"Did Max apologize yet?"

I arched a brow. "I think we both know that's never going to happen."

"I could... ugh, he's such a little shit." She forced herself to take a breath. "On behalf of our brother, I'm sorry he's such an asshole."

With a tight smile, I shouldered the door open and climbed out of the car, scanning the parking lot for Nate. Things were hazy from when we parted last night. He'd given me a ride back to the house, but I'd insisted he drop me off at the end of the driveway to avoid being seen together.

Fat lot of good that had done me.

We hadn't exchanged numbers or made any kind of promises to see each other again. Not that I wanted to. But I couldn't pinpoint his motivations.

Why had he helped me?

And would he expect me to pay him back somehow?

I pushed all thoughts of Nate out of my head. I had bigger things to worry about, like the delightful sneers being thrown my way from Marc, Angelica, and their group.

"Ignore them," Celeste said, coming around to lace her arm through mine.

"Good morning, my two favorite people." Miles bounded toward us wearing a goofy smile. He slung his arm around Celeste's shoulder. "What are we talking—" He spotted Marc and his friends, and said, "Say no more. Man, I really hate him."

"Join the club," I murmured.

We headed into school, and I stopped at my locker, leaving Celeste and Miles discussing our upcoming anti-pep rally. The details of which they were keeping to themselves. So long as it meant avoiding the actual pep rally at all costs, I was okay with whatever they had planned.

I yanked my locker open and grabbed a couple of textbooks I needed. When I closed the door, Nate grinned down at me. "Maguire."

My brows furrowed. "Uh, hello."

"Don't look so worried. I'm not here to suggest we cut class or anything. Which, by the way, Diego gave me a real roasting for. What's your punishment?"

"Punishment?" I frowned.

"Yeah, didn't he—of course he didn't. Guess it helps having a father who is a major school donor."

"Harleigh?" Celeste said, and I glanced at her. "We're heading to class if you're ready?"

"Go on ahead and I'll see you at lunch, okay?"

"You're sure?" Her eyes lingered on Nate.

"Relax, Rowe. I come in peace." He held up his hands.

"Okay, well, see you later." Celeste dragged a gawking Miles down the hall, and Nate let out a breathy chuckle.

"And here's me thinking Celeste was on my side."

"There are sides now?"

He gave me a half-hearted shrug. "How are you feeling this morning?"

"It took a while for me to get going. What are you doing, Nate?"

"Well, I thought I was saying hi. But I'm sensing I missed the mark."

"We're not friends," I said.

"You wound me, Maguire. I don't hotbox my car for anyone, you know." Amusement danced in his eyes, but I didn't return his smile.

"I'd prefer it if you kept our... interaction to yourself."

"Interaction? Is that what we're calling it? You know," he leaned in, lowering his voice, "some people might say I did you a favor."

"Hey, Miller," Marc's voice made my skin crawl. I took a step back, putting some space between us, and glowered at him.

"Your *friend* is calling," I said. "Better run along."

Nate's lips pursed as if he was considering his next words carefully. But they never came.

Instead, he gave me a small smirk and said, "See you around, Maguire," and he disappeared down the hall.

As I entered third period, a wall of muscle stepped into the doorway, refusing me entry.

"Seriously?" I snarled up at Marc.

"What's up with you and Miller?"

"What? Nothing."

"Don't act dumb, Maguire. I know you two cut class together yesterday. Ange said she saw him chase you out."

"Why don't you ask him since you're such good friends and all?"

"I did ask him, and he wouldn't tell me. So I'm asking you. Why the fuck would he come to *your* rescue?"

Nate hadn't told him. Interesting. He could have easily sold me out to them, giving them even more ammunition to come at me with.

But he hadn't.

I didn't know what to make of it, or him.

"Maybe he was feeling chivalrous."

"Or maybe you made it worth his while."

"What the hell is that supposed to mean?"

"You know—"

"Mr. Denby, Miss Rowe, I assume you're both about to go inside and take your seats?" The teacher glared at us both.

"Just swapping some notes, sir," Marc stepped aside and swept his arm out. "After you, Maguire."

I slipped into the room, pinning Marc with a terse glare. His dark chuckle followed me. "I'll be watching you, *Birdie*."

My heart faltered but I forced myself to keep walking. To ignore his eyes drilling holes into the back of my head.

"Seats, now please," the teacher boomed, and I dropped down into my chair.

"So," Ange said from somewhere behind me. "Did you find out what her and Nate were doing?"

"No, she wouldn't spill."

"She was probably sucking his dick for some pills. You know he can get a hold of anything."

"Yeah, maybe."

Maybe.

Anger flared inside me, but I bit the inside of my cheek to ground myself. If I didn't give them the power, they couldn't hurt me.

But it really was easier said than done.

enough. Worthy enough to wear a Hawks jersey and represent his team.

"We might be the underdogs, everyone might expect us to mess up again, but this is our season. I can feel it." He whipped off his ball cap and dragged his hand through his salt and pepper hair. "I want you to go out there tonight and soak it up. Your school is behind you. I'm behind you. You just have to believe you can do it. Hands in."

We all moved closer, shoulder to shoulder. Friends. Teammates. Brothers.

"Nix, son, you want to do the honors?"

Fuck.

Pressure closed in around me, making my lungs smart. I drew in a deep breath, shaking off the weight of expectation. Coach's. My teammates. The whole damn school's.

"Uh, yeah." I cleared my throat. "Coach is right, we came close last year." Too fucking close, but it had slipped through our fingers, and it was all my fault. Because I'd lost sight of the prize. "So this year we need to step up and make it ours. We're a good team, a strong fucking team, and we can do it. I know we can. Hawks on three. One... two... three... *Hawks.*"

My teammates' cheers rolled through me, boosting the adrenaline coursing through my veins. But when we burst through the doors and jogged into the gymnasium, a sinking feeling spread through me.

Because I knew if I looked into the bleachers, I wouldn't find her.

Harleigh was gone.

She was one of them now. She was where she'd always belonged.

And I needed to let her go.

But how did you give up a part of yourself—the better part?

She hadn't just been my best friend; she had been my conscience. My redemption. My anchor.

Harleigh Wren Maguire had been my reason for breathing. Without her, I was drifting. Lost in an angry sea that wanted to pull me under.

It had taken months, *months* for me to get back to a place where I could function without her. But now she was back. Right on the other side of the reservoir, living on her father's estate. And my heart, my heart couldn't fucking accept it.

Even if my head knew I had to let her go.

"Soak it up, Nix." Coach clapped me on the shoulder, jolting me from my reverie. "This is all for you, son. It's all for you."

"Yeah." I gave him a tight-lipped smile as he guided me toward the podium.

It was all for me...

They were all chanting my name.

Wilder.

Wilder.

Wilder.

I was their star player, their idol, their favorite...

But it didn't fill me with excitement anymore, it didn't

get my blood pumping, and my skin tingling. Something was missing.

She was missing.

And I didn't feel whole anymore.

The entire upperclassmen of Darling Hill High including some ninth and tenth graders had made it out to the reservoir to party. It had taken almost ten minutes to fight our way through the amped crowd, all eager to rub shoulders with the Hawks. Hench and Kye lapped it up, especially when it came to the attention from the girls. But Zane and I had pushed ahead, eager to get to our usual positions next to the bonfire.

Sure enough, no one had touched our rickety old garden chairs. Zane dropped two six packs of beer on the ground and sat down. "This place is carnage."

I surveyed the scene. Kids were already drunk or high, maybe even both. Dancing and goofing around on the vast stretch of derelict land next to the reservoir.

Zane handed me a beer and tipped his own bottle to where Kye had some girl pressed up against a tree. "He's such a dog."

"At least one of us is getting some."

"Plenty of girls here would be willing to bounce on your dick." Zane smirked, and I flipped him off.

"Not interested."

"Let me guess, your dick don't work right since finding out B is back."

"Can we not do this again?"

"Fine." He shrugged, leaning back in his chair. "So what do you think? Can we go all the way this season? Coach seems pretty certain we can."

"I mean, it's possible. The team is in good shape."

"But...?"

"I don't know, Z. I thought I'd want it. Senior year, our final season..."

"You always thought you'd be doing it with her by your side?"

I met his eyes, grimacing. It all came back to her.

Birdie.

My B.

"I took her for granted." I let out a heavy sigh. "She was always there, no matter what, and I... fuck, I messed up."

"It's life, Nix. Shit happens and then you die." He took a long pull on his beer. "If it bothers you that much, fix it. She's across the res, not dead."

I flinched at the honesty, and frustration, in his words.

"Nah, I need to cut her loose." I stared at the hypnotic flames, watching them as they licked the inky sky. "Let her fly free."

The Row had only ever clipped Birdie's wings. She wasn't made for a place like this. She wasn't made for a guy like me. Besides, too much had happened between us.

"So that's it? You're gonna move on and forget about

her? Just like that?" He snorted. "I'll believe that when I see it."

"Fucker," I muttered. "Miss Kyrie busted your balls about college applications yet?"

"We both know Darling Hill Community College is about as good as it gets for me. If I even bother."

"You could get help for her. See about—"

"No fucking way, Nix. She as good as raised me. I owe her everything."

It was true. Zane's grandma had raised him after his mom had died when he was just a kid, and his waste of space sperm donor hadn't cared enough to stick around. Mrs. Washington had always been a force to be reckoned with until the MS set in and began to ravage her body. On the days she needed it, Zane cared for her at home since their medical insurance didn't stretch to long stays in hospital. But it was hard on him, on them both.

"Yeah, Z. I know, I know..." I raked a hand down my face, blowing out a long breath. We were two guys stuck in impossible situations. He couldn't leave his gran, and I couldn't leave Jessa. People depended on us. People's *lives* depended on us. How the fuck were we supposed to chase our own dreams *and* protect the people we cared about?

The answer was... we couldn't.

The Row owned us.

Whether we liked it or not, The Row was our home. Our burden.

It was our motherfucking prison.

And there wasn't a damn thing we could do about it.

Nix

"WHAT'S UP YOUR ASS?" Zane climbed into the back seat and yanked the door closed.

I glanced back at him and shrugged. "Just the usual."

"Your old man being a dick?"

"Isn't he always?"

"What's up, fuckers?" Kye joined us, wearing a shit-eating grin. But his expression fell when he noticed the atmosphere in the car. "No, no, no. This will not do. It's Halloween, baby. Time to get fucked and get fucked up."

"I can't believe I let you talk me into this." Zane thrust his mask in the air. "Didn't we outgrow this shit two years ago?"

"Nah, Halloween is all about come as you aren't." Kye snickered. "That, B?" he motioned to my cell phone, and I nodded.

"Just texting her now."

Me: Trick or treat?

I smiled at Harleigh's instant reply.

B: Haha, funny. I'm almost ready.

Ignoring Zane and Kye discussing the game last weekend, I texted back.

Nix: Good, I'm ready to fuck things up.

I didn't give her a chance to reply before sending another message.

Nix: Your chariot awaits.

B: Two minutes.

I waited five before texting her again. If I knew anything about Harleigh, it was that she was never on time.

Nix: Kye is getting restless... are you coming?

Me: Leaving now.

The second she stepped out of her trailer, my heart catapulted into my throat.

What the hell was she wearing?

"You are so fucking screwed." Kye chuckled, clearly amused by the turn of events.

Zane caught my eye and shook his head as if to say, 'He's right.'

She climbed into the car, and Kye let out a low whistle. "Holy. Shit. Is that little Harleigh Wren?"

"Hey, guys." She tugged on the hem of her skirt, if you could call it that.

Fuck.

"Birdie," I whispered thickly, unable to stop my eyes roaming over her body. I didn't know where to look first, I'd never seen so much of her skin on display. My hands gripped the steering wheel tightly as I silently willed my pulse to calm the fuck down.

"What do you think?" she asked, peeking up at me through long, dark lashes.

"I... it's..." I cleared my throat. "It's a little... much, don't you think?"

She blanched and I felt like a total asshole, but I didn't know what else to say. Because holy fucking shit, she hardly resembled Harleigh.

My Harleigh.

"Dude." Kye leaned over from the back seat and smacked me upside the head. "A little much? Have you lost your goddamn mind? She looks hot as—" Zane elbowed him in the ribs, and he yelled. "Ow, fuck face, what the hell was that for?"

"We should go," I grumbled, stepping on the gas.

Harleigh was quiet, pressing her head against the cool glass, deep in thought.

Things were as awkward as fuck, but when she'd agreed to come tonight, I thought she would choose a safe costume. Something that covered her up and didn't make her stand out. Something that wouldn't require me to spend the night keeping guys away from her, guys thinking they could touch what wasn't theirs to touch.

"I heard that some of the academy kids might show," Zane said.

"Nah, no way," I replied. "They don't have big enough balls. Especially not after how we kicked their asses on the field last month."

"Only telling you what I heard, man."

"If they're stupid enough to wander into our territory, then they'd better be ready to pay the price." Anger zipped down my spine.

"Hell yeah." Zane leaned forward, chuckling, and we high-fived through the seats.

Harleigh had dressed up as Harley Quinn complete with pigtails. The three of us had stuck with our plain black hoodies and black jeans, adding LED neon masks.

She peeked over at me again and our gazes collided. Fuck, her eyes. They seemed to draw me in even more than usual. My jaw clenched as I sucked in a sharp breath and turned my attention back on the road.

"Nix, I—"

"Not now, B, yeah?" I said, a little harsher than intended, but I was a fucking mess. "Not now."

Out of the corner of my eye, I saw Harleigh sink further into her seat. And I hated that I'd made her doubt herself. But shit, if I wasn't having a real hard time reining in my emotions.

She looked... She looked like a total knockout. Not that I didn't think she was beautiful all the time, I did. But her costume was enticing to say the least. At least when she was in her normal everyday clothes, I could fight the urge to drag her into my arms and kiss the shit out of her.

But dressed like that, I wasn't sure I could behave.

Fuck.

I was in trouble.

So much fucking trouble.

Darling Hill Reservoir was the place to be tonight. Surrounded by the dense forest, it was the perfect place for teenagers to cause a little mayhem without upsetting the cops.

And tonight, it was party central. A huge bonfire crackled into the night as people danced and laughed, sipping warm beer and stolen liquor.

"Wilder, about time." Paul Odell, a senior from school, stalked over to us, fist bumping me then the guys. "Shit, Harleigh, is that you under all—"

"Don't go there, man," Kye murmured. "Not unless you want Nix to rip your head off."

Paul stepped back, smirking as he held up his hands. "I can see why it would be a problem." He glanced at Harleigh, and then back to me. "Shit, man." He chuckled, a knowing glint in his eye.

I glowered at him. *Back the fuck off, asshole.*

Harleigh shrank into herself, and I wanted to reassure her like I usually would, but I couldn't trust myself to speak.

Before I could figure out what the fuck to say, she cleared her throat and said, "I'm going to get a drink." She disappeared into the crowd and Kye let out a low whistle.

"I did not see that coming. She looks—"

"Carter," I warned.

"Yeah, yeah, I got the memo. But come on, Nix. Little Harleigh Wren is all grown up. And if you don't stake your claim tonight, someone will. Because holy shit... girl looks fine."

The knot in my stomach tightened. He wasn't wrong, Harleigh looked... fuck, she looked like sin and sex. Every guy's wet dream.

She'd knocked me on my fucking ass, and I didn't know how to get back up or what the hell to say to her.

Things were changing between us, had been for a while. We were juniors now, but I didn't want to rush her. I wasn't exactly a saint where girls were concerned, and until recently, I'd never allowed myself to even think that there might be a possibility of me and Harleigh taking things to the next level.

I knew she liked me. Knew she harbored feelings for me. But it had always been so innocent—*she* was so innocent—that I'd never acted on it.

Fuck, what was I talking about?

I wasn't good enough for her. I never would be. And there was no doubt in my mind that Harleigh was too good for a place like The Row. For a guy like me. She was quiet and kind and loyal. All she needed was the confidence to spread her wings and fly and she would never have to look back at this place.

My stomach sank. I couldn't imagine a world where I didn't have Harleigh by my side. She was my best friend. Every-fucking-thing to me. But she'd get out of The Row one day, she had to.

And although it would fucking kill me to set her free, I would.

Because that's what you did for the people you cared about.

The people you loved.
You let them go.

Harleigh

"TELL me again why he's here?" Celeste threw a displeased look at Nate, and then frowned back at me.

"He invited himself, what was I supposed to do?"

"Uh, I don't know," she whisper-hissed. "How about say no? Make up some excuse about why he couldn't possibly come with us. I'm sure you could have thought of something."

"You know, you could try speaking a little louder, Rowe." Nate chuckled from upfront. "Then I might actually hear what you're saying."

I suppressed a smile, but Celeste silently fumed.

"I think it's cool you're tagging along," Miles said. "Evens things out a little."

"What the hell, Miles?" Celeste leaned forward and tugged his hair. He yelped, trying to swat her away.

Nate caught my eye in the rearview mirror and arched his brow. "You good back there, Maguire?"

I nodded, moving my gaze to the window. But not

before I caught his smirk. I didn't know Nate's story, didn't want to know it, but Celeste was right, when he'd overheard us talking about ditching the pep rally, he'd asked to tag along. Had even gone so far as to offer to drive us somewhere we could hang out and have fun. Whatever that meant.

And I hadn't had it in me to tell him no.

"The reservoir?" Miles said and I bolted upright.

"No. Absolutely not."

It was one thing to come out here on an afternoon when no one was around. But it was the weekend.

"Relax, Maguire. We're not going across to their territory. It's a big place, we'll be good."

So why did it feel like tempting fate? It was Friday night. When I'd lived in The Row, every Friday was a party down at the res. Every weekend without fail.

I hadn't come down here much. The noise and crowd. All the alcohol and drugs. I didn't like it.

Celeste touched my arm, and asked, "Hey, you okay? We don't have to—"

"It's fine."

Fine.

The staple word of my vocabulary.

"Come on, you guys. I promised you a night of anti-pep rally fun. It'd be nice if you gave me a chance to deliver."

"What's in it for you, Miller?" Celeste drawled.

"Beats hanging out with Denby and his bunch of douchebag friends, or my brother and Max." He feigned a shudder.

"You're trying to tell me you and Marc aren't—"

"We're cousins."

"No shit," Miles said.

"It's not something either of us likes to advertise."

"Can't say I blame you there."

"But family politics can make things... difficult. Sometimes it's easier to keep the peace than rock the boat."

Nate pulled off the main road and followed a dirt road down toward the reservoir. It was a natural lake that had been siphoned off from the Hudson River. I had never seen it from this perspective though.

"Okay, so this is cool." Sarcasm dripped from Miles's words as he frowned.

"Look up." Nate leaned forward and pointed skyward.

"The water tank... no way."

"The view is pretty incredible."

"Is it safe?" Celeste asked.

Nate twisted around and shrugged. "Scared, Rowe?"

"I'm in," she said with mild confidence.

"Mulligan?"

"Hell yeah. Lead the way."

"Seriously?" I gawked at Celeste. "What happened to 'tell me why he's here again?'"

"We might as well check it out. It does look kind of cool."

With a shake of my head, I got out of the car. Right as Nate climbed out of the driver's seat. "I brought some treats." He winked.

"That was one time."

"If you say so." With a dismissive smirk he headed for Miles and Celeste who looked giddy about our strange adventure with the bad boy of DA.

I trudged after them; following them up the creaking, rusty stairs leading to the platform surrounding the tank. It was high, really high, the air thinning a little.

"Holy crap, the view is..." Celeste grinned, grabbing the handrail and taking in the sight.

"It's something," Nate said, lighting up a blunt. "You guys want in?" he asked Celeste and Miles.

"Nah, I'm good with beer."

"Me too," Celeste added, moving closer to Miles. He casually slung his arm over her shoulder, and I lifted a brow, noting the slight stain to her cheeks.

"Maguire, you in?"

I felt the heavy stares of my friends, their judgment brushing up against me. But I also knew how good it would feel.

Crap.

This was a bad idea.

"Does it react with your meds?" Celeste asked, a hint of concern in her voice.

"It... uh, didn't the other day," I admitted. "Not like the alcohol."

"I knew it. I knew you two had gotten high together."

"Listen, Celeste, I—"

"It's cool, I get." No judgment lingered in her expression, only sympathy. "At least, I'm trying to. If it takes the edge off and it's safe, then don't let me stop you."

Nate inhaled a deep hit and blew a wisp of smoke right at me. "What do you say, Maguire? Want to get high with me?"

I nodded. My body singing for the reprieve I knew he could offer me.

"Atta girl." He passed me the blunt. I glanced at Miles and Celeste, and they moved down the platform, sitting down to let their legs dangle over the edge. Nate did the same, patting the space next to him.

I dropped down, inhaling deeply on the blunt, letting the acrid smoke fill my lungs. It rolled through me, like a soft brush of a hand down my spine. Soothing. Comforting. Reassuring.

"Okay, okay, Maguire. Hand it back. We have all night."

Our eyes collided and something passed between us. It wasn't attraction or even friendship, but it was *something*. As if he knew what I needed because he needed it too.

My brows furrowed and I looked away, letting my gaze fall on the reservoir. At the vast stretch of water and the field and trees beyond it.

"Looks like your friends are partying," Nate said quietly.

Sure enough, there was a bonfire on the other side of the lake, faceless people moving around, their shadows dancing around like demons in the night.

"They're not my friends," I whispered.

They never were.

Only Nix and the guys, and I guess Kye's sister Chloe.

But we were less friends and more two girls stuck in a world that we didn't belong in.

For a second, I wondered if she was down there, partying with them. Getting drunk and making mistakes and being a normal seventeen-year-old. Nix wasn't the only one who had abandoned me last year—they all had.

My chest constricted but Nate said, "You know, sometimes, I think I was born on the wrong side of town."

"You don't mean that."

Sure, from up here it looked like a good time. It looked like a group of kids kicking back and enjoying their Friday night. But Nate didn't know what it was like for them. The shit they were dealing with day in, day out. The pain and trauma and burdens they carried.

"Sorry," he whispered. "That was a dickish thing to say."

"It's okay." I glanced up at him. "Everyone has their own stuff going on, Nate, and I know that money doesn't solve everything. It doesn't make people happy. But life in Old Darling Hill is worlds apart from life in The Row."

"This life carries its own burdens, Maguire." A shadow passed over his expression, and it was on the tip of my tongue to ask what he meant. But Celeste's laughter filled the air.

We both looked around at her and Miles sharing their own private joke.

"Something you want to share with the rest of us, Rowe?" Nate asked.

"No, no. We were just talking." She hiccoughed.

"Although this beer feels like it's going straight to my head. Did anyone bring any snacks?"

Nate dipped his hand into his jacket and pulled out a box of Swedish Fish. "Don't say I never give you anything." He threw it to her, and she grinned.

"Maybe I was wrong about you, Miller."

His eyes met mine, twinkling. "I'll take that as a compliment."

"What do you think they're doing up there?" I said, staring up at the blanket of stars as I laid on the hood of Nate's car.

We'd come down from the water tank earlier when I started to feel a little sick, but Celeste and Miles had decided to stay up there.

"If you have to ask, you probably don't want to know." Nate smirked. He'd retrieved a camping chair from his trunk. Just something he had lying around, he'd said.

"Celeste said she isn't interested in Miles like that."

"Haven't you ever fooled around with someone you're not interested in *like that*?"

I ducked my head, heat creeping into my cheeks and he chuckled. "Oh shit, you haven't, have you?"

"Is it really such a bad thing?"

"Not at all. I think it's admirable."

"Admirable," I murmured. "Yeah, right."

"So you and Wilder..."

"We are not having this conversation, Nate." Not now, not ever.

"He really hurt you, huh?"

I gave him a withering look and he blew out a thin breath. "Fine, Wilder is off-limits." His eyes went past me, over the car, as he said, "So I guess you won't want to know he's heading right this way."

"What?" I bolted upright and glanced behind me, my stomach plummeting into my toes. "Did he set you up to this?"

"No. No way. I had no idea he would wander over here. It's got to be almost a mile."

Tipping my head to the sky, I inhaled a deep breath.

"You," Nix said.

A chill ran through me at the sound of his voice, the anger there, sending shivers skittering down my spine.

"I come in peace, Wilder." Nate sipped on his beer.

"You shouldn't be here," Zane said.

It occurred to me they hadn't realized I was here. Crap.

"Just enjoying the view, man."

Nix and Zane emerged from the side of the car, closing in on Nate. He looked up at them, still drinking his beer. "Where are your friends?" Nix drawled.

I knew that drawl. He was drunk. Maybe a little high. But there was something else too, an undertone of anger that laced his words.

"I'm not looking for trouble. I'm here—"

"With me." I slid my legs off the hood and stood.

"Birdie," Nix whipped around. "What the actual fuck?"

"Hello, Phoenix."

I could have sworn he flinched, but a cool mask slid over his expression. "You're here with him? Are you fucking kidding me?"

"Celeste and Miles are here too."

"I don't see them anywhere, do you?" Zane said, glaring at me like I was the devil incarnate. But it was nothing compared to the way Nix looked at me.

Cold. Ruthless. Unforgiving.

"You two fucking?" he spat, his words lashing my insides.

"Come on, Wilder." Nate stood. "That's not—"

"Nobody asked you, asshole." Zane leveled him with an icy look.

"Okay, okay, enough with the territorial alpha guy bullshit. Nate is right, we didn't come here to cause trouble." My head swam and I lifted a hand to rub my temples. "It's not like we're anywhere near the party."

"Are you high?" Nix narrowed his eyes.

"That's none of your business."

"What the fuck, Birdie? You get high now? Is that what was wrong with you at the fair? Were you—"

"Stop. Just stop." I held up my hand, panting. "What I do with my life is none of your business, Nix. If you aren't going to leave, we will." I marched over to the water tank, ready to shout for Celeste and Miles to come down, but Nix grabbed my arm.

"Can we talk?"

"Talk?" I scoffed. "What could we possibly have to say to each other?"

"Birdie, come on... please?"

Tell him no. Just tell him no and leave. Leave, Harleigh.

But I couldn't do it. I couldn't say the words.

Instead, I said nothing. I *did* nothing as his hand slipped into mine and he started tugging me toward the trees.

Nix

"WE'LL BE BACK," I said over my shoulder to Miller and Zane.

"Ten minutes. You get ten minutes and then I'm coming after you," Zane grumbled.

The motherfucker meant it too.

Harleigh didn't resist when my hand slipped to hers, and I threaded our fingers together. I realized my error the second shivers ran through me. Touching her was like a zap of electricity rushing through my body, making my skin heat and my heart pound wildly in my chest.

It was probably all the alcohol and weed too, but everything was amplified with my hand wrapped around hers. It felt right. Normal. Nice. And I hated it. I hated that after all this time, she still wielded so much power over me.

"Where are we going?" she asked, with no trace of excitement or anticipation, just mild indifference.

"Just a little further," I said.

I really didn't want to have this conversation in front of Zane or Miller. Especially not Nate Miller.

Shit, hearing her voice and realizing she was out here with him, it had been like a punch to the gut. The idea that she had moved on, with some rich fucking prick who thought he was better than the likes of me.

Fuck.

"Nix." Harleigh yanked her hand free. "Stop, just stop."

I turned around, meeting her murderous gaze. She'd always been so soft, so quiet and shy. I wasn't used to seeing her like this... with this fight in her eyes.

But I liked it.

I really fucking liked it.

"Birdie, I—"

"Don't." She gritted out. "Don't call me that."

"How are you?"

"How am I?" Bitter laughter spilled from her. "What are you doing, Phoenix? At the fair you told Zane to get rid of me and now you want to what? Hang out? Catch up for old time's sake?"

"No, that's not... I... fuck." I dragged a hand through my hair and down the back of my neck. "You're with him?"

"I'm not with him. I'm just hanging out with him."

"Getting high..."

Who was this girl? Because she sure as shit wasn't the Harleigh I'd known most of my life.

"Like I said, it's none of your business."

I took a step forward. "I don't like it, B. This isn't you; it isn't—"

"You don't know anything about me anymore and you sure as hell don't get to swoop in and act like you still care. Not after what you did." A shudder ran through her, and I fought the urge to pull her into my arms and hold her.

"I can explain..." There was so much I needed to explain. "I can—"

"No, Nix. It's done. It's in the past. We're in the past. Zane was right." Conviction glittered in her murky eyes. "This, us, it isn't healthy. We can't keep doing this, torturing each other. Whatever we had, it's done. It's over."

"You don't mean that, B." Because it didn't feel over. It felt unresolved: a dark cloud lingering over us, a storm brewing. Circling. And until it exploded, it wouldn't pass.

She got right in my face, green eyes coolly assessing me. "I don't know how many more ways to say this. I. Hate. You. Everything we ever shared... It was a lie. I realize that now."

Anger vibrated through me, setting off a wildfire inside my chest. How could she say that? After everything we'd been through, how could she—

"This was a mistake," she said, going to walk away.

But I grabbed her arm, yanking her back to me.

We weren't done.

Not until—

"Get off me, you... you overbearing asshole," she spat with fire and fury.

The air crackled. My heart hammering against my chest, my pulse thudding in my ears.

This girl. She wasn't only my kryptonite, she was my addiction. The one bad habit I'd never fully succumbed to but had never been able to quit either.

She was the only girl in the entire world with the power to ruin me.

And she was staring at me as if she meant every word.

As if she truly hated me.

"Phoenix, I—"

I grabbed the back of her neck and crashed my lips down on hers, swallowing her hateful, spineless words. She could hate me. She could despise and resent me. But it didn't change the fact that I felt it.

I still felt the invisible tether binding us.

"Fuck, B," I breathed, sliding my hand into her hair and angling her face up to give me better access to her lips. To her goddamn delectable mouth. She pressed her lips into a tight line, refusing to give me entry.

I smirked. "You want to play it like that, huh?" I leaned in, licking the corner of her mouth, tracing my tongue along the seam of her lips. She tried to resist, thrashing against my hold, but I tightened my grip in her hair, holding her at my mercy.

She could fight me all she wanted, but I knew the truth. Her body betrayed the lies she had spewed.

Harleigh wanted me.

Even if she hated me.

And right now, I didn't care enough to stop.

"Open up for me, Birdie, let me in," I whispered, kissing the corner of her mouth.

Her eyes simmered with anger, and I pulled back slightly to look at her, really look at her. Maybe I'd misread things. Maybe I'd seen what I wanted to see. Because she was a statue in my hold. A silent storm, waiting to strike.

Fuck, I'd messed up. I'd—

She crashed into me, her hands going around my shoulders, her mouth fusing to mine. Devouring me. A breathy moan spilled from her, and need pulsed through me as I slid my hand down her spine, pressing her closer, erasing every inch of space between us. I needed to feel her, feel the soft curves of her body, her smooth skin. Feel the steady beat of her heart beneath my palm.

Kissing Birdie, breathing her air, her taste, it was like coming home. It was the thing that had been missing for the last nine months.

Her.

Me.

Us.

"Fuck, B," I breathed, cupping her face. Kissing her deeper, stroking my tongue against hers, exploring every inch of her mouth. Her skin.

I couldn't get enough.

She made the loud noises in my head quiet.

She made the beast inside me slumber.

She made the darkness circling me abate.

"Nix," she whispered, slowing the kiss.

"I'm here, B. I'm right fucking here."

Wetness coated my cheeks, confusing me. I pulled back slightly, touching my head to hers. My heart was a wild beating thing in my chest as I stared at her. Took in the tears, her broken expression.

"B-B?" I choked out, wiping away the tears with the pad of my thumb. "What is it? What's wrong?"

"This was a mistake." She stepped back, inhaling a ragged breath.

"A mistake?" My voice turned cold, my blood like ice in my veins. "Because you're too good for me now? That it?"

She stared at me, shuttering her expression. Refusing to let me see what really lay there in her green eyes.

"This was a mistake," she repeated, folding her arms over her chest, and touching a finger to her lips. Prodding. As if she was trying to remember if it had been real or not.

It had been real; the most fucking real I'd felt in weeks. Months. And she was going to pretend like it didn't matter.

"So that's it, huh?" Dejection coated my insides. Thick and sludgy, it filled my chest making it hard to breathe. "You don't even want to hear my side of the story?"

"I..." Hesitation flickered in her eyes. "It doesn't matter. Too much has happened." Her gaze dropped to the ground. "We can never go back."

I wanted to roar at her. Beg her to listen. To hear me out. But I wouldn't... I couldn't.

Not yet.

"The past doesn't define you, doesn't define who you are," I said. "That's what you used to tell me."

When I'd turn up on the door sporting another bruise

from my father that's what she'd say to me. Always trying to remind me that I wasn't like him, that I would never become him.

"And it doesn't." She met my heavy stare once more. "But this is different. We're different."

"So that's it? You just want to pretend like this didn't happen?"

"It shouldn't have happened," she said quietly, barely meeting my eyes.

"Such pretty lies, B." I closed the distance between us, reaching out to snag a strand of her hair. She pressed her lips together, refusing to answer. "It was always you, B," I admitted. "I know things are fucked up. I know I messed up... but so did you. This isn't over. We're not over. We're not—"

"Yo, Nix. We need to go." Zane burst through the trees, pale and wide-eyed.

I jerked away from Harleigh. "What happened?"

"Chloe."

"Fuck." I dragged a hand down my face.

"Kye needs us, man."

I glanced back at Harleigh, and her lips parted as if she was going to say something. But she thought better of it, snapping her lips closed.

Say it, I silently implored. *Ask me to stay*.

The words never came though. She just stood there, expressionless. Frozen. As if we hadn't just devoured each other with our teeth and tongues.

"Yeah, whatever. Let's go." I spun around and stormed

off, fighting my natural instinct to stay with her. To protect her.

"Hey, man. Where's Harleigh?" Miller asked as I blew past him. "Wilder, where's—"

But I was gone.

I needed to get the fuck out of here, anger descending over me like a red mist.

The whole situation was fucked.

"Whoa, Nix, calm down." Zane caught up with me as I followed the shadowy path back toward the party. We'd only wandered down here because Cherri turned up and decided to try to get a rise out of me by draping herself all over Hench.

I really didn't give a fuck who she did or didn't get with. But I couldn't stand his smug expression as they'd stood across the bonfire, practically dry-fucking. Zane had seen my fist clench, seen the anger build, and suggested we walk it off.

Movement over by the water tank had caught my eye and we'd decided to check it out. I'd never expected to find Birdie though. Hanging out with Nate Miller, her eyes bloodshot and constricted.

"Motherfucker." I kicked a stone, sending it flying across the ground.

"Feel better?" Zane snorted.

"Fuck you, Z. Fuck you."

"What happened?"

"A whole bunch of shit I'd rather not talk about."

He tsked. "Went that well, huh?"

"What happened with Chloe?"

"Kye got a message saying she needs bailing out from some party in Dartmouth."

A trickle of unease went through me. "She okay?"

"Not sure. He tried to call her back, but she wouldn't answer."

"Shit."

"Yeah, so we need to hurry the fuck up."

"What are we waiting for?"

Maybe I couldn't fix the shit with Harleigh, but I could be there for Kye and Chloe. She was as good as family. And if anyone had even tried to hurt...

Well, it wouldn't end well for them.

Harleigh

"WANT TO TALK ABOUT IT?" Nate asked as we waited for Celeste and Miles to finish up whatever the hell they were doing.

"Nope."

"Okay... although, you know it has been said, I'm a pretty good listener."

"What's with the change of heart all of a sudden?"

"Excuse me?" He blinked up at me.

"You were a sleazy asshole at the mixer. A total creep when you came over to hang out at the pool with Max and your brother. And now you what? You want to be my shoulder to cry on? I'm not buying it."

"That's fair. I was a dick." He ran a hand down his face. "Hell, I am a dick. But I figured we had something in common."

My eyes crinkled as I studied him. There was no hint of teasing. In fact, he almost seemed... sad.

"I know, Maguire. About what happened to you."

"I... I don't know what you mean."

"It's okay, your secret is safe with me. But I get it."

"I don't know what you think you get, but—"

"My sister." He glanced at the ground, kicking the gravel with his sneaker. "She... uh—"

Laughter floated over to us, Celeste and Miles emerging from the shadows.

"You two look... happy," I said dryly, arching my brow.

"She's drunk." Miles hugged her closer. "We should probably get her home."

"Yeah. It's getting late." Nate stood and folded his chair up. Part of me wanted to ask what he'd been about to tell me, but the other part was scared to walk that path with him.

I didn't want to bond over my trauma. Not with him. Not with anyone.

The scars from my past were mine and mine alone. Scratched onto my skin and etched onto my heart. They were my reminder of where I'd come from, where I'd been, and where I wanted to go. Sharing that felt... It felt wrong somehow.

So I was relieved when he gave me a small smile and ushered us to get into his car.

"What did you two get up to?" Celeste asked, shuffling into the back seat beside me.

"Talked mostly."

"Until Wilder and Zane Washington showed up."

I flashed Nate a murderous look in the rearview mirror.

"What?" Celeste gasped. "They were here? Are you okay?"

"I'm fine."

Liar.

Because the second Nix's lips had slammed down on mine, something inside me had cracked wide open. He'd kissed me. Pulled me under his spell, and I didn't feel wholly in control of myself.

But it was just a kiss.

Some unresolved bullshit we hadn't aired.

I knew firsthand when emotions ran high, people acted out of character. They did things they wouldn't usually do. I couldn't trust a single thing about that kiss—even if it had ruined me for all other kisses.

My fingers drifted to my mouth, prodding gently, in a feeble attempt to feel his mouth still on mine. *Damn you, Phoenix.*

He couldn't just leave me alone.

It made no sense when he'd walked away from me so easily last year.

I felt Celeste's heavy stare and thrust my hand under my thigh. "What aren't you telling me?" she whispered.

"What aren't *you* telling *me*?" I countered, and she flushed right to the tips of her ears.

'Later,' she mouthed.

"Fine." I leaned my head back against the seat and closed my eyes.

Tonight had been confusing. From Nate wanting to come with us, to Nix turning up and kissing me, to Nate's attempt at a heart-to-heart. I felt exhausted. My temporary high had slipped away the second Nix kissed me.

And now I was left with nothing but a gaping hole in my chest.

"Hey." Celeste slipped into my room and climbed into bed with me. "Can I stay in here?"

"Are you going to tell me what happened with Miles?"

"Oh God, Harleigh, it was... the biggest surprise of my life."

"So you two...?" I waggled my brows, surprised how easy this felt. Talking to her. Sharing secrets.

"We didn't fuck, if that's what you mean."

"You kiss your mother with that mouth?"

She balled up her fist and pressed it to her mouth, suppressing a smile.

"Celeste..."

"Fine, okay." She inhaled a deep breath. "We were talking and then he just looked at me, like really looked at me, and the air turned thick and my heart started beating so hard, and I knew. I knew he was going to kiss me... and I let him."

"And was it good?"

"So freaking good. And unexpected. I mean, it's Miles. He isn't exactly—"

"The bad boy from across the reservoir?" My brow

lifted and she rolled her eyes at me. "So, what else happened?"

"He touched me, *down there*. I swear to God, Harleigh, I came so freaking hard."

"Way to go Miles." I chuckled. "Did you reciprocate?"

"Of course I did." She shrugged. "And let me tell you, I was not disappointed."

"I'm happy for you, Celeste. Miles is a good guy and it's obvious he dotes on you."

A strange sensation snaked through me. I didn't want to think of it as jealousy because Celeste deserved this. She deserved to be happy with a guy who would treat her right. But she was the only real friend I had here. If the two of them started going steady, I'd find myself without an anchor. And maybe that made me a shitty person, but the truth was I was scared about drifting again. Scared of losing myself to the darkness.

"Harleigh, what is it?" Concern pinched her brows, but I couldn't tell her.

"Nothing." I forced my lips into a convincing smile. "I'm so happy for you."

"He asked me to Homecoming." A giddy expression washed over her. "I mean, I told him I'd think about it. I didn't want to seem too eager, you know? But it felt right, Harleigh. It felt... wonderful."

Guilt and shame rose inside me, choking the air from my lungs. God, I was a horrible person to make this about me. But I needed her. I needed Celeste more than I cared to admit. But I couldn't burst her bubble, I wouldn't.

"Anyway, if we do end up going together, we can all go. Maybe you can ask Nate or—"

"Nate?" My attention snagged on his name. "Why the hell would I ask Nate?"

"I don't know." She shrugged. "You two seemed kind of close tonight."

"Yeah, well we're not."

"Sorry, I just thought—"

"You don't have to worry about me, Celeste," I said, relieved it was dark enough to hide the truth in my eyes.

"Nothing will change," she said softly, cushioning the words with a half-promise.

Because we both knew love changed everything.

And not always for the better.

The next morning, I watched Celeste at breakfast, glued to her cell phone, a dreamy expression plastered on her face. And the pit in my stomach I'd fallen asleep with only grew.

It was already happening. It would start with some flirty texts back and forth, and then Miles would ask her out. Before long they would be inseparable, and I would be the third wheel to their fledgling relationship.

A burden that would eventually suffocate them.

"Who's that?" Max asked, flicking his head to his sister's cell phone.

"Miles."

"Please don't tell me you're finally giving Mulligan a shot?"

"What is that supposed to mean?"

"Oh come on, Sis. You're not that dumb. Mulligan has been trailing you around like a lost puppy since eighth grade." Her cheeks pinked as she muttered something under her breath, making Max chuckle. "So predictable. Shame you both have to babysit weirdo."

"Max!" Celeste fumed, sending me an apologetic smile that did nothing to ease the knot in my stomach.

She'd given him hell for revealing my secret to his friends but Sabrina had quickly put an end to their fighting. Not that I'd expected anything else.

"What?" He shrugged wearing a mask of innocence. "I'm only saying what we're all thinking. Although if the rumors are true, maybe Nate can keep her company."

Celeste came to my defense. "Shut up, Max. It's not even like that."

"Oh, come on—"

But I was already out of my seat, heading for the stairs and my room beyond that. I couldn't sit and listen to his cruel words, even if they held some degree of truth.

Tears stung my eyes as I headed straight for the roof terrace, slamming the door behind me. Going to the balustrade, I clenched my hand into a fist, hard enough that my nails cut into my palm. The pain was an instant relief, soothing the storm raging inside me.

I breathed in for four seconds, held it for seven, and exhaled for eight, repeating it over and over until the rapid beat of my heart slowed and the tremors running through me began to ebb away.

Of course Celeste wasn't going to be around forever. It was silly to think she would be. But she'd been my crutch ever since I'd gotten out of Albany Hills. It wasn't that we were half-sisters—that didn't really matter to me at all—it was that she had chosen to befriend me, to get to know me beyond the awful introduction we'd had last year, when I'd first moved here.

It was more than I could say for my father, Sabrina, and Max. Even Mrs. Beaker had kept her distance, acting polite but wary around me. And I got it, I did. I'd freaked out last November, and I'd scared them all. But I was trying to do better, trying not to lose myself to *those* thoughts again.

Stop. Breathe. Focus. Focus on something positive. A small achievable goal to give you purpose. But I couldn't see it. I couldn't find something in the shadows closing in around my thoughts, blotting out all the bursts of light. If I didn't do something, I'd quickly find myself at the bottom of a black hole so deep, I would never crawl back out.

Pulling my phone out of my back pocket, I scrolled through my short list of contacts and found her number, hitting call. It was early on a Saturday morning. She wouldn't answer, but that was okay. Things weren't at crisis point... yet.

Her automated message kicked in and I waited for the beep. "Hi, Dr. Katy. It's Harleigh. Harleigh Maguire. Something happened, and well, I think I need a session. I'm okay... but I feel... I feel restless. Anyway, I'll talk to you soon hopefully. Bye."

I hung up and stared out at the horizon. I didn't want to relapse. I didn't want to end up back in Albany Hills again. But it wasn't something I could necessarily control.

The emotional pain of finding my mom dead, of being ripped from my life in The Row, and being abandoned by Nix, was something I didn't allow myself to feel often. It creeped up on me sometimes though, striking without warning, like a huge weight being dropped on me, and no matter what I did, I couldn't escape out from under it. I'd gotten good at distracting myself from those intense feelings. Whether I refused to let them take root or focused on inane things instead, I'd learned to manage them.

To live with them.

But seeing Nix again, being forced to face the truth of the last nine months and having the intimate details of my life banded around school... it was too much, and slowly every defense I'd built over the last few months, even my coping mechanism, was being eroded away.

I wanted to be strong, to believe that I could do it. But the truth was, I was tired.

So freaking tired.

My finger ran absentmindedly over the ugly raised scar along my wrist. I didn't want to die. I didn't. I hadn't wanted to last year either, not really. But things had gotten too much to bear. The pain and grief and heartache had become a living breathing thing inside me, blotting out every shred of light until the darkness had slowly consumed me until I was desperate for a way out. A way to make it all stop. Just for a moment.

I wanted to believe that things would get better. That one day, when I was far far away from Darling Hill, I would be happy again.

But sometimes, I found myself wondering if maybe it would be just better to end it all.

Nix

"NIX, SWEETIE. WHAT THE HELL HAPPENED?"
Jessa picked up my hand, balking at the sight of my busted
knuckles. They had started to heal from my disastrous fight
with Meathead at Busters, but I'd split them open again,
teaching Chloe's *friend* Dan a thing or two about how not
to treat women.

He'd taken her to some party, gotten her wasted, and
tried to fuck her in the bathroom. When she kneed him the
balls, he'd gone and found another girl to stick his dick in.

I'd lost it.

Not even Zane could pull me off the asshole. I didn't
always get things right, but Chloe was as good as family
and the thought of some entitled douchebag putting his
hands on her was like a red flag to a bull.

"Don't worry about it," I pulled my hand away and
tucked it under the counter.

"I don't like the idea of you fighting, Nix. That's twice
in as many weeks."

"Relax. I said don't worry. So don't." I shoveled another spoonful of cinnamon crunch into my mouth.

"I hate that he did this to you." She brushed my cheek, the way she had when I was a young boy. "You have so much anger in you, Nix. It isn't health—"

"Spare me the lecture." She moved her hand from my face, stepping away. "It's The Row, Jessa. In case you haven't noticed, being angry is required body armor around here."

She leaned back against the counter and let out a heavy sigh. "You know, Nix. You can do so much better. Be so much better. I always thought you and Harleigh Wren would—"

"Don't." My body went rigid, my blood turning to ice. "Don't say her name."

Her brows knitted. "What happened?"

How did she do that? How did she know that something had happened?

She studied me quietly, the air thick, pressing in around us. "You saw her, didn't you?" It was a soft whisper full of sympathy and pity that made me bristle.

"How can you possibly know that?" I breathed.

"You've been different," she said. "I couldn't put my finger on it, but it all makes sense now. She's back."

"In a fashion," I murmured, trying not to think about her breathy moans as I'd kissed the shit out of her.

"What does that mean?"

"She lives across the res now, Jessa. Her life is there. Not here."

"I thought we'd decided that was a good thing? Her getting out of here, having the chance to make something of her life."

We had said that. Months ago, after I'd gotten into a fight after one of our games. She'd pulled me into her arms and held me like a baby, soothing me in the way only a mother could.

Except, she wasn't my mother.

I'd learned a long time ago that family wasn't always the people whose blood ran through your veins. Sometimes it was the people you chose. The people who were there, who showed up time and time again, despite the fact you didn't share DNA.

Jessa was family. Just like Zane and his gran, and Kye and Chloe were family.

Harleigh had been family too.

And since seeing her again, my head and heart couldn't accept that she was really gone.

"You know, Nix." Jessa laid her hand on my arm. "Sometimes the best thing we can do for the people we love is to set them free. She's always been your Birdie, sweetie. Maybe it's time for her to spread her wings and fly."

Damn, I fucking hated that she was right. Hated that no matter how much I rejected her words, I knew them to be true.

But I'd set Harleigh free once. I'd walked away, let her go, only to have her land back on my doorstep. So close... and yet, still so fucking far.

Sure, I didn't have to see her every day. Didn't have to

look into those jade green eyes and see the hatred simmering there, the pain and regret of what could have been. But it didn't stop my heart from wishing it could be different.

Wishing that I could be the type of guy who could give her everything she deserved, everything her heart desired.

A loud *thud* from the master bedroom had us both stiffening.

"Relax," Jessa said, giving me a small smile. "He was in a better mood last night."

I made some derisive noise. Joe Wilder didn't have a good mood. He had a bad mood and a downright fucking awful mood.

He appeared down the hall, wearing his trademark white wifebeater and a pair of black sweats. "What's for breakfast?" he grunted.

"Whatever you want, baby."

A little bit of puke rushed up my throat as I watched Jessa wrap her arms around him and pepper his harsh face with kisses. He grabbed a handful of her ass, nuzzling her neck. "Now feed me, woman." He slapped it for good measure and joined me at the breakfast counter.

"What the fuck is up with you?" he mumbled, accepting a fresh mug of coffee from Jessa.

"Nothing."

"Harleigh's back."

My eyes flew to Jessa. *What the fuck?*

Her expression softened. *Sorry.*

Yeah, sorry my ass. I loved Jessa like a mom but sometimes she was really fucking dense.

"If I've told you once, I've told you a hundred fucking times. No piece of ass is worth it."

"Joe," Jessa gasped, her expression wounded.

"You're different, baby" he said dismissively. "But girls like Harleigh Wren don't belong in a place like The Row. If you ask me, it was a blessing in disguise when her momma offed herself and—"

My fist crashed against the counter, pure rage shooting up my spine. "What the fuck did you say?"

He turned an unimpressed eye on me. "You heard me, kid. Trina Maguire checked out of life a long fucking time ago. She did everyone a favor, including Harl—"

Red exploded in my vision as I lunged for him, and we went down in a tangle of limbs and grunts.

"Don't. Please don't," Jessa yelled as I took a swing at my father, a man I hated more than life itself.

He was everything wrong with this fucking world. Selfish. Dirty. Always willing to screw people over. I'd stood by and watched him hurt Jessa time and time again. I had my own canvas of scars littering my body thanks to his preferred form of parental punishment. But hearing him talk shit about Harleigh and her mom... I couldn't do it.

"Don't ever fucking say—"

He bucked me off him, rolling us, and pinning me underneath him. His arm pressed tight against my throat, cutting off my air supply. My body trembled with anger, refusing to submit as I thrashed against him.

"Such a hot-tempered little shit." Spittle rained down on me, making bile wash in my stomach, and there wasn't an inch of me that didn't shake with visceral rage. But my old man was stacked and when his temper exploded, he was damn strong.

"Maybe I should really teach you a lesson if you think you can play with the big boys now." His lip curled with vicious intent. "Vince told me what you did, ya know? Told me how you stood up for Jessa. Always so fucking righteous."

He loosened his arm and I dragged in a deep breath, hating how he reduced me to... to this. Weak. Powerless. Completely at his mercy. "At least I tried to protect her," I snarled. "Where were you, huh, when he was here, raping—"

"*Nix!*" Jessa's voice broke, her sobs filling the trailer. And for a second, something like guilt flashed over my old man's face. He staggered off me and clambered to his feet.

"Jessa, baby." He went to her, but she shoved him off, rushing down the hall and into their bedroom. The door slammed behind her, echoing through my skull.

"Fuck... *fuck*." My father hissed, punching the flimsy wall.

I climbed to my feet, forcing myself to take a breath. Restrained anger still radiated inside me, making my skin vibrate. He stared at me with wild eyes. Eyes I knew we shared. I half-expected him to come at me and finish what he started on the floor. But he didn't. The air was thick, strained with the hatred between us.

"You're just like her, you know?" he said quietly.

No, I wanted to roar. *I'm just like you. Angry. Bitter. Broken.*

Swallowing the words, I lifted my chin in small defiance.

I couldn't remember a time when we didn't hate each other. The only difference was when I was a kid, part of me had craved his approval, his acceptance. I'd been desperate for whatever scraps of his attention I could get. But I quickly learned. I quickly learned that it was a fool's hope.

"I want you gone." His words were like a blow to the stomach.

"What the fuck do you mean, you want me gone?"

Jessa.

I couldn't leave Jessa. I wouldn't.

"After graduation, I want you out of here."

"You know I don't have anywhere to go. I don't—"

"Not my problem, kid. I'm done carrying your dead weight. Finish high school, figure out a plan, and get the fuck out of my life." He stared past me, through me.

"Jessa won't—"

"Jessa isn't your responsibility and it isn't her decision what happens in my fucking house," he spat the words, full of venom and fire. "She's mine, Nix. Mine. She isn't your mother, thank fuck for that. She's a good girl and I—"

"You don't deserve her." I stepped forward. "And you didn't deserve my mother."

"Watch it, kid," he sneered. "If it wasn't for Jessa you'd have been long gone by now."

It shouldn't have hurt. It shouldn't have mattered that the man I hated with every fiber of my being felt the same. But it cut like tiny knives, slowly slicing me open, and leaving me to bleed out.

My mother hadn't loved me enough to stay. And my father hated me enough to send me packing the minute he could.

Whoever said you could always count on family had clearly never met mine.

"Don't worry," I drawled, wrapping my words in false bravado. Because I would never—over my dead fucking body—let him see his words affected me. "I won't outstay my welcome."

"Good. And pull that shit with me again and you can pack your bag. We might not like each other, but this is my house and you will fucking respect that."

Go fuck yourself. I imagined myself screaming the words at him. Grabbing the nearest thing I could find and throwing it at his smug fucking face. But I didn't. I just stood there, teeth grinding behind pursed lips, glaring at him. Waiting for him to walk away. It wasn't exactly a small win. I'd still be homeless come graduation. But at least I stood my ground.

It worked. He blew out an exasperated breath and stormed off toward his bedroom, no doubt going to grovel to Jessa.

I grabbed my keys and cell phone and shoved my feet into my sneakers and left, wondering if I'd even make it to graduation. It was getting harder to bite my tongue, to rein in my fists. But I had nowhere else to go.

I'd never given much thought to what happened after graduation. I wanted to get out of The Row, of course I did. But it was a dream I couldn't afford to allow to take root. Because I had Jessa to think about. So I took each day as it came and hoped to God that one day she would wake up and smell the roses and leave my old man's sorry ass.

But maybe she was right. Maybe loving someone meant setting them free. Letting them choose their own path. Even if that path was steeped in mistakes and woven with pain.

Even if it meant that in the end, you lost them...

Forever.

Nix

"WHAT IS THIS PLACE?" Harleigh asked me as we drove in the darkness.

I was supposed to be driving her home, but after watching that fucker Denby taunt her at the party, I couldn't do it.

I needed a minute.

I needed her.

Fuck, it was getting harder and harder to deny her.

And that kiss earlier...

"Did I... do something wrong?" she asked, her voice a weak whisper.

But I couldn't tell her, I couldn't... fuck. Tonight had been a real test of my restraint.

"Harleigh, not here, not now." I let out an exasperated breath.

269

"What does that even mean? So I have done something? Is it the costume? Because I thought—"

"I can't do this right now." I snapped, storming off into the shadows.

But she followed. Of course she fucking followed me. Because that was Birdie, so willing to follow me into the dark.

"Don't you dare walk away from me," she shrieked. "We are talking about this. Right now."

I swung around, trying my damn hardest not to crack. "Harleigh—"

"Don't call me that." She flinched, pain etched into her features. "You never call me that."

True. I didn't. She was always Wren or Birdie or B. But I needed to put some space between us, some distance.

"Just tell me why you're being so... so weird."

Silence stretched out before us, the gentle rise and fall of her chest taunting me, drawing my eye to her amazing curves. That tempting, hot as fuck outfit that I'd tried my damnedest to ignore all night.

"I..." I dropped my gaze, a murmured cuss leaving my lips.

"Phoenix." She stepped forward. "Just talk to me, please." Harleigh reached for my hand, but I jerked back.

"Don't."

"I know I'm not like Cherri or—"

"Cherri?" I snorted. "You think this is about Cherri?"

"Well, her... girls like her."

"Birdie, that's not— fuck. Fuck." I jammed my fingers

into my hair and pulled the ends, frustration radiating from me.

"Nix, what's happening to us? I don't—" Crowding her against a tree, I leaned down and touched my head to hers.

"I..."

Fuck. This was dangerous territory. The line I'd drawn between us was right there... right fucking there, and if we crossed it, if I crossed it, nothing would ever be the same again.

"Do you have any idea what you're doing to me?" I whispered against the shell of her ear, feeling a shiver run through her.

"M-me?" she asked.

Harleigh pressed back into the tree trying to get a better look at my eyes. She went to speak, but I curved my hand around her throat, dragging my thumb over her bottom lip. "So fucking beautiful."

Surprise lit up her eyes. "Nix, w-what are you—"

"Sssh, B. I'm trying really fucking hard not to lose control right now."

A tremor ran through me. She was so close, too fucking close. Her scent. Her skin. Her delectable lips. How the fuck was I supposed to walk away without one taste?

One little taste.

"Why," she breathed. "What would happen if you lost control?"

"This."

My mouth crashed down on hers, hard and demanding.

She gasped at the sudden assault as my tongue snaked out, licking her lips.

I shouldn't have kissed her because now all I could think about was kissing her again. And again. Tasting her skin and mapping her sexy as fuck curves with my hands until I knew the shape of her body.

It was the worst kind of torture, having the one thing you wanted more than anything right there and be unable to take it.

Because I couldn't—could I?

"It's the old grain mill," I said.

"I've never been out here before."

"I come here sometimes. To get away from it all." The car rolled to a stop, and I cut the engine.

"You know, life won't be like this forever," Harleigh said.

"Yeah?" I glanced over at her, a weak smile playing on my lips. "You think we'll get out of The Row?"

"You don't?"

My shoulders lifted in a small shrug. "Kids like me... they don't get many opportunities, Wren."

"You have football. Coach Farringdon believes you could get a scholarship one day, and so do I. You just have to try to stay out of trouble."

I rolled my eyes. "Don't give me that look."

"What look?"

"You know who I am, B. What runs through my blood.

I'm not sure I'm cut out for college."

Her expression darkened. "His actions don't define you, Nix. You're more than just Joe Wilder's son."

"Maybe. Maybe not." I stared out at the darkness, wishing things were different. Wishing that I was just a boy and she was just a girl. But it wasn't that simple, because I was Joe Wilder's kid, and a small part of him lived inside me.

"Nix, I—"

I snatched her hand up in mine and gazed at her. "I need you to know that it's you, Birdie. It's always been you." My heart cracked, deep fissures spreading out through my chest, leaving me hollow. But I—"

"No." Her lip wobbled. "Don't do this."

God, I was a bastard. She thought the kiss earlier meant something more than it did. And I hated myself for it, but I would hate myself more if I took what she was willing to give me and ruined it.

"Don't you see, Wren? You deserve more than... than what I can give you. So fucking much more."

She let out a quiet, pained, bitter laugh. "I have spent years watching you with girls. Girls like Cherri. Girls who are everything I'm not. Yet, I still want you. I still want you to look at me the way you look at them. I wore this for you, you know?

"I wore this so for once, for one night, you'd look at me and see past the image you've formed of me. See me, Nix. Please just see me." Tears pricked the corners of her eyes.

"I see you, B. I've always fucking seen you, but it

doesn't change anything. I'm messed up, baby. Broken and scarred. Those girls are just a means to an end. But you, you'd be my ruin."

A tear broke free. And another. Until a river of tears streaked down her cheeks as all the words we hadn't said filled the space between us.

"I think you should take me home," she said, unable to look at me.

"Wren, please—"

"No, I can't do this. I need some time, Nix, take me—"

"Stop. Fuck. Just give me a minute, okay?"

She was crying now, sobbing as if her heart was fucking breaking. But didn't she realize mine echoed her pain? Because she was my mirror, the other half of my dirty fucking soul.

"Shit, B, don't cry. Please don't fucking cry."

Without thinking, I pulled her onto my lap, forcing her to straddle my legs.

"Let me go," she cried, smudging her Harley Quinn makeup. "Just let me—"

"Stubborn girl." I gripped her chin, forcing her to look at me. "You shouldn't give me your tears, Birdie, I don't deserve them."

"You're right, you don't."

"Tell me you'll always be mine. That I'll always own part of this." It was a shitty thing to say, to ask for, but I needed to hear her say it. Just once.

My hand dropped to her chest, right over her heart, begging her to say it.

"No."

"Say it."

She pressed her lips together, shaking her head.

Anger rolled through me, but I kept myself in check, as I said, "Yeah, guess I deserve that. Just promise me, whoever you give it up to will deserve you. Promise me, B."

"Fuck you," she sneered.

It was seven shades of messed up, but those words coming from her pouty mouth did things to me. Dark, devious things. My eyes dropped to her mouth and a low groan rumbled in my chest.

"Don't you dare—"

I wrapped a hand around her throat and crashed my mouth down on hers, taking what I needed.

Once.

Just this once.

"Need to touch you," I murmured between kisses. "Need to feel you, just once."

Harleigh melted into me, soft whimpers spilling from her lips.

"You taste so fucking good, why do you taste so fucking good?" I trailed hot open-mouthed kisses along her jaw, sucking the skin there, nipping and licking. She shifted above me, rolling her hips. The heat of her pussy turned my blood molten. I was so fucking gone for this girl.

"Keep doing that, B, and this is going to end with me buried deep inside you." I warned with a smirk.

"Is that a promise?" she whispered.

"Fuck, you can't say stuff like that to me."

Harleigh leaned down, scraping her nails along my jaw, tracing the seam of my lips with her tongue. I gritted my teeth at her, nipping the end of her tongue and then sucking it into my mouth. I couldn't get enough of her. My hands dropped down to her ass and started rocking her over me, back and forth, up and down.

"Does that feel good?"

She nodded, smothering a moan. "Touch me," she whispered against my neck. "I want you to touch me."

"One night," I said. "That's all this can be. Then things go back to how they've always been, Wren."

She nodded, her eyes fluttering as I thrust up against her, our bodies moving as if they knew exactly what to do.

"I'm serious, B." I gripped her chin again, pulling us eye to eye. "You're my best friend. My fucking ride or die. I can't lose you."

"Stop," she said, attempting to nuzzle my neck again. "Stop making everything so difficult. I want this, I want you."

Fuck.

Those words shattered something inside me, so I kissed her again, harder, pushing my tongue into her mouth. One of my hands slipped between us and I found the bare skin of her stomach, walking my fingers down to the waistband of her skirt.

"Nix." It was a breathy plea.

I watched her, soaking in every breath, sigh, every fucking thing as I dipped my fingers underneath her skirt and found her panties. "Fuck," I hissed. "You're soaked."

"For you. Only ever for you." She murmured the words as I stroked her over her panties. "More." She arched into my hand.

"Greedy little thing." I smirked, hooking two fingers inside her underwear and slowly sinking them into her tight wet heat.

"Oh God," Harleigh cried, anchoring her arms over my shoulders.

"Okay?" I asked, and she nodded. "You're so fucking tight, B." My thumb circled her clit in lazy slow circles. "Never gonna forget this."

I was entranced as I watched her fall. Bottling the sound of her breathy moans as she came around my fingers. She was perfect. So fucking perfect. And in a different time and place, she could have been mine.

But that wasn't our destiny.

Birdie would escape this place one day. She would leave, and I would let her. Because The Row was toxic and that shit would eat at your soul until there was nothing good left.

"Thank you," she smiled at me all dreamy-eyed and sated as she leaned in to kiss me.

Nothing had ever hurt me more than this moment. Knowing that's all it could ever be.

So I held her. Held on tight and for a few seconds I let myself believe that this was the start of something special. Something real.

Something I knew I'd never get to experience again.

Chapter
Twenty-Five

Harleigh

"MILES," Celeste giggled, nuzzling his arm as we sat outside in the yard. They were lost in their own little world. Had been all morning.

I'd wanted to stay in my room, but she'd refused to let me, insisting that they both wanted to hang out with me. But I'd barely said two words while they drifted deeper and deeper into their bubble.

It was cute, watching them. But it made my heart heavy.

"Sorry, Harleigh." He flashed me an apologetic smile. "I just can't believe this one"—he hugged Celeste into his side—"finally agreed to go out with me."

"Technically, you never asked."

"Because you've always kept me in the friend zone."

And they were off again, gazing at each other with those dreamy lust-filled expressions. Miles nipped Celeste's jaw, tenderly holding the back of her neck, teasing her with featherlight kisses that made her squirm and sigh.

My stomach curled, the bitter sting of jealousy shooting through me.

I'd never had that.

Never had anyone looked at me the way Miles was looking at Celeste right now.

Even when Nix had kissed me, he hadn't gazed at me like that. His eyes were always clouded with regret, his expression tortured. Because things were never simple between us. He'd put me on a pedestal. Treated me as if I was some kind of precious stone or rare bird, to be cherished and protected but never touched. He'd loved me, I never doubted that. Not for a second. But it wasn't the kind of love that consumed a person until they couldn't think of anything else but being with the object of their desire.

If it had been, he would never have left me.

He would never have willingly let me go.

Miles's cell phone chimed and he leaned over, snatching it off the small rattan and glass table.

"Who is it?" Celeste asked, trying to peer over his shoulder.

"No one." He batted her away, concealing his screen as he texted the no one back.

"Hmm, keeping secrets, Mulligan. I can probably think of a few ways to get them out of you." She latched her mouth onto his neck, sucking and kissing. A deep groan rumbled in Miles's throat, a breathy cuss falling from his lips.

Rolling my eyes, I clambered off the lounger and said, "I'm going to grab some more snacks from the kitchen."

The house was empty. My father and Sabrina were out of town with some business associates, and Max was off doing whatever Max did with his spare time. Ever since he'd outed me to his friends, he'd been avoiding me more than usual.

Good.

I wanted nothing to do with him.

I'd been here for weeks now. I knew what lay behind every door, around every corner, but it didn't feel like home. It never would. It was beautiful, sure. A light and airy canvas full of perfectly positioned vases full of fake, never wilting flowers; abstract wall art splashed with vibrant colors. Everything had its place, had been picked out to compliment the ambience. But what it had in style and aesthetic beauty, it lacked in feeling. And maybe it was weird, but I felt cold here. Empty.

Even my room didn't feel like my room. It felt borrowed. Temporary.

"Harleigh?" I turned to find Celeste frowning at me. "What are you doing?"

I hadn't even realized I'd wandered over to the sideboard and picked up a rare photograph of my father with his family—the one he'd wanted, the one he'd claimed for himself.

"Nothing," I said, placing it back down, ignoring the bitter sting of jealousy stabbing my insides.

"Are you okay?"

"Yeah. I'm fine."

"I'm sorry... about Miles. I know it's been like a day and we're already that annoying lovesick couple. I'll try and—"

"Celeste, I said I'm fine." I didn't meet her apologetic gaze. "You deserve to be happy."

"Yeah, but I don't want it to change things between us. I've really liked having you around, Harleigh. I don't make girlfriends easily, or at all, really." She toyed with the ties of her shorts.

"I'll be here," I said.

It's not like I had anywhere else to go.

"I think I'm going to head up to the roof."

"Are we that bad?" Guilt glittered in Celeste's eyes. But it really wasn't about her, it was about me.

"It's new and exciting and you don't want me cramping your style. Besides, I—"

The doorbell rang and we both glanced down the hall toward the door.

"Expecting someone?" I asked her, and she shook her head.

"I'll go see who it is."

I used the moment to grab a bottle of water and a granola bar and head for the stairs. But a voice gave me pause.

"Mulligan invited me."

"Nate?" I spun around and marched toward the door. "Seriously?"

"I'm guessing Mulligan didn't tell you he invited me."

"No, he didn't." I ground out, glancing at Celeste.

She balked. "Don't look at me, I had no idea either. But now that you're here, I guess you can—"

"Celeste!"

I didn't want to hang out with Nate again. Not after last night. But the overbearing ass stepped into the house and held up beers and a bag of snacks. "I grabbed a bunch of stuff."

"We have food, Nate." Celeste smothered a laugh.

"Yeah, but it's rude to turn up empty-handed."

They both looked at me expectantly.

"Fine." I blew out a frustrated breath. "Whatever."

"'Nice to see you too, Maguire." He smirked, slipping around me, and disappeared into the kitchen.

"Sorry. I didn't know," Celeste said.

"It's fine." It wasn't, but whatever.

Something told me even if I took off up to the roof, Nate would only follow me, so I let Celeste slip her arm through mine and lay her head on my shoulder. "He's not so bad."

"You've had a change of heart."

"Yeah, it's weird. I thought he was another Marc Denby type. But I don't know, there's something about him."

"Yeah, I know what you mean." It pained me to say the words, but she was right.

There was more to Nate Miller than met the eye.

I just didn't know if I wanted to find out what it was.

"So that's... gag-worthy," Nate said as the two of us lay on loungers, eating candy like it was going out of fashion.

"Yeah, they've been at it all morning," I said, barely glancing at Celeste and Miles making out in the shallow end of the pool.

"You sound thrilled."

"I'm happy for them. It's just..."

"Yeah, I get it."

I lifted my eyes to his. "Do you?"

"You've seen me around school, I'm not exactly Mr. Popular."

"You're an enigma, that's for sure."

"An enigma. Difficult to interpret or understand. Mysterious." His mouth quirked with amusement. "Sounds like a great t-shirt right there."

"Did you just quote the dictionary at me?"

"I didn't un-quote it." He grinned.

"You're a goofball."

"Better than some of the names I've been called in the past."

"So how is it you're Marc Denby's cousin and we had no idea?"

"It's a long story. But the short version... our families only recently buried the hatchet after some drama a few years back, so we didn't grow up close or anything."

"And now?"

Because I'd seen him and Marc together around school. They acted friendly.

"It's complicated." His lips flattened. "You know, I thought you might have something to say after our conversation last night..."

"I don't want to talk about it." My walls slammed up.

"Okay, but have you considered that maybe you need to talk about it?"

"And let me guess, you want to be my sounding board?" I shot him an incredulous look.

"I'm here, aren't I?"

"Why? Why do you even care?"

"Because I saw your scar, Harleigh. When I came over with my brother that day, I saw your wrist and figured out what had really happened to you last year."

"Y-you saw it?"

He nodded. "Do you want to talk about it?"

"I said I didn't."

"My sister... she uh... she killed herself."

My body began to tremble. "S-she did?"

"Almost ten years ago. She would have been twenty-eight this year."

"I didn't know."

"It's not something my family talks about. It isn't becoming of the Millers to discuss their failings." His expression tightened.

"I'm sorry."

"Yeah, me too. I was only eight at the time, her

annoying little brother. But she was my idol. I loved her so fucking much and one day, she was... gone."

"H-how did it happen?"

"Overdose. She went through some stuff in junior year and never recovered."

"What was her name?"

"Penny. Even now, after all this time, I still hear her yelling at me for going into her room without permission or for stealing the last bagel. Man, she loved a cream cheese bagel."

Silence hung between us. Thick and heavy with the pain of our pasts. I got it now—the strange affinity between us. Nate recognized the darkness living inside me and it called to me in kind. Our souls were the same. Dark. Damaged. Tainted.

"Have you ever—"

"No, no." He shook his head. "I'm a suffer-in-silence type of guy, but I'm not looking to permanently check out of life. What about you? Are you—"

"I know what you're doing." My voice cracked.

"Yeah? What am I doing?"

"Trying to reverse-psychology me into opening up about what happened."

"Is it working?"

"Not yet." A faint smile tugged at my mouth.

"Fair enough. I want you to know that I'm here, and I get it. Talk to me, don't talk to me, that's your prerogative, but I offer a non-judgmental safe space to talk."

"Thank you."

"I also offer some premium grade weed and witty conversation. In case you need persuading."

"You know, Celeste was right about you."

"Yeah?" His eyes twinkled.

"Yeah, you're not all bad, Miller. You're not all bad, at all."

"Likewise, Maguire." We shared a tentative smile. "Likewise."

"You two looked cozy earlier," Celeste said, nudging my shoulder as we ate our slices of pizza.

After spending the day out by the pool, we'd come down to the den to watch a film. The guys were busy arguing over the upcoming football season while we gorged ourselves on the copious amounts of food they'd ordered.

"It isn't like that between us."

"No... but could it be?"

Nate glanced up as if he felt us watching him. I smiled and he returned it with a blinding smile of his own. But there was no flutter of butterflies or tingles under my skin. Nothing except the comforting reassurance of having someone who got it. Who understood what it was like to be in my shoes.

"I don't think so."

"Because you're still hung up on—"

"Celeste." I let out a heavy sigh, the pain I was

accustomed to whenever Nix came up in conversation spreading through me.

"Sorry. I just want you to be happy."

"It's not something you can fix with a bit of attention from a guy."

"I know, I'm sorry. I'll drop it, I promise."

"Your guy looks lonely." I flicked my head over to Miles and he flashed her his best puppy dog eyes.

She made a quiet little simpering noise. "He's too freaking cute."

"Go, put him out of his misery."

"You're sure?"

"Go," I said.

She wiped her hands on a napkin and made a beeline for Miles, curling up on his lap and looping her arms around his neck.

Nate appeared, rolling his eyes at the lovesick puppies. He dropped down beside me and ran a hand down his face. "Want to get out here?" he asked.

"What did you have in mind?"

"Drive to the res and—"

"Anywhere but the reservoir," I said.

"Fine, I know a place. You in?"

"Yeah." I nodded. "I'm in."

Nix

"SERIOUSLY, CLO." Kye grumbled. "This is what you want to do?" He gawked up at the building.

"You said we could do whatever I wanted." She pouted. "And I'm in the mood to bowl." With a dismissive shrug, she marched toward Strike One and disappeared inside.

"Is it me, or is she more... Chloe than usual?" I asked.

After taking off this morning, I'd driven around for a little bit, trying to get my shit together.

So my old man wanted me gone after graduation? It wasn't like I wanted to stay. I just needed to figure out a plan. Get a real job. Save some cash. And if Jessa was dead set on staying with him, I needed to accept that. At least if I was still around, I could keep an eye on her.

"She's something," he muttered, taking off after his sister.

"Feels kind of weird being here," Zane said.

"Yeah, but we said we'd be his back up."

Chloe was acting weird, as if last night had never

happened. Mrs. Carter had asked Kye to keep an eye on her, and Chloe had interpreted that as Kye spending the afternoon with her.

"I've never bowled before," Zane added.

"Seems pretty simple to me. Roll the ball down the alley and hope for the best."

He smirked. "Fucking bowling. He owes us for this."

"Come on." I slung my arm around his shoulder and guided him inside.

Kye had already paid for our game by the time we reached them. "Courtesy of Mom," he said. "Come on, we're on lane five".

Kye and Zane went off toward the lanes but I hung back with Chloe.

"It's fancy here, I like it." She surveyed the warehouse. At least, that's what I imagined it had been once. "Thanks for coming with me," she added, dropping her gaze to my busted up knuckles. "And thanks for... you know."

"Anytime, Clo. You know that."

"I... I can't believe he did that. I thought... I thought he really liked me, but he only wanted to fuck me. I'm such an idiot."

"Guys will do that, Clo. Say all the right things, give you all the right signals..." A sticky trail of regret slithered through me. I'd done it enough. Whispered sweet nothings into a girl's ear to get what I wanted. But I never forced them to do anything they didn't want to.

I always, always fucking drew the line at that.

"He won't hurt you again," I said.

I'd fucked him up pretty bad.

"Yeah, I know. But it doesn't change how I feel, in here." She touched a hand to her chest. "He played me and I fell for it. Hook, line, and sinker."

"There'll be plenty more fish in the sea, Clo. Just maybe go easy for a while yeah? I'm not sure Kye will suit turning gray at eighteen."

"I don't know, he's cocky enough to make it work." She tipped her head over to where her brother was flirting with a girl playing on the lane beside us.

"Does he ever take a break?"

Chloe rolled her eyes, inhaled a deep breath and took off toward them. It didn't surprise me that she'd confided in me about Dan, rather than tell Kye. She didn't want to hurt him, to let him think it had affected her more than it had.

I wandered over and sunk down onto the leather seat of the booth. I'd only been here once before, when I'd followed Harleigh. It was strange being back. Part of me half expected to see her appear.

Of course, she didn't.

"Okay, let's do this," Kye said, picking up a bowling ball and skipping to the lane.

"You've got to avoid the gutters," Zane called, and Kye flipped him off over his shoulder, focusing on the lane.

"Ten bucks says he misses."

"Make it twenty." Chloe chuckled, flashing me an appreciative smile.

I gave her a small nod, scrubbing my jaw. Chloe was strong. She'd get over what happened with Dan and move onto the next guy. And if things went wrong again, hopefully she knew we'd always have her back.

"You know, Nix... if you ever want to talk to me about Harleigh... I'm here."

"I'm just here to bowl," I said, standing to take my turn.

Because I couldn't talk about Harleigh right now, not after last night, not without feeling that oppressive black cloud swarming me.

"Okay. I won't mention her again," she whispered, but I didn't reply.

What was there to say?

Harleigh hated me. The kind of hatred that embedded in your soul. There was clearly shit we needed to talk about. I didn't know her story and she sure as fuck didn't know mine. But would I ever get the chance to make her hear me out?

Did I even deserve it?

Watching Zane lose his shit over losing to Kye and Chloe was exactly the kind of distraction I needed.

"You are such a sore loser," I taunted, laughter rumbling in my chest.

"Fuck you, man. Fuck. You." He picked up the cap off one of our soda bottles and threw it at me. I ducked and it ricocheted off the leather banquette behind me.

"This place is all right," Kye said.

"Told you." Chloe grinned. She seemed better, back to

her usual snarky, sassy self. "They have a games room in the back. Want me to beat your ass at pool?"

"That was one time, Clo. One fucking time and you've never let me live it down."

"Damn right I haven't, brother." She glanced over at me. "We can play doubles?"

"I'm in." Zane stood, drained his soda and said, "Lead the way."

"I guess we're playing pool," I murmured. A couple of people playing on the next lane over watched us, the way people did whenever kids from The Row wandered across the border into Old Darling Hill. But I let their judgment roll off my back.

"What's up with you?" Kye asked as Chloe and Zane racked up the balls.

"My old man told me that he wants me gone after graduation."

"What the fuck?"

"Yeah." I blew out a steady breath. "We got into it... Thought he was going to beat the shit out of me. Instead, he told me he wants me gone."

"Shit, Nix, that's—"

"It is what it is." I raked a hand through my hair. "I always knew it would happen one day. Either that or we'd end up killing each other."

His expression turned grim. "Don't joke about that shit. It isn't funny."

"Who says I'm joking?"

"What are you two pussies talking about?" Zane joined us.

"Nix's old man wants him gone after graduation."

His eyes snapped to mine, narrowed and deadly, and I nodded.

"What are you going to do?"

"Try to get a decent job, save some cash, figure out a plan."

Sometimes, I fought for Bryson to earn a quick buck, but it was dangerous business and when Coach had found out about it last season, he'd lost his shit. If I wanted to stay on his team, I'd had to promise there would be no more illegal fights.

"Or..." Kye added. "Speak to Coach about Albany U. This is the perfect opportunity to get out of here, Nix."

"And leave Jessa? Leave you guys?"

"It's Albany. It isn't the other side of the country. It's what, a forty-minute ride at most? You wouldn't even have to move if you didn't want to."

"Can we not do this right now?" I said.

"When then?" Kye challenged. "When can we talk about it? Because burying your head in the sand isn't the way to go, Nix. You know—"

"Fuck's sake, Carter, I said drop it, okay?"

"Fine." He held up his hands. "But I think you're making a mistake ruling it out. This is your shot, man. Your chance to get out of this fucking place and make something of yourself. Why wouldn't you want that?"

I stared at him, one of my best friends in the whole world, and I didn't know what to say.

It would be easy to tell him I was scared. That I couldn't let myself believe I could make it out of The Row; because if I didn't make it, if something happened and my shot at getting out was ripped away from me, I wasn't sure I would fucking survive it.

Besides, what if I got to college and I wasn't good enough? What if I couldn't handle the pressure? The Row was lawless. People lived by their own codes and values. College wasn't like that. Especially college football where everyone was out to prove themselves.

Laughter floated over to us, and my body grew tense as I glanced over my shoulder to find Celeste Rowe and the Mulligan kid standing in the archway.

"Oh God," she said, her eyes darting from me to Zane and back again. "We didn't realize you'd be here. We'll go."

"She with you?" I asked, stopping them in their tracks.

"N-no. We're... we're on a date." She lifted her chin slightly and I frowned.

Why the fuck would I care if she was on a date?

But her gaze flicked back to Zane and realization hit me like a truck. The sister had a thing for my best friend.

Interesting.

If Zane noticed her lingering stare, he didn't react.

"Are you guys playing pool?" Mulligan asked with a nervous smile.

"Why, any good?" Zane quirked a brow, a faint smirk tracing his mouth.

So maybe he had noticed, after all.

"I'm decent."

"Let's see what you've got then, pussy boy." He grabbed a cue and thrust it at Mulligan.

Celeste frowned. "Miles, come on, we should lea—" But the asshole shrugged her off, joining Zane at the pool table.

"Hi, I'm Chloe."

"Celeste." She gave Chloe a tight smile.

"So you're Harleigh's half-sister?"

She nodded, keeping one eye on her date and Zane. "Did you know Harleigh, from before?"

"Yeah." Chloe looked at me with a sad smile. "I'm Kye's sister. We weren't friends exactly, but I liked her."

Fuck this.

I didn't want to stand around and get to know the half-sister and her guy. And yet, questions teetered on the tip of my tongue—questions I had no fucking right to ask.

"We can go," Celeste said, noticing my expression. "This probably isn't a good idea."

"Worried your guy will get his ass handed to him by Z?" My words were an icy cold warning, but it was hard not to resent her. To hate her for the simple fact she got to be around Harleigh day in, day out, when all I had were a bunch of hazy memories.

"N-no... that's not..." She rolled her eyes, moving away from us to watch the pool game.

"What's that about?" Kye asked me while Chloe went to talk to her. No doubt fishing for details about Harleigh.

moment, waking up with little to no memory of the night before, surrounded by half-dressed dudes and a bunch of empty bottles, beer cans, and ashtrays. But I'd needed to get out of my head. Before I did something really fucking stupid like drive over to Harleigh's trailer and bury myself deep inside her.

"Come on, let's get out of here."

Kye skulked over to us. "My insides feel wrong. What the fuck was in that shit?"

"You guys leaving already?" Paul said. "Stay. I can get my mom to cook some—"

"Nah, man. I need a shower and my own bed."

"Cool, bro. Cool. See you next time."

When I would never touch his shit again. My brain felt like it had blended in a food processor.

The ride back to The Row was somber. Kye dozed on the back seat while Zane messed with my radio.

"Last night was some bad shit."

"Yeah, remind me never to trust Odell again."

"You okay?" he asked me.

"I will be once I speak to B."

After what felt like an eternity, I turned into The Row and dropped Kye and Zane off at their trailers before heading to mine.

"Nix, sweetie, thank God." Jessa came running out of the trailer as I was climbing out of the car.

"What happened?" My body tensed the second I heard the panic in her voice.

"It's Wren, sweetie."

"Wren?" The world grew small, my heart crashing wildly in my chest. "Is she okay?"

"Trina... she, uh, she's gone, Nix." Tears rolled down her cheeks. "She's gone."

"What?" I staggered back, reaching out for something to break my fall.

Trina was gone.

Harleigh's mom.

No.

Fuck no.

"I need to find Wren. I need—"

"They took her, sweetie. Mrs. Feeley saw the whole thing. The cops took her away and—"

I was already gone, jogging over to Harleigh's trailer. "Wren." I hammered the front door. "Open up, Wren. Come on."

She wasn't gone.

No way.

"Birdie, it's me. Open up..."

"She's not in there."

Mrs. Feeley's voice penetrated the blind panic ravaging my insides.

"She's gone?" I asked, defeat slamming into me.

"Left about four thirty this morning. I was about to come out and see what all the commotion was about when I saw the police cruiser leave."

"She's at the station?"

"I don't know, Phoenix. But she's going to need you, son. Now more than ever."

"Y-yeah." I swallowed over the giant fucking lump in my throat. "I gotta go, Mrs. Feeley."

"Go get our girl, Nix. You get her and hold on tight."

I ran back to my trailer, blowing through the place to my bedroom. Grabbing the phone charger cable, I shoved it into the end and waited.

But when my cell phone came back to life, the message thread waiting for me almost sent me off the edge.

B: She's gone, Nix. My mom is gone.

B: She was just lying there. I thought she was sleeping... Call me as soon as you get this. I need you, Nix. Please... call me.

B: Where are you? I've been calling you and the guys for hours. I'm scared, Nix. I'm at the police station and they won't let me come home. What am I going to do? She's gone and I... God, I can't believe this is happening. How can the best night of my life become the worst? I hate it... Please, call me.

B: Nix... you're scaring me. Why aren't you answering me?

Then the most recent message, sent almost thirty minutes after all the others.

B: Nix, where are you? I need you. A man came to get me. He claims he's my father. He wants to take me home with him. He wants to take me away. Nix... I know things are weird between us, but I need you... please.

Father?

What the actual fuck?

Harleigh didn't have a father... She'd never even met her piece of shit sperm donor.

I checked the time.

Almost ten thirty.

It had already been almost four hours since she'd sent her last message.

Fuck. Fuck. Fuck.

My fist flew out connecting with the wall and pain ricocheted up my arm.

"Nix?" Jessa rushed into the room, clapping a hand over her mouth. "Oh, Nix," she cried, dropping onto the edge of the bed, and pulling me into her arms.

"She's gone." My voice cracked. I didn't accept that, couldn't accept it.

"We'll figure it out," she said. "I promise."

Chapter Twenty-Seven

Harleigh

"HARLEIGH, COME ON, OPEN THE DOOR."

Nate's voice echoed around his family's bathroom. It was a small room downstairs. I hadn't even known where I was going when I got the text message from an unknown number, but I'd found myself in here and locked him out.

"Harleigh..." His bangs grew more insistent, each one reverberating through me, making me flinch.

"Stop," I murmured, hands pressed to my ears. "Stop, stop, stop."

I couldn't breathe. My lungs were so tight they burned as I tried to force air into them. Inhale. Hold. Exhale. Inhale. Hold. Exhale. Inhale. Hold—

"Harleigh, I swear to God—"

"Leave me alone," I shrieked, laying down on the cool smooth tile. I couldn't breathe. I couldn't make my lungs work. "Just... just leave me alone."

Clutching my cell phone, I read the text message again.

The hateful, cruel words taunting me. Seeping into every crack and insecurity I had.

Unknown: Why don't you just do us all a favor and go back to wherever you came from, piece of trailer trash whore. Or better yet, end it properly this time. No one wants you here. You think Miller gives a shit about you... He doesn't. He feels sorry for you. Has some weird need to save you. But he doesn't care about you. Nobody does. Your mom did the world a favor... Now why don't you?

Bile rushed up my throat and I had to press a fist to my mouth, forcing myself to swallow it back down. My head swam with dark, dark thoughts; not helped by all the drugs in my system. The benzos. Nate's really strong weed.

I probably shouldn't have gotten so high, but when he'd lit up a blunt, I'd craved it. The momentary peace I knew it would bring me.

Surviving my new life in Old Darling Hill was exhausting. Keeping up pretenses, acting like everything was okay so I didn't draw too much attention to myself. Every day was like wading through mud, and some days it was almost impossible to keep moving.

But I did it.

I kept pushing forward.

Even when Nix had showed up again, I'd kept putting one foot in front of the other and moving forward.

Because the choice was simple. Continue to exist—to try and find myself again in all the heartache and pain—or give up.

And I knew what lay at the end of that choice, and it was a place I didn't ever want to revisit.

"Maguire, come on, open the door and let me in. We can figure it out, I swear. Just don't do anything stupid."

Stupid.

Because that's what it was to people on the outside. A stupid, reckless, spur of the moment decision. It couldn't possibly be the final straw. A moment born out of pure desperation and hopelessness. A moment when everything felt impossible, the obstacles simply too insurmountable.

A moment when choosing to end it felt like the easier option than sticking around to fight.

Unless somebody had been in that situation, they couldn't begin to imagine what it was like to be in that headspace. To truly believe that it was the only answer.

My breaths came in short sharp bursts as I drowned in the darkness. It swept in, unyielding and unforgiving, enveloping me in its ironclad grip. It would be so easy to close my eyes and surrender. To let it wash me away until there was nothing left.

"Harleigh... Fuck." Nate's footsteps receded, fading into the distance.

A whimper spilled out of me as I tucked my knees up and squeezed my eyes shut.

"Harleigh? Harleigh!"

My eyes flew open. Had I fallen to sleep? Was I dreaming?

"I swear to God, B, if you don't open this door right—"

"N-Nix?" My voice was barely a whisper, my limbs heavy and head too clouded to focus.

"No, Wilder. You can't—"

"Watch me."

The door splintered in on itself, crashing against the wall.

"Birdie, shit." He rushed to my side, crouching over me. "What—"

"I'm okay," I sniffled, dragging a deep breath into my tight, aching lungs. "I..."

"Come on, up we go." He slid his arm under my legs and one around my back and lifted me up with ease.

"Harleigh, oh my God." Celeste appeared. Miles and Nate too.

"Is she okay?" someone asked.

"I don't know. Can I take her somewhere?"

"Yeah, my room. Up the stairs, first door on the—"

"Somewhere else," Nix said, his grip on me tightening.

"The games room. Come on."

I clung to his shoulders as he carried me down the hall, following Nate. The oppressive black cloud slowly began to dissipate until I could breathe again. But another wave crashed over me, this time one of shame and embarrassment. I buried my face into Nix's hoodie, letting his familiar scent calm me.

He'd always felt like home to me, still did.

But he wasn't my home, not anymore.

A tremor ripped through me, and another. Aftershocks of the panic attack that had paralyzed me.

"I got you," he whispered into my hair. "I got you, B."

The air rushed past me as he lowered me down onto the couch, and someone tucked a pillow under my head.

"Hey, you're okay." Celeste's face appeared. "You're okay, Harleigh." She brushed the stray hairs out of my face. "Do you want to tell me what happened?"

"I... I—"

"What is this?" Nix appeared with my cell phone in his hand. "What the fuck is this?"

"Whoa, man. Calm down." Nate held up his hands, slowly approaching Phoenix.

"Celeste," I cried, grabbing her hand. I didn't want anyone to fight, not over me. But I couldn't find the words or energy... completely wrung dry.

"Stop. Both of you. You're scaring her."

"Did you send this?" Nix ground out, thrusting the cell phone at Nate.

"Send what?" The color drained from Nate's face as he read the screen. "No. I have no idea— fuck. I didn't know. I swear I didn't..."

"Harleigh." Nate approached, crouching beside me. "When did you get this?"

"E-earlier, when we were talking."

"This is why you locked yourself in the bathroom? Why you freaked out?"

"She didn't freak out, idiot." Celeste said. "She had a panic attack. You all need to go. Get out and give her some space."

"I'm not leaving." Nix planted himself there, folding his arms across his chest.

"Nix, come on," Celeste hissed. "She doesn't need this right now."

"Celeste," I croaked. "It's okay. He can stay."

"Harleigh, you don't—"

"I said it's okay."

I just wanted them to stop. To stop arguing and stop looking at me like I was a freak show.

She gave me a tight-lipped smile. "Do you need anything?"

Such a loaded question.

I needed things to go back to how they used to be. When my mom was alive, and Nix was my whole world. When life was hard, but it was also safe and familiar and predictable. When people didn't hate me because of where I came from.

But she couldn't give me any of those things, so I shook my head gently and whispered, "No, thank you."

"Okay. I'm going to let Miles and Chloe know you're okay."

"Chloe's here?"

"Yeah. She was worried."

Exhaustion rolled through me. I wanted to close my eyes and erase this moment from my mind.

"I'll be back soon," Celeste added, leaving the room.

"If you need anything," Nate said.

"Thanks."

He followed her out, leaving me alone with Nix.

He didn't move closer, just stood there in the middle of the room, staring at me.

"Nix..." I whispered.

"I need a second, B." Pain was woven into every word. He released a heavy sigh, the air shifting around him. Thick and oppressive and suffocating. "I'm trying to understand what the fuck is going on... but I'm coming up empty."

"You weren't supposed to see me like that."

"And at the fair? Was that whatever this is?" There was an angry edge to his words.

"Kind of."

"What the fuck does that mean?"

"It means it's not something I can control, Nix. You think I like being like this? Not knowing from one minute to the next when something is going to set me off?"

"I-I don't get it. What happened to you? What—"

His words hit me like a wrecking ball, shattering something inside me. And all I could do in its wake was let out a bitter, broken laugh. "You. You happened."

He went deathly still, his gunmetal eyes fixed on my face, searching for what, I didn't know. "M-me?"

"You heard me." Venom coated my words, but I was tired, so freaking tired of everything.

"Birdie, I don't—"

"Don't call me that," I shrieked. "Don't ever call me that. I'm not yours, Nix. I never was."

He stalked toward me and dropped to his knees. "You're so fucking righteous, acting like I'm the only one who fucked up. But what about you, huh? You chose this, B. And I get it, I do. Why would you possibly want to stay in The Row when you can have all... all *this*." His eyes turned darker, anger swirling in their depths as his chest heaved.

"Y-you think I chose this?" My voice was quiet, thick with disbelief.

"You told me to stay away. You told me to give you space. And then you fucking left without so much as a trace. So if anyone should be feeling screwed over here, it's me."

"What?" My blood ran cold.

He stared at me, eyes clouding with confusion. His mouth twisted. "You heard me, B. I fucked up; I get it. You needed me and I wasn't there. But you left me. You walked away. You decided I wasn't—"

No.

No.

That's not how it happened. That's not—

I searched my mind for the memories, trying to sort through what was the truth and what was lies. But I couldn't do it, everything was too hazy.

Nix stood, taking the air with him. My lungs smarted, barely recovered from my panic attack in Nate's bathroom.

"You know, I always imagined it would be you and me until the end. That nothing, no one, would ever come between us. It was you, Wren. It was always fucking you."

"Lies," I spat. "Stop lying to me. It isn't fair," I screeched, hands fisting the couch.

"Fair?" He seethed, his face red with anger. "I'll tell you what's not fair, B. Realizing you have everything you ever wanted and knowing you're a selfish son of a bitch if you take it. I wanted you that night. I wanted you so fucking much, but things were moving too fast. I wanted you to be sure. I didn't want you to hate me. So I let you walk away. I let you walk away angry at me and everything went to shit... and you left me."

"Stop saying I left you." My hands balled into fists as frustration welled inside me, tears leaking down my face. "I didn't leave you; I didn't have a choice."

Nix ripped his cell phone out of his pocket and ran his thumb over the screen. "Just stop with the lies. It's done. You chose this life and maybe it's for the best." He looked right through me. "Maybe it was always supposed to be this way."

Celeste crept closer, perching on the arm of one of the chairs.

"Can I trust you?" I said.

"Excuse me?"

"It's a simple question. Can I trust you?"

"What happened?"

"Your father happened."

"I... I don't understand." She paled.

"Did you know? That he tried to keep us apart?"

Surprise glinted in her eyes quickly followed by a flash of anger. "No, I didn't," she said.

"Yeah. Turns out daddy dearest didn't like Harleigh having any ties to The Row, so he severed them." I motioned to my cell phone. "Read it."

She picked it up with shaky fingers and I barked out my PIN number. The second the screen lit up, her eyes ran over the text. "You're saying my father sent this?"

"Seems the most likely culprit given that when I turned up at your house a month after that message was sent, he threatened to have me thrown in jail if I ever came near her again."

I could still remember the pure hatred on his face as he confronted me. The disgust in his eyes that his daughter could possibly love a guy like me.

"He wouldn't—"

"Wouldn't he?" I countered.

I knew men like Michael Rowe. Rich men who were used to getting their own way. Men who liked order and control. Men who, if you didn't fit into their neat little box, would cast you aside without a second thought. Harleigh was his blood. His daughter. His legacy. He could bend her to his will, shape her into one of his puppets. But he couldn't do it if she had one foot in The Row.

Because The Row was beneath a man like Michael Rowe and he wouldn't ever want his precious daughter tarnished by someone like me.

"You know, when I went down to the police department, one of the officers told me to leave it alone. Said that I was out of my league and should let it go. I thought he was just pulling rank and being an asshole but maybe he was warning me."

"You're deluded."

I arched a brow. "You sure about that? How well do you know daddy dearest?"

"Stop calling him that." She chewed on the end of her thumb, contemplating something. "It makes no sense. You tried to reach her that day?"

"Multiple times."

"But she said you never returned her calls or messages."

"He must have deleted the messages and flashed her phone or something. I don't know how he did it but what I do know is that B needed me. She fucking needed me, and he kept her from me. And she... she hurt herself because she thought I'd abandoned her."

Fuck, those words hurt. Cut so fucking deep the air sucked clean from my lungs. How was I ever going to move past the fact she'd tried to hurt herself... because she thought I'd left her.

"How bad was it?" I pushed the words past the giant lump in my throat as I ran my thumb over the jagged scar on Harleigh's wrist. A soft murmur left her lips and I soaked up the sight of her sleeping. Peaceful.

Alive.

I didn't want to know. The thought of Harleigh ever hurting herself because of me was too much to bear, but I *needed* to know.

The blood drained from Celeste's cheeks. "It was bad; really bad."

"Fuck," I hissed, running my eyes over Harleigh's sleeping form. She looked so small and fragile. So peaceful.

I would never forgive her father for his scheming that led us to this point. That led Harleigh to believing I'd abandoned her during the darkest day of her life.

"She still loves you, you know?" My eyes snapped to Celeste's and she gave me a sad smile. "When she told me about you, about what happened, I said it didn't make any sense... But she's broken, Nix. She's so broken that she couldn't see past all the lies and half-truths. I'm sorry. If what you say is true, then I'm sorry. For all of it."

"It isn't your fault."

"I know. But she's my sister. I care about her. And I hate the idea that our father was somehow involved...." Anger flared in her eyes again.

Good, get angry, girl. Because I'm fucking furious.

"I visited her in Albany Hills. I was the only visitor she would allow."

"Albany Hills?"

Guilt washed over her, and she murmured, "She didn't tell you..."

"We have a lot to talk about," I admitted. "What is it? Some kind of rehab center?"

"An inpatient facility on the outskirts of Albany."

"That's where she was?"

She nodded. "The first month she lived with us, Harleigh was completely checked out. She wouldn't eat, barely drank. She didn't leave her bedroom unless my parents forced her to. The family doctor said she was severely depressed and started her on medication but it only seemed to make her worse. She was like a ghost, Nix. It was horrible. After she tried to..." Agony etched into her features. "My parents sent her to Albany Hills. She was there for six months."

Six months.

My stomach dropped into my toes.

"When she got out, she was... different. I can't really explain it. It's like she had this calmness about her, but it felt forced. I've tried really hard to break through her defenses, Nix. To be someone she can trust and lean on. But she hates life here. It clings to her like a second skin; you can literally see her writhing around in it. Repelling it. But she won't talk about it. She won't—"

"C-Celeste?" Harleigh's eyes fluttered open, and she gazed up at me, her brows drawn together. "Nix?"

"Yeah, B. I'm here."

"I thought... It wasn't a dream?"

"No, it wasn't a dream." I smoothed my thumb over her cheek.

"I'm sorry you had to see me like that." Her eyes darted away, but I gently gripped her chin, forcing her to look at me.

"Listen to me, and listen good, Birdie. Never shy away from me. Ever. I see you, B. I've always fucking seen you. And nothing about you scares me. Not a damn thing."

Tears clung to her lashes as she swallowed hard. "You came," she whispered.

"I meant what I said, B. I'll always come for you. No matter where you are, or where I am, I'll always come for you."

Because she was mine.

And nothing or no one was ever going to come between us again.

refusing to answer him. "Let me make one thing clear, Birdie. I want you. I have wanted you for as long as I can remember. But things between us have always been complicated..." He let out a small sigh. "It's important to me we get them right this time, because I have no intention of giving you up."

Nix dropped a kiss on my forehead. "Now stop sulking and let's go make sure Miller is in one piece."

"I thought you hated Nate?"

"Oh, I do. But he's been there for you when I couldn't be. So I owe him." Nix got up, tugging me alongside him. His arms slipped around me and he gazed down at me. "I promise not to hurt him so long as he promises not to go after what's mine."

"It isn't like that between us."

"Let's hope he knows that."

I swatted Nix's chest, but he snagged my wrist, yanking me forward so I tumbled into him.

"You're mine, Harleigh Wren Maguire," he whispered against my ear, the words filling the cracks inside me. "Then. Now. Forever."

Just as Celeste said, we found everyone in the kitchen. Nate's eyes immediately went to my hand, the one currently clasped in Nix's. But I found no jealousy in his eyes, only gentle understanding.

"I see you two sorted out your differences," he said.

"Watch it, Miller," Nix drawled. "I haven't decided if I like you or not yet."

Zane snorted at that, his hard gaze sliding to mine. "Sorry, B, about before, at the fair." His expression softened slightly, and I knew we needed to talk. But I wasn't ready to face the firing line, not yet. So a small nod was my only answer.

"Oh my God, Harleigh. It's so good to see you." Chloe rushed over to me and pulled me into her arms. "I'm sorry about your mom. I know it was a while ago, but I never got to say it."

"Thank you." My eyes shuttered as I hugged her back.

When we let go, Celeste caught my eye, smiling. Miles looked less thrilled; a weary expression plastered on his face. But I didn't blame him. Things were tense around Nix and his friends.

Always had been.

"Looking good, B." Kye grinned in that easy way of his. "I'd hug you but I'm not sure Wilder will let me get close enough."

Nix muttered something that sounded like 'damn right,' and I rolled my eyes.

"Liar," I said to Kye. "I look like I had a panic attack and passed out on my... on Nix." I cleared my throat, hoping no one noticed my slip of the tongue.

But Nix pulled me back into his chest, wrapping his arms around me, oblivious to the strange looks our friends were giving us. "Your what, B?"

I heard the smirk in his voice and elbowed him in the ribs, making him grunt in pain.

"Remind me never to get on your wrong side." Kye chuckled.

"Nate, can we talk a second?" I tried to pull away from Nix, but he tightened his grip on me. Zane and Kye both smirked and I glowered at them.

"Not helpful," I murmured, peeling Nix's hands from my stomach.

"It's okay, Maguire, we can talk another time."

"You should listen to him, B," Nix whispered. "The guy talks a lot of sense."

Celeste and Chloe suppressed their own smiles. I twisted my face to Nix and pinned him with a serious look. "I'll be right back. But I am going to talk to Nate."

His jaw ticked but he relented. "Fine. Go. I've got my eye on you though, Miller."

"I would expect nothing less." Nate jammed his hands in his pockets and flicked his head toward the back door. I followed him outside, aware of the six pairs of eyes watching us.

"How are you feeling?" he asked.

"Like I owe you a huge apology."

"No, Harleigh. Don't even think that. I had no idea about the text message. I swear to God... My cousin is a real asshole."

"You think it was Marc?"

He frowned. "You don't?"

"I guess it makes sense." Marc or Angelica.

"I'll talk to him—"

"No, no. You shouldn't get in the middle of it, it will only make things worse. I can block the number."

"Harleigh." He gave me a sympathetic smile. "You locked yourself in the bathroom and had a panic attack."

"I know..." Shame pressed in on me. "I ... it's been hard, you know? Trying to pretend I'm okay, putting on a brave face."

"But you and Wilder figured things out?"

"I think so."

"That's good, right?"

"I... I mean, yeah. But a lot has happened." We weren't the same people anymore. At least, I wasn't. And I knew Nix wouldn't wait long for answers. He wouldn't rest until he knew every detail about what had happened to me.

I wasn't sure I wanted to relive it though, to dredge up all those dark and desolate memories. Not to mention the fact that the more Nix knew, the angrier he would be about my father.

My father.

God, there was a lot to unpack there.

I was choosing denial for the moment though. Because if I let myself think about it, if I let myself go there...

"I know we didn't get off to a great start, Nate. But I wanted to say thank you. For being there for me even when I didn't want you to be. You're a good friend."

"Friend... yeah." He ran a hand up and down his face, and a strange sensation took root in my stomach.

"Nate, what—"

There was a commotion over by the door and Nix appeared. "Okay, time's up, Miller." He stalked toward us, and Nate laughed.

"Good luck with that." He gave me a small nod and headed back inside.

"You couldn't give us five minutes?"

"What can I say, Birdie, I'm a possessive idiot." He hooked his arm around my waist and drew me into his chest. "You two clear the air?"

"I guess."

"And did you make it clear that you're mine?"

"Nix..." I sighed.

Guilt flashed in his gray eyes. "Shit, sorry, I'm being an ass. I... I didn't think we'd ever be like this again. And now I have you back, I don't ever want to let you out of my sight."

But that was impossible.

Because we lived on opposite sides of town now, and the reservoir might as well have been a vast unpredictable ocean between us.

"B, what is it?" he asked, noticing my solemn expression.

"Nothing." I forced a smile, unwilling to burst his bubble. He looked so happy, like the boy I'd grown up adoring.

I didn't want to take that away from him.

Not in this moment.

Nix

"ARE we going to talk about the fact this is as weird as fuck?" Zane said as we sat in Miller's kitchen, waiting for him to return with pizza for everyone.

The girls were sitting over on the sectional talking. I wasn't surprised how easily Celeste and Chloe slotted in beside Harleigh. They were both similar. Feisty. Sassy. Fiercely protective. Harleigh needed people like that in her life. Especially after—

Fuck, I couldn't go there.

Couldn't let myself think about her trying to hurt herself because she thought I'd abandoned her. It was too much of a mind fuck.

"Breathe, Nix," Kye whispered, motioning to my hand as I white-knuckled the edge of the counter.

"You good?" Zane asked, and I nodded, forcing myself to take a deep breath. "Maybe we should—"

"No. I'm not leaving. Not yet."

"And I get it, man. I do. But what's the plan here? She

lives with her old man now. She's a minor. You know what happened last time you tried to go after her. If he finds..."

"Z." Kye shook his head. "Ease up for a second, yeah? I'm sure Nix has a plan."

But that was just it, I didn't.

I lived my life from day to day, never letting myself think too far ahead. Hopes and dreams were a dangerous notion in my world, because the consequences of chasing them meant leaving Jessa behind. It meant leaving Zane and his grandma, and Kye and Chloe behind.

How could I do that?

How could I put myself first when Jessa's life depended on me?

It wasn't like Harleigh could come and stay with me. Not after the shit that had gone down with me and my old man. And Zane had a point. If she tried to run, Michael would come after her. Probably make good on his word and come after me. She was a minor, at least for another few weeks.

Even if she wanted to run, what did I have to offer her?

Nothing.

I had nothing.

My fist clenched against my thigh, tension mounting inside me. When I'd first found out Harleigh was back, I hadn't let myself imagine a scenario where we found our way back together. So much time had passed. Too much shit had happened. But now she was here and I was here and all I wanted to do was pull her into my arms and reassure her that nothing would hurt her again.

I couldn't do it though.

I couldn't make promises I had no way of keeping, not after everything.

I needed more time. Time to figure out a plan that gave us a way to be together. Because that's the only thing that mattered. Us. Together. Her safe by my side.

But could I really do it? Could I bind her to my life again? Clip her wings and ask her to stay by my side, wherever that took us?

As if she heard my thoughts, Harleigh glanced over and gave me a small uncertain smile. Fuck, there had been a time I'd lived for those smiles. Always so shy and unsure of herself.

I smiled back, and Zane snorted. "It's been what, an hour," he said, "and you're already making moon eyes at each other."

"Fuck off," I growled.

"Okay, food's up." Miller appeared, pizza boxes piled high in his arms.

"What do we make of him?" Zane asked under his breath, watching with cool assessment as Miller dropped them on the opposite end of the counter.

"He seems okay," Kye said with a small shrug.

"You think we can trust him?"

My eyes snapped to Zane, understanding passing between us. He was wary about how quickly things were moving with me and Harleigh, and I didn't blame him. He was first and foremost my best friend. But I also knew he'd welcome her back into the fold without question. Because she'd always been mine. And therefore, she'd always been his too.

"Harleigh trusts him, that's good enough for me," I said, pushing down all the reservations I had.

Zane snorted, seeing straight through me. "We'll assume he's friendly... for now."

"You guys want pizza?" the guy in question called.

"Hell yes." Kye bounced over to them, unaffected by Miller's big, excessive house.

It wasn't as big as Harleigh's old man's place, but it was still impressive to three kids who had been dragged up in The Row.

"Where did you say your parents are again?" I asked him, moving over to the pizza.

Harleigh joined me, wrapping her arm around my waist and laying her head on my arm.

"Hungry, B?" I asked her, aware of Miller watching us.

"No, but you should eat."

"Oh yeah?" My brow lifted, innuendo dripping from my words.

Her cheeks flushed, eyes widening with surprise and something I wanted to believe was lust, too.

"Gross," Chloe muttered, shouldering past us to get to the pizza. "Thanks for this," she said to Nate.

"No problem. As for my parents, they're out of town with my brother until tomorrow night."

An idea started formulating in my head. "You cool with us hanging out here tonight?"

"Nix," Harleigh said, tugging at my hoodie.

I dipped my head and brought my mouth to her ear. "It's not like I can bring you back to The Row or you can bring me home to daddy dearest." She went rigid at the mention of her father. "We can hang out here tonight, figure out a plan..."

I needed this. I needed tonight with her. One night before shit undoubtedly hit the fan.

She pulled back to look me in the eye, searching my face for what, I didn't know. Her gaze flicked over to Nate, and I fucking hated that he was somehow involved in this. But I wasn't letting my stubbornness prevent me from taking advantage of his hospitality.

"You guys in?" I asked everyone else.

"Sounds good to me," Celeste said. "Mom and Dad are out of town for the night anyway."

"What about Max?" Harleigh asked.

"Max will be off doing whatever Max does. It's cool. I'll tell him we're stopping over at Miles's house. Right, babe?" She glanced at Mulligan and he gave her a nervous smile.

"Sure."

"Sounds good to me." Miller shrugged. "It isn't like I usually have anyone to hang out with when they're away. It's kinda neat to have company for once." Miller grabbed another slice of pizza and headed for the couch.

"What the fuck?" Zane caught my eye, and I shrugged, glancing back at Miller.

He wasn't looking at us though. He was staring off at nothing. But Chloe joined him, whispering something to him that made him smile.

"Oh fuck no," Kye muttered.

"Good luck with that, bro." I chuckled.

"Why do I feel like I'm missing something?" Harleigh pinched my side, and I dropped a kiss on her head.

"There's a lot to fill you in on, B," I said, one-handedly adding pizza slices onto a plate.

"Everything," she breathed, gazing up at me. "I want to know everything."

"Okay, I take it back," Zane said. "This is pretty fucking epic."

We'd moved things outside, to Miller's patio. There was a decent sized pool, and a hot tub on the corner of the deck, surrounded by a gazebo strung with twinkle lights. Miller had turned it on earlier when the girls said they wanted to take a dip later.

Zane was sprawled out on a heated lounger, drinking Miller's beer and eating his snacks. The fact he was high on Miller's weed probably had something to do with his good mood.

Harleigh nuzzled my neck, wrapping herself tighter around my body. She'd barely left my side, some part of her always touching some part of me. Not that I was complaining.

"Please tell me you're not planning on going in there with the girls," I whispered, running my hand down her spine, loving how she shuddered beneath my touch.

"I don't have a swimsuit."

"Neither do they." I flicked my head to where Celeste and Chloe were half-naked, sitting on the edge of the pool.

Kye grumbled something under his breath, and Harleigh chuckled.

"At least she's safe here. She could be at some party, drunk, taking off her clothes—"

"Whoa, whoa whoa, B, that's my little sister you're talking about."

"Doesn't look so little to me anymore."

"B has a point," I added with a smirk.

Kye flipped me off and got up. "I need another drink."

"Mulligan doesn't seem so happy that his girl is enjoying herself."

Zane looked over, shrugging. "They can both go fuck themselves."

"Yeah, okay. Because you aren't—"

"I swear to fucking God, Nix. Just because I'm flying right now doesn't mean I won't kick your ass six ways from Sunday."

"I'd like to see you try."

"Your boy's weed is some good shit, B."

Anger zipped down my spine and Zane grinned. Even high, the fucker knew exactly what he was doing.

"Nix," Harleigh said, her lips so close to my jaw it felt like she was kissing me. I stilled, my heart racing, my fingers digging into her hip as she hovered there, taunting me.

"Yeah, B?" I said, unflinching as the air crackled around us.

"He's not my boy, you know." Her voice was low, sultry, doing all kinds of weird shit to my insides.

"Oh yeah, how's that?"

I wasn't breathing or I was pretty sure I couldn't breathe as the seconds ticked by, each one slower than before.

"Because..." she whispered the word onto my jaw, ghosting her lips over my skin. "You're my boy, you always have been."

Fuck.

She was going to kill me.

Every defense, every wall I'd ever built against this girl was being shattered wide open.

A splash sounded behind us and I glanced over to see Chloe in the water. Miller went next, taking a run and jump as he cannonballed in.

"Come on," I said, taking her hand. "Z, I know you're high as fuck, but keep everyone away from the hot tub, yeah?"

Zane glared at me. "Seriously, you're going to fuck—"

"*Talk*, asshole. We're going to talk."

"Yeah, whatever," he grumbled.

But I didn't let his bad mood stop me as I tugged Harleigh over to the hot tub. It was pretty private, only the corner opening out to overlook the rest of the yard, which meant if I pulled her to the back, no one would even be able to see us.

"I'm not getting in there," she said, a hesitant expression pinching her brows.

"No? That's a shame." I hooked my hands into my hoodie and pulled it clean off with my t-shirt. Harleigh's breath caught as she ran her eyes over my body. I looked good, I knew that. I'd always liked working out, running drills on the football field. I liked the rush of adrenaline, the tingle of exertion deep in my muscles. But it was nothing compared to the way I felt with her eyes drinking me in, running over every single inch of me as if she was memorizing the lines of my body.

"You're hurt." She reached out and traced one of the fading bruises from Meathead's beating a couple of weeks ago.

"I'm fine." I snagged her wrist and pulled her further under the gazebo. "I've been waiting all night to get you alone."

"You have?" A faint smile traced her lips.

"Yeah. I can't believe you're here." I ran my finger along her forehead and down her nose, painting it across her lips and along her collarbone. Harleigh's eyes fluttered, soft moans falling from her lips as I touched her.

When they opened again, settling on my face, my heart stuttered against my rib cage.

God, she was beautiful.

I'd never allowed myself to see it before, not like this. Not without all the expectations and consequences of our friendship stacked up between us. But too much happened to go back to that place.

"You have more tattoos," she said awed as she reached for my body, tracing the swathes of ink marking my skin.

"I like the pain."

"I've thought about getting one but I don't think I could do it."

"Of course you could, B. You can do anything you set your mind to."

A coy smile played on her lips. "Maybe one day you can take me?"

"I can make that happen." I ran my hand along her neck and cupped her nape. "Come in the hot tub with me, Birdie."

Harleigh nodded, stepping back a little. Slowly, she stripped out of her shorts and t-shirt, left standing in nothing but a plain black bra and panties. There wasn't anything special about it, but on her it could have been expensive lace, she looked that fucking good.

"Look at you," I drawled, running my hand down her side and drawing her back into me. "You're so fucking beautiful, B." Gently, I gripped her wrist and brought it to my lips, kissing the scar there.

Her body trembled as my lips hovered, a silent apology for everything that had happened. "Never again, B," I said thickly, my heart in my throat. "Never fucking again."

Tears glistened in her eyes. "I promise," she whispered.

I knew it wasn't that simple, knew that mental health wasn't something to be downplayed or ignored. But it was a promise I planned on helping her keep.

Somehow, I'd find a way to fix everything.

Starting with right now.

Kicking off my sneakers, I loosened the drawstring on

my sweats and pushed them down my hips, kicking out of them. Without warning, I grabbed the back of Harleigh's thighs and lifted her up my body. She wrapped her legs around my waist, shrieking as I climbed the steps to the sunken hot tub and got in, submerging us both.

The water was hot, bubbling around us, but it was nothing compared to the way she felt pressed up against me.

"Fuck, B," I breathed, gathering her hair off her neck and winding it around my fist. "Is this real?"

She took my hand and pressed it over her breastbone, right above her heart. "Does it feel real to you?"

It raced under my touch like a runaway train. "You're nervous?" I asked.

"I was always nervous around you, Nix."

Tugging gently on her hair, I tilted Harleigh's head back, giving me those deep green eyes I'd always found myself so weak for. "And now?"

"I don't know what I feel," she admitted.

"Feel this." My other hand slipped down her spine under the water and curved around her hip, dragging her down on me. "Feel that. Feel what you do to me, B. What you've always done..."

Harleigh rolled her hips slowly, the friction damn near perfect as I thrust up against her. Eyes at half-mast, lips parted on a small whimper, a deep crimson flush smattered along her cheeks. She looked so fucking sexy, I had to refrain from tearing her panties off and burying myself deep inside her.

"Nix..." She moaned my name, rocking above me, dragging her pussy right over me.

"Use me to get off, B." I buried my face in her neck and licked her damp skin. "Take what you need."

"Everyone is—"

My eyes snapped to hers. "Nobody is watching you but me."

"We shouldn't..." She bit down on her lip.

"Yeah, we really fucking should." My mouth came down on hers, hard and demanding. Needing to taste her while she got herself off on my dick.

Her hands slid over my shoulders, nails digging in and making it hurt. But the flash of pain only amped me up.

"It feels good." The breathy moan made me grip her harder, erasing every sliver of space between us. Any closer and I would have been inside her, fucking her, owning her.

But this wasn't about me. It was about her. About *her* taking what *she* needed.

"Fuck..." I choked out as she started circling her hips, grinding right down on me.

"God, Nix... God."

I couldn't take my eyes off her. I'd only ever seen her come undone like this once before and I'd felt too fucking guilty then to enjoy it.

That night I'd allowed myself one taste, one touch... but I had no plan of walking away this time.

Consequences be damned.

Chapter Thirty-One

Harleigh

AN INTENSE WAVE rose inside me, spreading through me like wildfire until I was moaning his name over and over.

Nix... Nix... Nix.

"Shh." He nipped my jaw before kissing me deeply and swallowing my little cries of pleasure.

I was flying, soaring out of my body as the ripples went through me. Nix didn't just kiss me, he fucked me with his tongue. Long deep licks alternated with quick shallow thrusts. I was drunk on him, completely and utterly wrecked.

When he let me up for air, I buried my face in his neck, too embarrassed to look at him.

"Don't ever hide from me, B." He coaxed me out and forced my eyes to his. "You're so fucking beautiful when you come."

"I... I can't believe I did that."

"Wait until I'm inside you." My thighs clenched and

his brow quirked up, a knowing smirk on his face. "You like the idea of that, B? My dick buried deep inside you?"

"Nix..."

"Don't be embarrassed, Birdie. We've waited a long time to get here."

Here.

He said the word as if it had always been inevitable. Part of me liked to think that maybe he was right, that we'd had to endure all the pain and heartache, trials and tribulations to get to this point. Because how could you ever truly know if something was meant to be if it hadn't been tested to its limits?

But when he took my wrist and gently pressed his mouth to my scar, something inside me shattered.

"Shit, B, don't cry." Nix wiped away the tears rolling down my cheeks. "Do you want to talk about it?"

I pressed my lips together and shook my head.

"Come here." He wound his arms around me and drew me into his chest, the steady beat of his heart like my own personal lullaby.

"I got you, B. I got you."

The tears came harder... wracking my body as I sobbed into his shoulder. But Nix didn't recoil, he didn't demand answers, or try to get me to stop. He simply held me again, as he'd done in the games room.

And his patience, his willingness to give me space meant everything to me.

He was *everything*.

"Tonight has been fun," Celeste whispered as we dried off in one of Nate's guest rooms while the boys set up the movie and snacks downstairs.

"Miles didn't look too impressed," I said.

"He's cute," Chloe added. "Not as cute as Nate, but he has that whole hot geek thing working for him."

"Miles is... a good guy." There was a slight hesitation in Celeste's voice that had me wondering if a certain brooding bad boy from The Row had caught her attention tonight.

"So Nate..." Chloe wore a sly smile. "Is he seeing anyone?"

"Clo," I warned. "I'm not sure Kye would—"

"Kye Smye. I'm not looking to marry the guy. But he's hot and guys back home aren't exactly..." She stopped herself, gawking at me. "I mean guys except Nix."

"Mm-hmm," I murmured, not wanting to think about Nix like that. With other girls.

With Cherri.

My stomach sank, the question crawling up my throat and onto my tongue. *Don't do it. Don't ask.* But I couldn't do it, I needed to know.

"Were Nix and Cherri ... together?"

Chloe froze as she towel-dried her hair, telling me all I needed to know. "You should probably ask Nix about that."

God, I hated the sympathy in her eyes. The sheer pity.

"I'm asking you." I choked out.

"They hooked up a lot over the summer. You know what Cherri is like; it's always meant more to her than it ever has Nix. He doesn't care about her like that, Harleigh. Not the way he cares about you."

True.

But I hated that he'd been with her, turned to her over the last few months. When he should have been with me.

Cherri Jardin had always been a thorn in my side, a festering wound I couldn't heal. Because she was exactly the type of girl Nix went for. Bold, brave, and sexy. I'd never been any of those things. She was a bright red rose in a bed of thorns, and I was an insipid flower wilting in the shadows.

My heart sank.

"Oh no, Harleigh. Don't you dare think whatever you're thinking right now. Cherri isn't important to Nix, you have to know that."

And I did. Somewhere under the years' worth of self-doubt and second guessing. But she was everything I would never be. And they had history, sexual history.

I dropped down on the end of the bed, curling my fingers into the soft coverlet.

"Harleigh." Celeste sat beside me. "I don't know who Cherri is—"

"Total bitch," Chloe interrupted. "Sorry, continue."

"But Chloe is right. Anyone can see how much Nix cares about you. The way he literally crashed through Nate's bathroom door to get to you... we're talking action movie hotness level right there."

A small smile tugged at my mouth. "I know. It's been a long time though."

She nudged me gently with her shoulder. "And you have a lot to work through. But don't doubt him before you've even given him a chance."

"You're really okay with this?" I gawked at her. She knew some of the history. Knew who Nix was to me.

Celeste's brows pinched. "You love him."

"You know Michael won't—"

"Screw Dad." Anger flashed in her eyes. "He is the last person I want to talk about right now."

"Same," I sighed. But the truth was, I couldn't ignore him. He would never accept my relationship with Nix. Not in a million years.

Celeste took my hand in hers and squeezed gently. "We'll figure it out."

"I hope so." I swallowed the lump in my throat.

I couldn't lose Nix, not again.

It was bad enough thinking about returning to the house soon and leaving him.

"Well, this is as good as it's going to get." Chloe tamed the damp hair out of her face. "I look like a drowned rat but whatever."

"It was fun though," Celeste said.

The girls shared a secretive smile and Chloe nodded. "Yeah, it was."

"Does this feel weird to you?" I whispered into the dark.

Everyone had found somewhere to sleep a while ago. Nate was in his room, hopefully not with Chloe. Although after the way she'd cuddled up beside him during the scary movie, I wouldn't be surprised. Zane and Kye had crashed on the sectional in the games room, and I had no idea where Miles and Celeste had disappeared to.

"You're supposed to be sleeping," Nix said, his voice gravelly as if I'd woken him.

"My mind is too busy."

He shifted onto his side, toying with the ends of my hair. "Want to talk about it?"

"I thought we agreed no talking tonight?"

"Technically it's a new day." I heard the smirk in his voice.

"Technically, I said I didn't want to talk about it *yet*."

"B?" He pressed a finger against my mouth.

"Yeah?" I breathed, my heart beating furiously in my chest.

"Stop talking."

"Okay." Rolling away from him, I shrieked when he banded his arm around my waist and rolled me underneath him.

"Hi," he said, his eyes twinkling in the dark.

"Hi." I felt giddy. Drunk on him. On lying here with him in the shadows.

Leaning down, he ghosted his mouth over mine, a whisper of a kiss.

"Tease," I said, a little breathless.

"You're right, we should get some sleep." He started to roll away from me. "It's late and I—"

I grabbed his arm and pulled him down on top of me, wrapping my legs around his waist.

"B..." he warned, his voice cracked with lust.

"I want you, Nix. More than anything."

I'd spent the last nine months uncertain of everything. The people around me. The staff at Albany Hills. My own thoughts and emotions. I'd almost forgotten what it felt like to believe in something real. To want something so much you felt like you wouldn't survive without it.

"Not like this, not in Miller's fucking guest room."

"Please..." I lifted my hips, rubbing the growing bulge in his boxer briefs.

"Who's the tease now?" He gently nipped my bottom lip, grazing it with his teeth, sending a violent shiver down my spine.

"This feels right," I admitted, pressing my hand to his heart. "Me. You. Together in the dark."

His eyes narrowed, a conflicted expression there. "You deserve to live in the light, B."

"Maybe, one day. Now make love to me, Phoenix Wilder. Make me yours."

"Fuck," he breathed, sliding one of his hands down my waist and clamping it around my hip. "You deserve better, B. So much fucking better."

I laid my palm against his cheek, and said, "It's not about what I deserve, it's about what I want. What I *need*, Nix. And it's you. It's always been you."

Nix kissed me, sliding his hand in my hair and angling my face right where he wanted me. I loved the weight of his body on mine, the way our legs tangled, how hard he felt at my stomach. A thrill went through me as I glided my hands over his shoulders and down his back, feeling his muscles ripple and contract beneath my touch.

"Do you have any idea how many times I imagined this?" He stared down at me.

"Show me," I breathed. "Show me everything."

"Fuck, B." His hand slipped between our bodies finding my center. "You're so wet for me," he rasped, sliding his fingers over my damp underwear. "I need to feel you."

I nodded, lifting my hips slightly, silently showing him what I wanted.

Hooking the material aside, he pressed two fingers into me. A whimper spilled from my lips as he curled them deep. Nix watched me, every moan and whispered plea, as he worked me with his fingers. But it wasn't enough. I wanted to feel him. I wanted him with me, inside me.

"Nix," I said, breathless. "I want... you. Please. I need to feel you." Curling my fingers around his wrist, I pulled his hand away. His eyes darkened, blown with lust as I stroked him through his boxers.

Nix grabbed my hands, pinning them on either side of my head as he rocked his hips into me.

"God, Nix." I pressed my lips together, trapping the moans.

One of his hands slipped under my t-shirt, sliding up my stomach to cup my breast. "You are so fucking beautiful." He leaned down, brushing his mouth over mine, teasing me with little kisses.

"Nix..." Frustration coated my voice.

"What do you want, B?"

"You. All of you."

Some indecipherable emotion lit up his eyes and he pressed a quick kiss to my lips before climbing off me and padding over to his jeans. He pulled a foil wrapper out of his wallet and I arched a brow.

"Do I even want to know?" My stomach sank, but he stalked toward me, the intensity in his gaze breathtaking.

"Let me make one thing clear, B," he said, inching my panties down until they slipped free of my legs. My t-shirt went next and then his, until we were both naked, nothing but skin and scars between us.

Nix tore open the wrapper and rolled the latex over himself, crawling over me. "It's you. It's always been you. I was too scared back then to take what I wanted. I'm not good enough for you, B."

"Nix, that's—"

"Shh." He brushed his lips over mine again. "It's the truth. Life by my side won't be easy. It won't be like... this." His eyes scanned the guest room. "But I'm done fighting it. I lost you once, Birdie. I won't lose you again."

His words sank into me, stitching my heart back together.

Nothing would ever wholly fix me; I knew that. But being here with Nix was more than I could have ever hoped for.

His eyes met mine, his body trembling above me as he gripped my hip and slowly inched into me. "Okay?"

I nodded, clutching his shoulders as he filled me.

"Fuck, B. *Fuuuuck.*" He dropped his face to my neck, stilling inside me.

"N-Nix?" I croaked.

"Just... give me a second, yeah?"

My heart was a wild beating thing inside my chest. This was happening. Me and Nix.

Me and Nix.

And it felt so right, so inevitable, that a rush of emotion rose in my chest and exploded as he pulled out of me and slammed home.

Home.

Nix was my home, he always had been.

Harleigh

THE NEXT MORNING, Celeste and Miles left together to get breakfast.

Zane glared at their car as it disappeared down the street.

"Why are you acting so weird?" Chloe said, and he threw her a dirty look before storming off toward Nix's car.

"Was it something I said?" She chuckled, but no one else laughed. "Harleigh Wren, don't be a stranger." She came over and hugged me. "You've got my number, use it."

Oddly, her and Celeste had also traded numbers. But they had hit it off, the two of them more similar than I'd ever realized.

"Thank you." I hugged her back before Nix grew impatient and tugged me into his arms.

"I'll be there in a minute," he said to Kye and Chloe.

"Clo is right." Kye grinned as if the past was already erased between us and everything was normal again. "It's good to have you back, B." The two of them got in Nix's car leaving me, Nix, and Nate.

"I'll... uh, wait in the car," he said.

"I fucking hate this," Nix breathed, pulling me into his arms. "I should be the one driving you home, not Miller."

"It's just a ride home."

His eyes narrowed, swirling with anger. "Still don't like it. You're mine, B. Last night was... fuck, it was everything."

It had been. Falling asleep in his arms, sleepy and sated. Waking up to his intense gray eyes watching me, kissing him good morning, feeling the heat of his body pressed against mine.

I couldn't remember sleeping that well in a really long time.

"This is our reality, Nix. I live here now. And you—"

"Don't." He huffed. "Don't worry, B, I haven't forgotten where I come from."

"Please." I tugged on his hoodie. "Don't do this. I don't want us to argue before I have to go back there."

"Shit, B. I'm sorry." He dipped his head, touching it to mine, and breathing me in. "I know this isn't going to be easy. I just need you to stick with me, Birdie. Can you do that?"

I slid my hands up his chest, fighting back the tears burning the backs of my eyes, and nodded.

"Now kiss me like you mean it," he said, his voice low and husky, hitting me straight in the stomach. "I want to be able to taste you all day."

Our lips met as silent tears rolled down my cheeks.

God, I hated this. I didn't want to say goodbye. Not now, not ever. But things were different. And I didn't doubt Michael would go to great lengths to keep us apart if he'd already intervened last year.

Nix pulled away first, kissing me once. Twice. Dropping a final kiss on my forehead. "Text me as soon as you can, okay?"

I nodded, stepping back and wrapping my arms around myself, trying to hold in my tears. My broken bloody heart.

It wasn't fair.

Nothing about this was.

And as I watched him walk backwards to his car, his eyes never once leaving mine, the harsh truth slammed into me.

I'd spent the last nine months hating him and it was nothing but a dirty lie.

The sun was cresting on the horizon, as Nate pulled up outside my father's estate.

"Thanks for the ride, and for... everything." I unbuckled my belt.

"Listen, I know last night was intense. If you ever need to talk... and I don't mean in a creepy way. But I get it, at least, part of me does. I'm here, always."

"I appreciate it, I do. I'm just really overwhelmed right now."

"Of course." He ran a hand down his face. "I'll see you tomorrow at school."

With a small nod, I climbed out of his car and made my way up to the house. Nate waited until I went inside to leave and part of me liked him even more for it. Nix was going to have to accept that Nate was my friend. Something I was going to need to survive the rest of my year at DA. Especially after the text I received last night.

Inhaling a shuddering breath, I headed for the kitchen to grab a bottle of water before heading to my room to grab a couple hours of sleep before Michael and Sabrina returned home from their trip.

My eyes shuttered as a heavy weight settled over me. My father couldn't know about Nix, not yet. Not until we'd figured out some kind of plan.

I dipped my hand into my pocket and pulled out my cell phone, opening a new message.

Me: I'm back.

Nix replied immediately. I smiled at the nickname he'd entered into my cell.

Hot Tub Guy: I'm already thinking about when I can see you again...

My heart strained. I wanted that, I did. But there was so much to consider and now that we were apart again, things seemed insurmountable.

Me: Soon.

Hot Tub Guy: When? And why do I feel like you're already checking out on me?

Me: I'm not... I promise. I'm just overwhelmed.

My cell phone started vibrating and I answered. "Hello."

"I needed to hear your voice." His voice was distant. Cold. "Are you alone?"

"I'm in the kitchen, getting a drink."

"Is anyone there?"

"Celeste isn't back yet and Max must be sleeping still, but this is... risky."

"Yeah," he blew out a frustrated breath. "I know. But I needed to hear your voice, to know we're okay. We are okay, aren't we, B?"

"Yeah, we're okay. We're more than okay."

His sigh of relief settled deep inside me. "Try to get

some rest. I'm going to figure out a plan for us, you hear me?"

"I hear you."

"You know, last night... it meant something to me, B. Something real."

His words fisted my heart as tears rushed up my throat. "Me too."

"I'll talk to you soon, B."

"Bye," I whispered, hanging up.

"Who was that?"

My heart almost lurched out of my chest as I whirled around to find Max glaring at me. "No one."

"Didn't sound like no one to me. Where were you all night?"

"Where were you?" I countered, noticing he was dressed in yesterday's clothes.

He smirked. "That's for me to know..."

"Don't you have someone else to annoy?" I scoffed, trying to calm my racing heart.

"When it's so much fun getting under your skin? Nope."

"Whatever, Max. I'm going to my room." I moved around him, toward the stairs. But he grabbed my arm. "Don't touch me." A lick of fear ran down my spine.

"Or what, Harleigh Wren?" He stepped up to me, contempt shining in his eyes.

"Why do you hate me so much?" The words tumbled from my lips.

"Hate you? I don't hate you, I pity you. Trying to fit in a

place that will never accept you. It's sad really. You're pathetic, Maguire. Nothing but a piece of trailer trash who doesn't belong here."

Tears of anger stung my eyes, but I refused to let them fall, reminding myself that Max was just a spoiled kid who had grown up with Michael and Sabrina, two emotionally stunted people, for parents. Although they couldn't be held entirely responsible for his vile personality, I didn't doubt it had a big impact.

"Trust me," I snarled, "I want to be here about as much as you want me here." Shoving past him, I stomped upstairs.

But his voice gave me pause. "I wonder what Dad would think of you spending the night with Phoenix Wilder."

No.

No.

My blood turned to ice as I glanced back at him and forced my expression into complete neutrality. "I don't know what you're talking about."

"No? Huh." Amusement glinted in his eyes. "I must have gotten it wrong then."

A beat passed. The air crackling around us.

He knew.

Somehow Max knew.

Had Nate told someone about last night? His brother? Or Marc? I didn't think he would betray me, but what if he'd accidentally slipped and someone told Max?

Before I could figure out what to say, how to fix it, he

shrugged and said, "Well, I've got shit to do," and walked off as if he hadn't just dropped an undetonated bomb at my feet.

I all but ran up to my room, slamming the door behind me. This place had always felt like a prison. Cold. Unforgiving. Soulless. But I'd tolerated it, found peace in the little things. The roof terrace, Celeste, my bedroom, the huge yard.

It had been enough, a means to an end. Get through senior year, get my diploma, and then run far, far away from Darling Hill.

But now that I knew what lay beyond the gates, now that I knew Nix was out there, waiting for me... This prison, this gilded cage, suddenly felt like a small room, the walls pressing in on me, taking the air with them.

And I knew it wouldn't be long until I suffocated.

But if Max knew, if he'd somehow seen me with Nix...

Things had just got a hell of a lot more complicated.

PLAYLIST

Tear Myself Apart – Tate McRae
Everything I Wanted – Billie Eilish
Wandering Romance – LIE NING
Bleed Out – Isak Danielson
NDA – Billie Eilish
Lost My Mind – FINNEAS
He Don't Love Me – Winona Oak
Power – Isak Danielson
I Don't Think I Love You Anymore – Alaina Castillo
Safe – Olivia Grace
Break My Broken Heart – Winona Oak
Hands – ORKID
Young and Free – Dermot Kennedy
Hurricane – Kayne West, The Weeknd, Lil Baby
Two Weeks – FKA Twiggs
Between The Wars – Allman Brown

If You Leave, I'm Coming With You – The Wombats
Stay – Gracie Abrams
Lovely – Lauren Babic, Seraphim
Cosmic Love – Florence and the Machine

AUTHOR'S NOTE

Ahhh finally, Nix and Birdie's story has arrived. When I wrote their prequel *These Dark Hearts* I had some idea of how their duet might go ... of course, they proved why I should never get too far ahead of myself. But a huge part of my process is trusting my characters and letting them take me on **their** journey. And what a journey it was.

Nix and his Birdie are flawed. They're broken and hurting but they're also resilient and strong and I can't wait to watch them fight for their well-deserved HEA!

As always, I need to thank my team for helping me put the finishing touches on this story. Andrea (aka editor-extraordinaire, I feel like a broken record but you always go above and beyond for me and my utter chaos, I owe you! Amanda and Bree, thank you for beta reading and providing me with your constructive feedback. Darlene and Athena, thank you for your eagle-eyed proofreading. Candi Kane PR, thank you for all of your support with the release and keeping me on track. To all the book bloggers who took the time to read an advance copy of *These Dirty Lies* your support, reviews, and messages, are everything.

And finally to you, the reader, thank you for giving my stories a chance.

Until next time,
    L. A. xo

ABOUT THE AUTHOR

Angsty. Edgy. Addictive Romance

USA Today and *Wall Street Journal* bestselling author of over forty mature young adult and new adult novels, L. A. is happiest writing the kind of books she loves to read: addictive stories full of teenage angst, tension, twists and turns.

Home is a small town in the middle of England where she currently juggles being a full-time writer with being a mother/referee to two little people. In her spare time (and when she's not camped out in front of the laptop) you'll most likely find L. A. immersed in a book, escaping the chaos that is life.

L. A. loves connecting with readers.

The best places to find her are:
www.lacotton.com

Printed in Great Britain
by Amazon